Is
Underground

Is

Underground

Joan Aiken

A YEARLING BOOK

Published by
Bantam Doubleday Dell Books for Young Readers
a division of
Bantam Doubleday Dell Publishing Group, Inc.
1540 Broadway
New York, New York 10036

ISBN: 0-440-41068-1

Reprinted by arrangement with Delacorte Press
Printed in the United States of America

August 1995

10 9 8 7 6 5 4 3 2 1

OPM

Is
Underground

THE PLAYLANDERS came to Winchelsea
With flags flying
And Gold Kingy's standerd flying in the midil medil midill
And with a rush
The Playlanders came to batal
And sixty were killed at the furst shot from John's canan
And with a great noyse all the Playlander army
Fell backwards down the hill
And they met the other fruntgard of the rill army
And tumbeld it all about and shouted "you noty men
What are you trying to do?
You noty raskles
What do you think you are?
Shouting flee!
Ealce we will kill you all."
But John's men lathted at this
And John shouted "fire the canans
And your rifuls
And out with the standerd of luck.
Now men fight bravely
For you now
That the Playland army
is larger than ours."
The mane army came rushing up the hill
With Gold Kingy shouting
Ahoy! Ahoy!
Flee! Flee! becoz the mane army is coming up the hill.
And the Playlanders fled down the hill
In great disorder
And they tumbeld tumbold over one another
And shreeked, and got all mixt up . . .

One day some Playlander warships
Were sailing saling in the sea
And they saw a lovly lovely island
In the Mediterrranean sea
With blew blewe rivers in it
And buttful pine foristes in it
And they sailed to its shores
And when they got there
They saw a buttful lake lak among the montens
And there was one montenn witch they called Juhuhooa
Witch was larger than all the others
With lovly beards berds beairds in it
And buttfull beests that would come
When you called them
And buttfull cats that would come in your window
And lovly froats and flowres flowrs
Witch would flowr all the year round.

Jane Aiken

This poem was written by my sister Jane when she was seven, or there-abouts, and if she was not sure how to spell a word, she put in all the possible alternatives. I am grateful to her for letting me use part of it, and to the Huntington Library, San Marino, California, for providing a copy.

Note: The details about coal-mining conditions in the nineteenth century are factual, and I am grateful to the Caphouse Colliery Museum and the Halifax Industrial Museum for information acquired there. But of course workers were allowed to leave the mines at night.

The chapter headings are taken from the *Oxford Nursery Rhyme Book.*

The action of this story begins a few years after the end of my book *Dido and Pa,* and a few of the characters in that and earlier books are mentioned. But this is a separate story, and you don't need to have read my earlier books to follow it.

1

Oh where and oh where . . . ?

ON A CLEAR EVENING IN NOVEMBER, NEARLY A HUNDRED YEARS ago, frost lay like thick white fur over the ancient thorn trees on the crest of Blackheath Edge, some miles south of London town. The birds had long since hushed their faint murmurs. And farther south, in the forests of Chislehurst and Petts Wood, the last few leaves were dropping fast from giant oaks, and glistening with frost as they fell.

A tall woman, hoisting a pail of water from a well in a clearing of Blackheath Wood, turned her head sharply as she heard the faint wail of wolves in the distance.

She called, "Is? Are you close at hand, Is?"

A girl came running toward the well. She was small in build, but quick and alert. Her breeches and jacket were made of wolfskin, with the fur left on. She carried a large basket of chestnuts.

"What is it, Penny?"

Penny said, "You best get indoors. I heard wolves."

"Already?" Is stood still to listen. "Wonder what brings 'em out. They ain't often as early as this."

"Never mind that, you get indoors. Where's the blessed cat?"

"He's not far. Figgin, Figgin!"

A large, scrawny, bony cat came bounding through the frosted clumps of grass. In his mouth he carried a fieldmouse with long, dangling tail. At a louder howl from the wolves in the distance he dropped the mouse, ate it in two hasty bites, then snarled out a long, angry, defiant answer to the wolves' chorus:

"Morow—wow—wow—wow—wow!"

"Don't be silly, Figgin, you can't take on a whole wolf pack! Come on inside."

Cat and females vanished into a long, low barn that had been turned into a comfortable dwelling by the addition of a cot bed, table, stools made from sawn-up tree trunks, and a log fire that smoldered inside a knee-high ring of brick. The floor, too, was paved with brick. Two small windows were uncurtained, for who was there to look in?

Penny dumped her pail of water under a shelf that held bowls and pans, then barred the door with an oak beam which could be slid through two hoops. She was a lean, pale person, aged about thirty, with straw-colored hair tied in a tight knot, and a sour expression. She wore a sacking dress. The look on her face did not alter as she spoke to the girl—it was fixed by years of habit—but her voice was friendly enough as she said, "You and that dratted cat! You'd take on all the wolves of Kent if I was to let you." ·

"Pesky things! Hark—they're a-coming this way," from Is, intently listening. "They're after summat, I guess."

"Never mind them." Penny had started cutting up vegetables for soup. Is began to pull off the prickly outer casings of the chestnuts in her basket and toss them onto the fire, where they burned with a smoky crackle.

"Tell us a story, Pen, do," she said hopefully. "Tell the one about the harp o' fishbones. That's one o' my fav—"

"Hush!"

Penny held up a warning finger. The two stood silent. Figgin growled. They all strained their ears and, after a minute, began to catch an irregular thump-thump of footsteps on the hard ground—not those of wolves—which seemed to grow louder and then die away again, as if the runner were following an uncertain, frantic course: now coming closer, then veering off in a different direction.

Penny bit her lip and glanced doubtfully at the door.

"Tricky if we open up—we don't want to let *them* in."

"But if there's a poor cove out there in the wood with the wolves arter him—Pen, we *can't* jist leave him to be guzzled up!" urged Is.

From the far end of the barn she fetched a long, thin bundle of hazel twigs tied together with most of the leaves still on, and thrust the leafy tips into the fire until they began to blaze.

Penny, worried and frowning, rolled a tree stump close behind the door so that it could not be opened wide; then, from the hook where it hung on the wall, took down a blunderbuss, an ancient weapon, but clean and well greased.

It was already loaded.

Now they heard a voice outside the window that cried faintly, "Help! Does anybody hear? I'm in sore straits!"

"Is—you stand there by the wall!" ordered Penny. "Hold the poker and—when I say—shove the door beam back, while I ready myself here with the gun."

They took up their stations, Is against the wall with poker and blazing sheaf of twigs, Penny facing the point where the door would begin to open when Is thrust back the beam.

Outside, the snarls and howls of the wolves increased to a mad triumph; it seemed they had caught up with their quarry and were fighting each other for a chance to get at him.

"Now, Is!"

Is shoved back the beam, Penny dragged open the door.

A wolf catapulted inside, but was instantly driven out again by Is, twirling her burning faggot in its face. Then she knelt in the crack of the door, waving the improvised torch so as to give light while Penny stood guard over her with the gun, aimed high; next moment she fired, and in the startled silence that followed the blast, gave her order:

"*Quick*, Is—grab his arm, he's done in!"

Penny leaned the gun against the wall, Is hurled her fire-brand through the doorway among the disconcerted wolf pack, which sprang back a few paces; and their intended victim was hurriedly half dragged, half lifted through the narrow crack of doorway and left unceremoniously lying on the floor while Penny hastily refastened the door and Is, with rapid care, reloaded the gun. Not until this was done did they turn to examine the person they had rescued.

He proved to be a thin, worn-looking man with scanty gray hair and a wispy gray beard; his face was dreadfully pale and his clothes were mostly in tatters. He bled from a score of wounds on his neck, arms and back, some of them quite deep. He had fainted, probably from loss of blood.

"Marvel he's still living!" said Penny. "Looks as if they been arter him for miles, poor devil. Give us a hand, Is, to hoist him on the bed."

He was so thin and worn that they could easily lift him.

"Where are *we* going to sleep?" demanded Is, when he was stretched out on the bed, a wooden frame with cords and canvas slung across it.

"On the floor, where else? You *would* bring him in," Penny told her. "Save us, those wounds look nasty. Set a pan of water on the fire, Is. Too bad we've no brandy; he'll have to make do with mint tea. Drop in a bunch of leaves to steep, will you, while I get these togs off him. Queer, he don't look like a tramp, though he's so ragged."

"Hark at them outside!" said Is, balancing a copper pan across two logs.

The wolves, deprived of their supper, had not given up. Half a hundred of them must have been out there, howling and scrabbling at the wooden walls. Figgin the cat crouched on a high shelf, his fur all on end, his eyes rings of green fire with huge black pupils.

"Keep your fur on, Figgin, they can't get in. Pay them no mind; they'll give over by and by."

It took a long time to wash the stranger's dripping and filthy gashes; meanwhile he lay limply in a half sleep of total exhaustion.

At last Penny wrapped him in a man's old flannel shirt, worn but clean, which she took down from a nail on the wall.

"Lucky van Doon left it behind," she remarked with a sour quirk of her mouth.

"Poor Mr. van Doon," said Is. "D'you reckon he'll ever come back?"

"Leyden's a long way off," said Penny shortly. "And two years is a long time. Here, take the cup and spoon and try if you can get the cove to swaller."

With a good deal of trouble, Is managed to trickle a few spoonfuls of the hot aromatic brew down the man's throat.

"Reckon that's all he'll take," she said at length. "He jist wants to sleep."

"Oh well, leave him be, then. We might as well have our soup and get some rest."

They made up a pallet for themselves on the floor with two extra blankets and what spare clothes they had. The fire was banked to stay in till morning. Figgin came down from his high shelf and huddled against Is while she and Penny lay down to such rest as they might hope for, with the wolves clamoring outside and their uninvited guest moaning on the bed.

Toward morning the wolves finally gave up, and went in search of other prey. But the hurt man, instead of getting better, grew feverish and wild; he suddenly sat up with a flushed face and blazing eyes, which seemed to take in nothing of what lay around him.

"Arun! Arun!" he cried hoarsely. "Where are you? Your mother wants you! She is going to the shore for cockles! She wants you! Where are you, boy?"

"Be quiet! Lie down!" exclaimed Penny crossly. "Isn't it enough that we give up our bed to you, but you must keep us awake with your potherings? There's no Arran here, whosoever he be! And if you throw off the covers, you'll only take a chill. Lie down, do, for mercy's sake!"

But the stranger, ignoring Penny completely, continued to call for "Arun! Arun!" in heartbroken tones.

"His head's as hot as fire," muttered Penny, frowning, feeling his brow. "*And* his hands. And I don't like the look of those wounds. Wolf bites can turn right nasty. And some of them go deep."

"What can we do? We washed 'em as best we could," said Is.

"Even so. Reckon I oughta go for Doc Spiddle at Lewisham."

Is thrust out her lower lip, wholly disliking this plan.

"That's an hour's walk, Pen. Suppose the wolves is still around?"

"They'll not come back this way. They never do. And it'll be daylight in an hour."

"How'll we pay old Doc Spiddle?"

"I'll give him a couple of toys for his grandchildren," said Penny with a brief, sour smile, and she glanced at the shelves where rows of dolls and toy animals were stacked. "Dear knows we've plenty, the way sales are falling off."

"Maybe he won't come."

"He'll come. I'll roust him outa his dozy old bed. You mind the sick cove while I'm gone. Keep him covered, don't let him get chilled."

After wrapping herself up in various hoods and shawls, Penny set out. She did not take the gun, for it was too cumbrous to carry any distance, but armed herself with a knobbed, spiked stick of thornwood.

"Bar up after me and don't open to strangers."

"As if I would!" said Is.

When she had slid the beam across the door again and fed the fire till it blazed, Is settled herself cross-legged on a big tree-trunk stool and listened to the sounds of the night, with Figgin vigilant beside her.

"Arun, Arun!" pleaded the sick man again, imploringly.

"There bain't no Arran here, mister; there's only me. Here, swig a mouthful of mint tea."

She tilted the cup to his lips. This time his eyes focused, and he seemed to take in the fact of her existence.

"No more!" he said faintly. "That's enough. Who are you? Where am I? There were wolves—they mauled me badly—I ran for hours, it seemed . . ."

He stared about the place, puzzled.

"You're on Blackheath Edge, mister."

"I was looking for Arun."

"There's no one of that name in these parts. There's no one but me and my sister Penny."

"He ran away. My boy Arun. He ran away a year ago."

"Why look for him on Blackheath Edge?"

"It was London. He had spoken of—threatened to run to London. Where godless songs are sung. I have walked to London over thirty times—every second week—since he ran away; I have stood by Charing Cross, asking all the passersby if they have beheld him."

Is stared at the stranger with scorn and pity. She had spent the first nine years of her life in London, scurrying about its crowded streets, and could imagine the total unconcern that such an inquiry would receive from the hustling, jostling mob around Charing Cross.

"Why ask there, mister?"

"Charing Cross is the center of London, I have heard. Is it not so? Sooner or later, somebody there must have seen my son."

"Humph." Is did not argue this, but asked, "Did he have a trade, your boy?"

"He—that is—we had apprenticed him to a wig-maker. An honest, *useful* trade. But he was not grateful!" declared the sick man in trembling, bewildered tones. "In ten years he would have become a journeyman, in fifteen a master wig-maker . . . Who knows, he could have made wigs for the Duke of Kent—even for His Majesty, perhaps."

"Wigs?" said Is doubtfully. "Does the king wear a wig?"

"The boy left a note. He wished for songs. My pouch—" The man looked about him anxiously.

Among his tattered clothes had been a small leather satchel. Is passed it to him and he fumbled with the strap. After rummaging through its contents he pulled out a scrap of gray paper—damp, now, and stained with blood.

Is, who had been taught reading by Penny, slowly made out the unevenly printed words on it.

> "Breath is
>   for speech
>   to teach
> Silence
>   is death
> Wigs
>   are for pigs."

"Did your boy write that?" asked Is, much struck.

"Ay. Our silence, it seems, distressed him. We belong, you must understand, my wife and I, to the Silent Sect. But Arun always wished to ask questions."

"Can't blame him," muttered Is. "You gotta find out. Don't you?"

"All our acquaintances, in Folkestone, are of the Silent Sect. Amos Furze, the wig-maker, is one, of course—Chief Elder. They are devout, good folk," said the stranger chidingly, and coughed. Is passed him the mug of mint tea.

"So your boy run off to the Smoke, to get the answers to his questions? He wanted *songs,* you said?"

"His mother has wept her eyes out, every night since. When he was at home he could *not* be prevented from singing in his bedrooom—*singing!*—though we told him, over and over, that song is an offense against the Holy Quiet. Now, Ruth wishes that she had not reprimanded him."

"Eh, me," said Is. "Reckon you'd best give up hunting for that boy, mister. He'll not be back."

"Child! Do not say so! Ruth would never lift up her head again. She had—has—a fondness for the lad. Of course she would never, never show it."

"Why not?"

"That is not our way."

Is made no comment but, getting up, put more wood on the fire. Then she said, "Could you take a bite, mister? Soup? Mouthful o' bread?"

He shook his head weakly.

"No victuals. I could not swallow bread . . ."

"What fetched you up on Blackheath Edge, then?" asked Is, after a pause, in which, far far away, they heard the faint, triumphant cry of a cock, on some outlying farm where woods gave way to plowland.

"I fancy my younger brother once dwelled hereabouts. Long ago when he first married. In truth I do not know if he is still living—it is many years since we communicated. Our minds were not in tune. But—having failed yet again in my quest—I bethought me to seek him out and take counsel of him. He was a man shrewd in the ways of the city. And he knew many songs. My boy might—"

"What's his name, your brother?" Is inquired, yawning as she dribbled more tea into the mug.

"Abednego Twite."

Is let fall the pan from which she had been pouring. A puddle of green tea spread over the bricks.

At this moment a sharp rap on the door made itself heard. Penelope's voice called: "Hey, in there! Open up!"

Is ran to unbar the door and let in her sister. Ice-cold air came in as well, like a wrapping round Penny. The frost on the ground lay thicker than ever.

"Deliver us! That's sharp!"

Penny knelt by the hearth to warm her blue hands. "Lucky you kept a good fire up, Is."

"Where's the doc, then?"

"Had a lying-in at Hilly Fields. Said he'll be along by and by. *In* his own good time," said Penny, with a lift of the lip. "But he gave me this flask of tincture for the cove." She got up and walked toward the bed. "How's he been? How are you, mister?"

"Pen," hissed Is, pulling her back, "that chap's our *uncle!*"

Pen slowly turned round.

"How d'you figure that?"

"He said he was looking for his brother, Abednego Twite. There couldn't be *two*."

"He's a mite late," remarked Penny dryly, after a moment or two.

She approached the stranger.

"Mister? Here's some jossop for you, from the sawbones." She uncorked the little flask and obliged the stranger to swallow a mouthful. When he had done so, and lain down again, not visibly benefited by it: "You say your brother was Abednego Twite?" she demanded, in a voice that entirely lacked any warmth.

"Ay, that's him. Abednego Twite the hoboy player. He makes up sinful songs as well. Sometimes I believe he calls himself Desmond. But music is the devil's voice," muttered the sick man. "Only in total silence may we hear the Word of Truth. Why, daughter, are you acquainted with the man Twite, my brother?"

"Only since I was born. He was my father," said Penny shortly. "But he's dead. Some years past. The wolves got him. *And* it was a fitting end for him," she added in an undertone.

The stranger did not seem surprised, or much moved, by this news. He sighed.

"Dead; doubtless with his sins upon him. He was not a right-thinking man. So you are my niece then. Dido, is it?"

"Penelope," she snapped. "And this here's another—so far's we know, that is. Is."

"Is," he murmured. "That would be from her great-grandmother—Isabett. From Brittany, she was. My boy Arun will therefore be your cousin."

"He lost his boy," Is muttered to Penny. "Ran off to Lunnon. Liked songs, the boy did. Been a-searching for 'im ever since."

"A lot more runs off than ever comes back," commented Penny. "Why the pize did you get the notion my dad might help you, mister—Uncle? My dad never helped anybody in his whole life unless it was by mistake."

"Abednego was a musician," weakly explained the injured man. "My boy Arun liked to make up songs—ungodly songs."

"So you thought he—I see. Then you must be our uncle Hosiah from Dover."

"Folkestone," he fretfully corrected her. "Can you—will you find my boy Arun for me? His mother is so—is so grievously distressed. Much more than is reasonable, I fear. And what can I do? Thirty times I have walked to Charing Cross and back—asking—asking—"

He began to cough, and did not stop until Penny had given him some more of the doctor's mixture.

"Perhaps—" he gasped, "perhaps the boy went in search of his other uncle—the one in the north country, up in Blastburn."

"We got another uncle up north? I never knew; Dad wasn't a one for family connections. But why would the boy do so?" snapped Penny. "Boy runs off from home, he don't run to his *uncle*. 'Sides, the north country is all foreign land these days—cut off. You can't get up that way no more. The boundary's closed. Didn't you know that?"

Hosiah Twite did not seem to follow her. He repeated weakly, "Will you find my boy Arun? For his poor mother? Who is brought so low?"

His eyes fell on Is, who was offering him another mug of mint tea. He said, with a faint flicker of hope, "*You* would be able to seek him out for me, I feel sure, my child. For—now I come to observe you in the dawn light—you have quite a look of my boy Arun, indeed you do—"

He stopped speaking, and a look of queer concentration came over his face.

He said, once again, "Find him! I beg you, I beg you to find him!" then coughed a little blood, lay back, and died.

"There! Now I've bin and fetched the doctor here all for

nothing," said Penny crossly, as a horse's hoofbeats began to be heard in the wood outside.

Journal of Is

Me an Penny as bin R guing 4 days sins we berried Uncle Hose. (That was a hard old job count o the ground bein so friz.) We R guing about me findin the boy. I sez you gotta pay heed to sum wun when they dyin. Pen sez No one ever dun her a Good turn why should she oblije a Cove she never saw in her hole life? Well I sez Ill go, you helped me Pen and tort me ritin and readin, now Ill find Unk Hoses Boy. Pen aint best pleezed. Spose I baint here wen U gets bak she sez. Spose I dont get bak at al I sez. So we R gues 4 days an days. In the end I sez well Ill go for a munth. Pen sez oh very well N she rrites to Misiis Hose Twite in Folks Town a tellin her Unk Hoze took an dyed in R house an Im alookin for his boy Arn in Lunnon.

2

As I was going by Charing Cross
I saw a black man upon a black horse . . .

WHEN IS FIRST SET OUT FOR LONDON, IT WAS WITH A HEAVY heart. First, there was the parting from Figgin. He had been used to accompanying Is wherever she went in the woods and, because of his quick hearing and sharp eyes, had often warned her about distant dangers. Now he could not understand why he was forbidden to come with her, and started off with her several times, in his regular way, until at last he had to be shut up in the house with Penny; the sound of his indignant caterwaulings followed Is down the track. This was hard enough; but Penny, too, had been in a bad mood at being left. She did not consider this a sensible errand.

"You'll never find that boy," she had said harshly, over and over. "And if you do, what then? He won't agree to go back. And his da's dead—his ma, too, like enough, by now. Folks *don't* go back—not once they've left."

Thinking of Mr. van Doon, who had stayed with them in the forest for a couple of years, had then set off to look for his lost family in Leyden and had never returned, Is could see that this was probably true in most cases. But she repeated stubbornly, "I promised, Pen. You make a promise to a cove what's dying, you gotta keep it."

"Well *go*. Go, then, and see if I care." And Penny, pinching her lips together, had rapidly stitched a doll's wig onto a bald pink crown.

Walking down the north-facing slope of Blackheath Edge, Is looked at the distant smoky skyline without pleasure. London seemed like an immense gray shroud lying over the land ahead of her.

Is had spent her first nine years in the city and had been totally wretched: poor, overworked, abused, always hungry, dressed in greasy rags. Her life there now seemed like a bad dream, compared to her present freedom in the woods and Penny's sharp, but not ill-natured, company. Still, she had made one or two friends in London, and hoped to find them again.

Having crossed the river Thames by Tower Bridge, she turned eastward toward Wapping and Shadwell, threaded a network of narrow alleys near Shadwell Dock, going past roperies, tanyards, breweries, and wharves, until she reached a large warehouse. Here, tapping on a small hatch door set into a great gate, she was asked her business.

By now, dusk was falling.

"I'm a-looking for Dido Twite!"

At once the door was thrown open. The big, cheerful, cross-eyed boy who let her in studied Is carefully, and then, grinning, said, "*I* know who you are! You're the liddle 'un who used to live with Dido's da near Farthing Fields. But you've grown plenty since them days. *Is*—that was your name."

"Still Is."

His, she remembered, was Wally Greenaway, and he had kept a coffee stall in Wapping High Street. He also had grown, was now the size of a man, but still cross-eyed.

He nodded at her in a friendly fashion and said, "But you're out of luck, young 'un. Dido's gone out o' the country."

"Out o' the country? Where to?"

"Oh, not for good," he said soothingly, observing her disappointment. "Went to see friends in Nantucket. She'll be back by spring. But come in, anyways. We can find ye a bed —my dad'll put you up. He'll be right glad to hear your voice."

Is considered.

"Thanks, cully, I'd be right pleased. For a night, anyway. I'm looking for a boy."

Wally's face clouded with a queer, troubled look. He said, "Best ye come inside and talk to my dad about whatever it is. No sense telling your business to the whole of Shadwell." And he glanced about the muddy docks, which seemed empty and quiet enough at this hour of the evening.

Drawing Is inside, he shut the door, and led her through warm, spice-scented darkness.

"Go carefully, there's a deal of barrels and crates everywhere. Just you follow me."

His hand drew her on. Sometimes she stubbed her toe on a chest, or tripped over a rope. Ahead, she began to see the glow of a fire, and then a very large, silent man sitting by it on a massive seat, fashioned to fit him out of a huge cask.

"Guess who's here, Dad," said Wally. " 'Tis young Is, what used to live with Dido and Mr. Twite."

Wally's dad could not see, Is remembered; he was blind. But he put out a hand the size of a saddle—and hard as one —saying kindly, "Any kin of Dido's is welcome as daffs in spring. Come and sit ye down, my dearie, and Wally'll fetch ye a bite and sup."

After providing bread, ham, and apples, Wally said, "The liddle 'un's looking for a boy, Dad."

At these words, Is noticed the same doubtful, grave expression settle for a moment on the large, calm countenance of Mr. Greenaway.

"A *boy*, ye say, daughter? What boy would that be?"

Is explained her errand. Father and son were silent for a moment or two.

Then Mr. Greenaway said, "The Baron'll be here in a brace of shakes, Wal. I wonder now . . ."

Wally frowned. "Dad! You can't think—"

A tap was heard on the outer door.

Mr. Greenaway cocked his head.

"That's him now. I reckon this is a Sending, Wally. Without any question at all. A Sending. Go let him in, boy. And take a torch along."

Shaking his head, Wally obeyed. While he was threading his way through the contents of the great dark storage place, Mr. Greenaway said to Is, "Let me have your hand again for a moment, my dearie."

Puzzled, Is laid her small paw once again in his great leathery palm. With fingers the size of balusters he carefully and delicately traced the lines on her hand, then touched the tips of her fingers in turn. Finally he said, " 'Tis just as I thought. You were Sent here, my liddle 'un."

"I was?" said Is.

"Ay. Where did ye come from? Today?"

"Blackheath Edge."

"There be a line, straight from there to here, my maid. Ah, and another one, going on northward—"

"*Northward?*"

Now Wally came back, carefully leading a slight, spare, white-headed gentleman who was all dressed in black velvet. He looked, Is thought, inexpressibly sad. Wally and his father both treated the visitor with signs of the greatest respect, settling him in a comfortable seat, padding it with hanks of cotton, arranging a footstool for his feet (in silver-buckled shoes) and supplying him with a mug of apple punch which had been warmed by having a red-hot poker thrust into it.

"Who's the wee lassie?" he inquired, but without any great interest.

He spoke, Is noticed, with a Scottish accent.

"She's come to us out of Kent. We'll speak of her later." And Mr. Greenaway began putting slow, careful questions to the visitor about his health and state of mind. His voice was so kind, so deep, wise, and concerned, that Is thought, I wisht Penny had a cove like that to talk to. That's what she needs . . .

Then, being extremely tired from her long day's walk, Is, without at all meaning to do so, dropped off to sleep, curled up on the warm hearthstones with her head pillowed on a bale of sacking.

Mr. Greenaway smiled, tilting his head.

"The young 'un's all tuckered out. We'll let her rest

awhile. Now tell me, sir, have ye heard any news from the boy Simon—His Grace the Dook?"

"He reached Bremen in safety and began to make his inquiries—I have heard no more since then."

"And ye are doing the breathing exercises as I bade ye—fifty times in front of an open window facing south?"

"Och, aye—but my heart's no' in it . . ."

The quiet voices above her head, talking about things that did not seem to concern her, wove into her dreams like the pattern on a bed hanging, and finally woke Is, when Mr. Greenaway remarked, in a grave, sad tone, "Ay, dear knows, a lost child is the hardest care of all."

At that, Is started up, still half under the spell of a dream in which she had been searching through a pitch-dark forest.

"The lost boy!" she cried. "Arran! Yes! We have to find him before the floodwater comes. The whole country is going to tilt sideways—"

Then she realized that she had been talking nonsense, related to her dream, and stopped, much abashed. But the unknown white-haired gentleman was staring at her with a strange fixety.

"*You* know this, my child? About my lost boy?"

"N-n-no, sir," she stammered. "*Your* lost boy? No—I was having a dream about my cousin Arran—"

"Arun? She is looking for a boy called Arun?"

Now the white-haired stranger was even more intent.

"Ay, my—sir. She is that."

"There are not many boys of that name."

"Not that I ever come across," agreed Wally.

"My Davie had a friend of whom he sometimes spoke. Not a school friend. A lad that he had met in—in London.

Arun was the name. A boy, he said, who sometimes made up songs—"

Songs? Is pricked up her ears. Now it was her turn to look intent. Uncle Hosiah had told of his boy singing songs, rebelling against the Holy Silence.

"She is seeking her lost cousin," Mr. Greenaway said gently, above her head. "She made a promise to her dying uncle to find him—a promise that she feels she must hold to . . ."

There was a long silence, which puzzled Is, while the two men and Wally considered. Then Wally said, as if someone had argued with him, "She's so *little*."

"That'd be in her favor, I reckon," said his father. "Nobody'd suspicion *her*. Special if she's a-hunting for her cousin."

The white-haired man said thoughtfully, "She is the sister of Dido Twite?"

"So we understand, sir."

Now all three of them were smiling, though the smile on the face of the guest passed away quickly, like the last gleam before a storm.

"That says much in her favor," he remarked, but then added, "Just the same, it is a heavy burden to lay on a child."

"That's what *I* say!" struck in Wally.

But his father said patiently, "No one *but* a child will do."

"Ay—that's so, indeed," sighed the white-haired man. "And yet, my mind misgives me sair—"

Now Is became impatient. "Beg parding, but what the *clunch* is all this about? You talking about me? Then will you kindly tell me what's up? You know summat about Arun? Is that his name? Arun Twite?"

"Not about him, no, my dearie," said Mr. Greenaway.

"Except that he perhaps was a friend o' this gentleman's son. But, ye see, there's other boys been lost as well. And gals, as well. And his m—this gentleman here, his own boy has gone missing, and he's grieved to death about it, as ye may well guess."

"That's too bad, mister," said Is with ready sympathy. "I'm right sorry for ye. But—I reckon boys is allus liable to take a fancy to cut and run."

"But, you see, my child," said the white-haired man heavily, "it is worse than that. More than just my own son, though that is like to be a mortal blow to me, since his mother—" He stopped, took a firm grip of his voice, and began again. "There are *too many* boys lost. Altogether too many."

"In fact," explained Wally, "more'n *half the kids in Lunnon town* is missing."

"You're gamming!" Is gaped at him in disbelief. "You've gotta be!"

"No. 'Tis so," confirmed Mr. Greenaway gravely.

"And," went on Wally, who seemed to have decided that he was the best person to explain matters to Is, "besides naturally wanting to get the kids back, besides his m—the Baron's own trouble about his boy, he's afeered that a panic might soon start—if folks get putting their heads together and counting how many's gone."

"Where?" demanded Is. "Where can they all have gone?"

"Ah. That's the puzzle. We can guess. But we don't know for sure. Nor how they go."

Is remembered a story—one of the hundreds that had been told her by Penny—about a wonderful piper, who lured all the children away from a town . . .

"Hanover," she murmured.

"No, ducky," said Wally. "Not Hanover. Hanover and this land is friendly these days. Ever since King Richard married Princess Adelaide of Thuringia—"

The white-haired man flinched. Wally went on quickly and gently. "Everybody was right sorry when she died. 'Twas a dreadful pity. Anyhows, the Hanoverians are our pals nowadays. *They* wouldn't nab our young 'uns. Though Simon Battersea has gone over there, just to make sure young Davie didn't take a fancy to cross the German Water just for a caper, like. But what's more likely is that those coves up in the Northlands of *this* country—"

"Northlands." Is recalled her uncle Hosiah referring to another uncle in the north country, in Blastburn.

"In the north," she repeated slowly.

"You know?" said Wally. "You been hearing the news, living hid away in those woods, in Kent? You heard that the folk in the Northlands have cut loose and made theirselves into a separate kingdom? And won't have naught to do with us no more? You heard that?"

"Yus. We heard summat about it, from peddlers and such," said Is. "But—would King Richard *let* them? Couldn't he stop them?"

She felt the white-haired man flinch again.

"He couldn't, duck," Wally said quickly. "He'd a peck of trouble himself at the time, acos of the death of Queen Adelaide and the Chinese wars, and a row of bad harvests. And then, they are rich, up in those northern parts—most o' the coal mines and all the iron foundries and potteries are up there. So 'twas a blow when all the north-country shires banded together and said they wouldn't have no more dealings wi' the south. And now they call theirselves the Kingdom of Humberland. And the town what used to be Blastburn has had its name changed to Holdernesse."

"Blastburn," murmured Is. "That's where my uncle lives. Or did live. So t'other uncle said."

A quick look of interest flashed over the faces of her listeners.

"Your *uncle*? Would that be your father's brother?"

"Reckon so," said Is. "Ma—if Mrs. Bloodvessel was my ma—had no kin. But I never met this cove. Don't even know his name. My uncle Hosiah spoke of him—the cove what died. Arun's father."

"If she were attempting to visit an uncle in those parts—that would lend plausibility . . ." murmured the gentleman.

Is wanted to know more about the northern shires.

"Who's boss up there, then?"

"They have a leader called—so we understand—Gold Kingy."

"Gold Kingy!" Is exclaimed. "Well I never! What imperence!"

A faint wry smile flitted across the face of the visitor.

At that moment a knock was heard on the warehouse door. Wally made haste to answer it, and Is heard him mutter to the would-be-caller, "Not tonight, Sam. Baron Renfrew's here."

The door shut again and Sam, whoever he was, went away.

By the time that Wally returned, Is had been putting two and two together.

"What you think is, those coves up there, in the northern parts, are waylaying the young 'uns from hereabouts, or 'ticing and snatching 'em?"

"That could be so," said Mr. Greenaway cautiously. "It'd be one explanation."

"But you got no clue at all?"

"Ne'er a clue," said the gentleman called Baron Renfrew. "Our police agents have made countless inquiries—so have the Bow Street Runners—we have placed detective officers all over London, but a' to nae purpose at a'. One of our canniest agents believed he was on to something at last—but he was found, puir fellow, last month, stabbed and dying in Kingsway. All he could gasp out was *Euston Green*."

"Croopus," said Is quietly.

A thoughtful silence fell, then the Baron began, "So you see, my bairn, why I feel this is no ploy for a young lass to get imbrangled in—" when he was interrupted by Is.

"Begging your parding, sir, mister, but that's jist what it is. *Now* I twig your lay," she said to Mr. Greenaway. "Now I see why you sez no one but a young 'un 'ud do. If a grown feller ast too many questions, he get a shiv through the gizzard. Like the cove that was found in Kingsway. But if *I* was to ast—for instince—I'd jist get took off to where the others was took."

"Ay, that's it," said the Baron unhappily. "And you might then vanish and share their fate, whitever it be—and we cannot but fear sairly for them."

"Ah, but," said Is in triumph, "*I'd* have all me wits about me, wouldn't I? And *I* ain't no gull, nor no greenpea, I can tell you that! *I've* cut me wisdoms! Anyone who lived around Farden Fields and Shadwell Docks when they was a kinchin —let alone old Ma Bloodvessel—is up to all the jigs. *Now* I see why you reckons I was Sent," she said to Mr. Greenaway, "and I reckon you wasn't wrong, neether, mister. I can look for me cousin Arun and this gent's boy at one and the same time. Might I ask, sir, what was your boy's name?" she politely addressed the white-haired gentleman, who gave a slight start, and after a moment's hesitation, answered.

"He—that is to say, we used to call him Davie. But, of course, who knows . . ."

"He might've changed his monacker? Call hisself summat else up there?"

"Perhaps. Yes."

Is sat brooding, staring into the fire, elbows on knees, chin on fists. The other three sat waiting in silence.

At last she said, "The okkard business, as I see it, is how, once I've been 'ticed off, how I'm to get word back to you. Nobody comes and goes betwixt here and Humberland no more?"

"No, my dearie. 'Tis all closed off, like as if 'twas a foreign land. They've builded a great wall, and where there's rivers, they've blown up most o' the bridges, and the others is guarded. But there *are* boats, ships, that still ply along the coast. And many sailormen are my friends," said Mr. Greenaway. "Contraband goods will allus find a market."

"Ah, that's a thought," agreed Is. "If I could get a missidge to a jack tar on a boat . . . What *kind* of kids is missing?"

"Kind?"

"Yobs or toffs? Rich or poor?"

"Since his—" began Wally warmly, but the visitor interrupted in his soft Scots voice.

"Every kind, my child. Of the poor children who throng the streets we do not know how many are gone; but we do know that now many from weel-kenspeckit families are missing."

Maybe they got a monster up there, reflected Is, recalling

one of Penny's tales about a glass dragon with three heads that needed to be fed a victim every day. She did not mention this theory, however, for fear of upsetting the poor Scottish gentleman. She was busy, too, trying to work out why his voice seemed faintly familiar. Had she heard it before? *Where* could she have heard it before?

"You will undertake this task, then, my lassie? You will search for these boys?"

"I was a-going to anyways, wasn't I?" retorted Is.

The visitor rose to his feet, and the Greenaways instantly jumped up.

"Will you remain with good Mr. Greenaway another night, my bairnie? I've a notion to give ye a token by which my boy—should you chance to come across him—will ken for certain that ye come from me." His voice wavered, then strengthened. "Also—also it may perhaps help you in trouble."

"Or may do jist the opposite," Wally muttered, but only Is heard him. Next moment he was carefully piloting the visitor to the outer door amid friendly good-night greetings.

When Wally returned, "Who *was* that feller?" demanded Is. "Somehow—I dunno why—his voice put me in mind of Mr. van Doon, what used to lodge with me and Penny."

The two others gave this some thought. Then—

"She'll have to know," said Wally.

"I reckon so," agreed his father. "Daughter, that was His Majesty."

"The king himself!" breathed Is. "Old King Dick! Well I never!"

"Since his wife died he don't have no fancy for public doings," explained Wally. "But he's took a rare shine to my da, likes to come around every week or so for a chinwag.

And—now his boy's run off too—there ain't much heart left at all in the poor cove."

"Reckon he's just pining away," agreed Mr. Greenaway, sighing. "So you see, my dearie, there's a rare need to seek out that young rapscallion. First, to keep his poor da from dying—"

"And 'cos he's the prince? The next king? Croopus, I should justabout think so. You'd think his dad'd have all the army out searching—offer half his crown—summat like that."

"No, child. He daren't. He daren't let it be known that the prince is lost. For then there'd be threats, once it's out—demands for ransom, real or false."

"But how could he jist *go*?"

"He always liked to dress as an ordinary boy, go to an ordinary school, have friends who weren't lords or princes, but just boys he met in the street."

"Same as his dad," commented Is. "I get it. The poor gemman's in a real fix. Can't even stand asking at Charing Cross, like Uncle Hose."

"But if the boy is not found soon—and suppose His Majesty should die of grief, which I reckon could happen . . ."

"What did the queen die of?" Is demanded.

"Oh, she died of measles, poor lady, before the boy vanished. She was a deal younger than the king—he was very fond of her. He's a lonesome chap."

"Lucky he can doddle round here for a bit of cheer," remarked Is, and gave a great yawn. Suddenly she felt lonely herself, and missed Figgin dreadfully.

"You're fit for bed, daughter," said Mr. Greenaway kindly, and Wally expertly prepared her a nest of tow, packed into a sail slung between two joists. "Where," as he explained, "the rats won't bother ye."

Journal of Is

Well, fancy me bein ast to find His Nab's boy. Fat ol chans, I rekin. Like lookin fer a woodlows in a timber yard. Wally an his da seem rite desint coves too bad I kint stop here but seems I gotto go on Northards. Wonder how? On a ship mebbe. Hope Figin don't pine & Pen feeds him enuf. That poor king lookt reel sad.

3

Boys and girls come out to play
The moon is shining as bright as day
Up the ladder and over the wall
A halfpenny loaf will serve us all . . .

IS, NEXT DAY, WAS EAGER TO SET OUT ON HER JOURNEY TO THE north country, and somewhat irked that both Greenaways, father and son, insisted that she must remain with them until the king had sent around his token.

Meanwhile, though, it was agreed that she might as well roam the streets of London, keeping her eyes and ears wide open, dropping questions here and there about her cousin Arun, picking up any hints or clues that might possibly come her way relating to the unknown fate of the missing children.

As Uncle Hose had done, she began at Charing Cross. There she loitered for several hours, studying all the people who hurried by, on foot, on horseback, in cabs, or in coaches.

One thing struck her at once, and this was how very, very

few children there were to be seen, in comparison with the days when she had lived in London. She recalled then, that on her household errands through the streets, children had been everywhere, swarming like ants: ragged sharp-eyed brats, the active ones earning pennies by holding horses, or sweeping the mud from street crossings, running messages, picking pockets, shouting their small, shabby wares, bundles of matches or bunches of cress; and sick, shrunken, starved ones sitting listlessly on doorsteps or curled under bridges, waiting for death to come and solve their problems.

But now all these seemed to have vanished altogether. In London there were hardly any children visible; the hurrying crowds in the street were all adults, going about their adult affairs.

Croopus, where have all the kinchins got to? Is asked herself. It sure is a mystery! Funny no one's wondered about it sooner. Nobody cares above half, I reckon. Streets look tidier without kids all about. Some folks likes it better that way, I daresay.

"You seen a boy called Arun Twite, mister—missis?" she demanded over and over, but very few people even troubled to reply.

Asking, listening, watching, Is drifted northward, up Charing Cross Road, up Tottenham Court Road. Near here, in a small public garden by Whitefields Tabernacle, she found a street fair; if two or three meager stalls and a shabby Punch and Judy could be said to constitute a street fair. Dingy flags and bunting hung between the stalls, and a doleful-looking man played alternately on a set of panpipes and a tabor. The stalls offered a few playthings for sale: whistles, tops, hoops, balls, one or two dolls and toy animals. None of them so well made, Is noticed with a critical eye, as those produced by Penny and herself. But she remembered, now, Penny's recent grumbles about the fall in the sale of toys. And no wonder, thought Is, if more than half the young 'uns are missing.

The Punch play was drawing to a close; Punch had murdered most of his family and was singing a loud, boastful song of self-praise:

> "Ha ha ha, hee hee hee,
> Oh, Mr. Punch, what a clever boy you be!"

Is recognized the tune as one made up by her father: "The Day Before the Day Before May Day." Many of his songs were still to be heard about the streets and countryside, sung or whistled or chanted. Funny how tunes can stop in folks' heads long after the person who made them up is dead and gone, thought Is; and funny how he could make up such gladsome tunes when he hisself was such a no-good.

At this moment, under cover of the music, she heard a voice whisper sharply in her ear: *"How about a trip to Playland? Kids get a real good time in Playland!"*

Startled, Is glanced back over her shoulder. A crowd of twenty or so people had collected in the little space; which of these could have spoken to her? It had sounded like a man's voice. Several men stood near her. Was it the merry little character with black curls and whiskers, a velvet waistcoat and kerseymere breeches? Or the tall, lugubrious fellow in a striped jacket who looked like a waiter from a tavern? Or the man in a leather apron who offered to grind people's knives and scissors at the top of his lungs, as he wove among the crowd? Or the thin white-haired man who stood near Is with a bundle of books under his arm?

"Where's Playland, mister?" Is asked him, but he gave her a severe look and replied sternly,

"*Playland?* There is no such place. And a child your age ought to be at work, not idling about asking foolish questions in the public street."

A boy caught her eye and seemed as if he were about to say something, but the Punch show came to its end just then, the crowd quickly scattered, and the boy vanished from view.

Is began to make her way back to Shadwell, taking a circuitous route by Seven Dials and Piccadilly Circus, along the Strand, past St. Paul's Cathedral and the Tower of London. Once again, as she stood in a crowd near Piccadilly, watching the antics of a man walking on stilts, she heard a soft murmur in her ear: *"How about a trip to Playland, eh?"* But, as before, when she looked around, nobody near at hand seemed likely to be the person who had spoken.

Still, she felt that she had been given some clue at least. Tired, but not disheartened, she went back to Mr. Greenaway's warehouse.

While she was out, a messenger had brought the token from St. James's Palace.

"It's might puny," observed Is, studying it without excitement.

"All the easier to carry on your travels," pointed out Wally.

The token was a tiny disc, not much bigger than a silver fourpenny piece, made from slivers of black and green stone, cunningly carved and fitted together, so that on one side of the disc appeared a green lion rampant on a black background, and on the reverse side a black lion set against green. Mr. Greenaway, feeling and turning it most delicately with his enormous rugged fingers, remarked that it felt to him as if it were carved out of jade and jet, a wondrous clever piece of work, not fashioned in this land, he'd reckon, but in Chiny or Peru, some such place where they'd craftsmen that'd take years over a job like this.

"If I was you, dearie, I'd sew it, case an' all, into the hem of your jacket, where it'll be safe and won't slip out, accidental-like, into somebody's view. For in the parts you might be off to, jist having a token like that in your keeping might go agin ye."

"Might be the end of her," said Wally gloomily, frying sausages for supper.

Is thought Mr. Greenaway's advice was worth following, and unpicked an inch of jacket lining. While she was sewing the disc, in its tiny chamois-leather pouch, safely out of sight, she asked, "Mr. Greenaway, did you ever hear tell of Playland?"

Mr. Greenaway shook his head, but Wally said at once, "Don't you remember, Is, there used to be a song of your da's that went, 'If I could find my way to Playland, you'd never see me no more; Playland, the happy and gay land, where nobody is poor, and no apple ever has a core . . .'?"

"I'd forgotten," said Is slowly, "but now I remember. Is there really sich a place?"

"Not as I ever heard tell on."

Wally served the sausages, for simplicity's sake, on a slice of bread.

"Best eat hearty while you can, young 'un," he said.

Mr. Greenaway munched his in silence with a troubled expression on his face. It was plain that, while from various points of view he felt it proper for Is to undertake this errand, he was not very happy about the plan.

"I sent a message to His Majesty," he said, "by the chap as brought the token, to say as how, if you don't come back—suppose some mischief was to come to ye—your sister Penny should be took care of. Benefit, like."

"Care of Penny?" said Is, surprised. "Why, she's allus taken pretty sharp care of herself. There's not many—and that goes for wolves, too—as comes out on top of Penny. Why should she be took care of?"

"Well, dearie, as you're, in a manner o' speaking, doing a job of work for His Grace, 'tis only right that you, or anyway your kin, should be the better for it."

"I haven't *found* His Grace's boy yet," Is pointed out. "And may never do. Still"—thinking it over—"that ain't a bad notion. Poor old Penny-lope hain't had much luck up to now. The Dutchman went off and left her . . . Mind you" —bursting out laughing—"I'd be sorry for the chap as took Penny the Benefit. He's like to get his ears trimmed."

But still, it gave Is a feeling of comfort, as she climbed into her hammock, to think that Penny, who had argued so fiercely against her going and been so surly on leave-taking, might possibly derive some good from the business. You never knew, after all.

Is fell asleep, and instantly began to dream about a black, black forest, with water trickling among the roots of the trees. And there were voices calling for help . . .

On the third day of her wanderings about the streets of London, Is heard Playland mentioned again. She was at Covent Garden market, very early, before daybreak, watching great trays of fruit and flowers being unloaded from the carters' wagons, sniffing with relish at the fresh, earthy scent of leaves and roots, which, for an hour or so, prevailed over that of the acrid, coaly, pea-soup fog thickening the air and making it hard to see across the street.

A few children were to be seen hereabouts, running across the slippery cobbles with baskets and trays balanced on their heads, weaving among the sharp-faced buyers from fruit stalls and taverns and hotels.

Is had edged among the group surrounding a hot-pie booth. She was listening to the shouts of the pie-man: "Hot eels! All hot! Penny pies! Penny Jennies! Trotters here a farden!" when she heard a voice in her ear:

"Hey—missy!" whispered the voice. *"How about a ride on the Playland Express?"*

And, at the same moment, she felt something gently slipped into her pocket.

She looked around swiftly, but nobody near at hand seemed to be displaying the least interest in her.

Drifting around a corner into a narrow alleyway, Is carefully investigated the contents of her pocket. Her first expectation was that she had been used as a cat's-paw for some stolen article that a pickpocket needed to get rid of in a hurry.

But, to her great surprise, what she found was a species of wafer or pancake, very popular just at that season, and to be bought off pastry-cooks' barrows all over London. They were sold in stacks called Quires of Paper, or singly, at a cost of about a ha'penny apiece.

Written across this particular pancake in pink sugar-icing letters was the message: PLAYLAND EXPRESS EUSTON GREEN MIDNITE TONITE.

"Croopus!" said Is, much impressed.

Although strongly tempted to eat the pancake (they were

delicious, she had heard, flavored with orange and nutmeg), she slid it back into her pocket, glanced about her warily to make certain that she was not the target for anyone's special attention, and then set off, at a casual-seeming yet rapid saunter, for Shadwell.

There, in the High Street, she found Wally at his usual post, selling tea, coffee, and hot rolls. Even here, in Shadwell, the children who had once been in charge of the other market stalls, offering apples, whelks, household articles, and cheap clothing, had all been replaced by adults.

"Toss you for a mug of hot!" Is said pertly to Wally.

"No charge, matey, it's on the house!" And he handed her a mug of brown, steaming liquid; hot, certainly, and tasting of the brown powder used for scouring cooks' knives.

"I got news!" murmured Is, leaning close and blowing the steam from her mug.

"I'll be home at noon," murmured Wally in return.

Back, therefore, in the privacy of the warehouse, Is showed her edible message to Wally and his father.

"Now ain't that cunning!" mused Mr. Greenaway, carefully investigating the cake with his big clever hands. "No wonder the constables and Bow Street chaps never picks up any clues. Here's a billy-doo that ninety-nine boys and gals out of a hundred will gobble down as soon's they done reading it—and then, where's your evidence? That's a real mob's trick, and makes me even more positive this game is run by some big mogul who's up to all the dodges. A devilish clever one. You got to watch yourself, dearie, every step of the way."

"Euston Green, at midnight," said Wally thoughtfully. "Seems to me I did hear tell of some goings-on up that way; there was a big clog factory on the edge o' town, got burned

out and, on account of some law business, it can't be re-
builded till they get it argued out. So there it stands to this
day, empty and ruined and locked up. Just north o' the
Green, 'tis—and beyond it there's a big old graveyard, all
filled up with graves and supposed to be haunted. So no one
goes nigh it."

"Well, I reckon I'll doddle up there at midnight," said Is,
"and see what's to be seen."

Wally at once offered to come, too, but she would not
allow him.

"Whatever it is might not happen if there was two of us.
'Sides, you're too big, Wally. You'd show up. You ain't a kid
no more. Anyhows, you got your da to look out for. But
keep the pancake. And if I don't come back, show it to King
Dick."

At eleven o'clock, therefore, she hugged them both good-
bye, said, rather gruffly, "You might send my love to Pen if I
ain't home by Christmas," and set off to walk to Euston
Green.

The streets were mostly empty at that time of night, and
her way, through Cheapside and Holborn and Farringdon
Street, took her less time than she had reckoned; she reached
the neighborhood of Euston Green at about twenty minutes
before midnight.

It was a rough, wild area, still more or less on the edge of
town, with unbuilt-on land stretching away to the north,
which could not properly be called country, for it was covered with vegetable gardens, and sheds, and brick-works,
tanneries, livery stables, and great mounds of rubbish.

Making a slow and cautious approach to the north end of
Euston Green (a patch of unkempt weeds grazed by geese
and costermongers' donkeys), Is located the big warehouse

of which Wally had spoken. It was a massive, partly ruined building, at least three stories high. Against a sky now blazing with wintry stars it showed up as an irregular, gaunt shape, somber and spiky. In front of it lay a patch of inky shadow and, edging warily closer, Is found that this piece of shade was entirely packed with silent children. There must have been several hundred of them, all totally quiet. So far as could be made out in the dark, they were of every possible kind. Large, small, some decently clad, some ragged and dirty. All they had in common was their complete silence.

On the stroke of midnight—clanged out by not-too-far-distant St. Pancras Church—the very faintest of creaks could be heard, and the crowd shifted a little, softly and expectantly. Then, unit by unit, Is realized that it was beginning to diminish. She was on the southernmost edge of the group, and felt that everybody was moving north, inchmeal, drifting by scarcely noticeable stages toward the black wall of the factory building. A narrow hatch, she presently saw, had slightly opened and, one after another, children from the crowd were slipping inside, without making the least sound. Is, lingering on the outskirts, came last of all, and stepped through the wicket from darkness into deeper darkness.

"You the finish?" demanded a voice in a whisper.

"Yus, I reckon."

There was a pause, while she felt somebody brush past her and look out, presumably to check her statement. Next she was searched, not roughly but thoroughly, the contents of her pockets removed, inspected, put back. Lucky I tucked that token into my lining, she thought. After that, she was given a gentle push into what seemed to be a passage with canvas walls, the darkness giving place to dim light as she passed along. Then she stumbled down a flight of stone steps, holding on to a wooden rail, passed through a door—and suddenly emerged into a place of dazzling light and color.

It was also shatteringly noisy—so much so that, for several minutes, she stood with her eyes shut and hands clapped over her ears. Then, opening her eyes, she took careful stock of her surroundings.

She found that she was standing in a large, high hall. Far above her head, the domed ceiling appeared to be made of glass, which threw back reflections from rows of gaseliers giving light along the walls. These walls were painted in gaudy colors with crude pictures of birds and trees, dancers, toys, colorful goodies and cakes piled in dishes, also trumpets, drums, ribbons, and flags. Here and there, man-sized capital letters proclaimed: HUZZA, YOU ARE OFF TO PLAYLAND! HAPPY JOURNEY! NOW YOU WILL HAVE ALL THE FUN IN THE WORLD! GOLD KINGY IS WAITING TO WELCOME YOU!

Gold Kingy! thought Is. 'Aha! Then we are going to Blastburn! The north country must be Playland. But how are they a-going to get us there?

Now her dazzled eyes, slowly adjusting to the brilliance of the light and the shifting, excited crowd of children around her, became aware of what lay alongside the crowd, and was the source of the deafening noise, topping the shrill voices of the expectant travelers.

A train, like an immense red-and-gold snake, was drawn up along one side of the hall, stretching far away into the shadows at the distant end. Upon the train's side were written in fiery letters the words PLAYLAND EXPRESS, over and over. Two gigantic engines, one at the front and one at the rear, emitted fierce whistles, jets of sizzling steam, and sulphurous smoke.

Men in red jackets were already busy hushing the children, moving them forward, and marshaling them on board.

"*Plen-ty* of room for all—don't shove—just move along this way—pass along the platform, *if* you please. Don't push, don't shove, there's *plen-ty* of seats for everybody. Easy does it! Gently does it!"

Is hung back, watchfully. Loitering at the near end of the platform, she thought, once I'm aboard that train there won't be *no* way of sending back a message about all this.

She glanced behind her, but the entrance through which she had come was already closed. One of the red-coated men slammed a door, locked it, and put the key in his pocket.

Is said to him urgently, "Mister! Listen! I was waiting for me brother. He ain't come yet. Could you take back a message for him? To say I've gone on ahead?"

He said, "Can't be done, kid. It'd be as much as I'm worth. I won't tell you a lie; I couldn't do it. Your brother can come next month."

She stared at him, dismayed by the look on his face. He was pale and haggard, with black rings under his eyes. Like a picture of a monkey, Is thought. In his red jacket he looks jist like the toy monkeys Penny makes.

"You'd best hop on the train now, missy," the man said hoarsely. "They'll be ready to start in a minute."

Is made her way, not hurrying, toward the rear of the train, where the second great engine steamed and hissed and chuntered to itself. She was impressed by its size; she had never seen such a thing before. There were two drivers on it, she saw, standing by the footplate and talking; one of them was short, lame, and one-eyed, the other tall and redheaded. They wore frock jackets and black velveteen caps. One held something in his arms.

There was a freight car next to the engine, just one. Wonder what they carry in it, Is thought. Men were dragging carts loaded with sacks across the platform, and hurling the sacks through the open doorway of the baggage car.

As one of the carts rolled toward her, screeching and grinding over the stone-paved floor, Is was astonished to notice a small yellow cat come scampering in her direction, visibly panicked by all the noise and confusion. Narrowly avoiding the iron wheels of the cart, it swerved toward her; instinctively, Is knelt and grabbed it, and it clung to her with all its claws, terror-stricken; she could feel its tiny heart pounding against her own. It was hardly more than a well-grown kitten, with soft, ginger-color fur, thick as lamb's fleece.

Thinking of Figgin, she hugged it reassuringly, then looked about her, wondering if it had an owner somewhere among the throng of children now piling on to the train. Their voices were all around her:

"Mind your silly self, don't shove so! — Coo-er, I can't wait to get on board, can you? See what's there! — D'you think they'll give us dinner? Breakfast? I'm something hungry! — How long does it take to get there? — Mom, Mom, I don't want to go, I want to go home, I want Mom! — Don't be a stupid crybaby, you know Mom don't want us at home. And you can't go back to the workshop, now you've run off, Mrs. Poss 'ud beat you till you couldn't stand up."

In all this chatter and hubbub, Is, unused to crowds, felt very much alone.

"I like *you* better than all of them," she told the ginger cat, still looking about for its owner. "Which one of them do you belong to?"

"Hey—you—young 'un!" shouted a harsh voice behind her. "That's my Ginge you got there!"

Turning, she saw one of the men jump down from the engine cab. He was the tall carroty-headed driver. He came toward her, scowling.

"This kitty—yours?" said Is distrustfully, still cradling the little cat protectively inside her crossed arms. But there was no mistaking the way in which, as soon as it saw the red-haired man, the kitten greeted him joyfully, leaping across onto his shoulder, then burrowing down into what was plainly its regular place, an inner pocket of his black jacket.

"If he's yours, you oughta take better care of him, mister!" snapped Is. "That cart nearly flattened him."

"One o' the kids knocked him off me shoulder, time they all come scampering in," said the man defensively. "I was on the lookout for 'im. Anyway, you best get on board. We'll be starting in a brace of shakes."

He added after a moment, in a lower voice, "Thanks, anyway, kid. I'd not want to lose him, he brings me luck. And he sure wouldn't ha' took to everyone the way he done to you"—glancing past her warily as if to make sure they were not overheard.

"I got one, too, called Figgin," said Is. And then, as she clambered onto the step of the last car before the freight car, she turned and asked, "Hey, mister—you go back and forth on this train? Any chance of sending summat back—a message—about *my* cat?"

He shook his head quickly, violently, then leaned closer to her and murmured—while his eyes still continued to dart about the crowd—"Can't be done, young 'un. There's spies everywhere. The only cove I heard on what took back a message, he fell off the footboard while the train was goin' acrost the Wash bridge—that was the end of him. I dassn't do it, see, kid?"

And he quickly walked away from Is, back to the engine and his one-eyed mate.

Very thoughtful indeed, Is pulled herself up the steps and entered the train.

Inside, she saw, the passenger car was gaily decorated in the same style as the station hall—in gaudy reds, blues, yellows, and greens, with pictures of palm trees waving, dishes of greasy-looking tropical fruits, golden crowns, and butterflies.

YOU ARE ON YOUR WAY TO PLAYLAND said a sign. There were brass fittings and pink-shaded lamps, and the seats, set in alternately facing rows with an aisle down the middle, were covered in red canvas. On the floor was a red Turkey carpet, very much worn and spotted with grease.

Is, who had never seen a train before, let alone traveled on one, found everything remarkable.

"Why ain't there any windows?" she asked one of the red-coated men as he passed by, making sure that everybody was fitted into a seat somewhere.

"Why," he replied, looking somewhat startled, as if no one had ever asked such a question before, "it's because . . . that is to say . . . this train only travels by night . . . in the dark . . . so there'd be no point in having windows." And he went quickly on his way.

"How long does the trip take?" she called after him, but got no answer.

Is found an empty seat beside a shabbily dressed, dirty-faced, yellow-haired girl, who looked pretty, knowing, and stupid. She was already giggling and winking at the two boys in the facing seats opposite.

"What's yer name?" the girl asked Is.

"Is."

"Is? *That's* a crummy kind o' monackèr! Mine's Mary-Ann. What did you work at? Where're you from?"

"Blackheath," said Is, not bothering to answer the first question.

"Blackheath? I never been south o' the river," said the girl, as if this was a virtue. "I was a milliner's 'prentice in Spitalfields. My mom 'prenticed me when I was six, 'cos there's ten of us at home. It was crool long hours, I can tell you: start at eight, most nights we wan't done till two or three. Stitch-stitch-stitch, all day long, only bread and taties to eat, an' not much o' them. So I made up me mind to cut an' run. How d'you hear tell of Playland?"

"From a fellow in the street."

"One o' the other gals told me," went on Mary-Ann, paying little attention to what Is said. "It's a reel prime place, she sez; all you want to eat all day long, no work to do unless you fancies workin', fun an' frolic an' dancin' every night, every gal has a room of her own with her own *bed*. Ooooh! I jist can't wait to get there." And she hugged herself and wriggled joyfully on her seat.

"What about the girl who told you?"

"Susie? She went off three weeks ago an' I never saw her no more."

"If nobody works in Playland, unless they want to," said Is doubtfully, "how can they make it pay?"

Mary-Ann stared at her. "*I* dunno! I don't worrit me head about stuff like that." And she tossed her yellow head, which did not, indeed, look as if it were capable of worrying much about anything. She caught the eye of the boy opposite, gave him a grin, and said, "What's your name? Mine's Mary-Ann."

"Abel," he said. "And my friend's Tod."

With a gentle jerk, the train started on its way. Once it was rolling along, it made remarkably little sound, above a regular thud-thud-thud from the engine.

"Ain't it quiet," said Is.

"That's acos they got the wheels wrapped in felt," explained Abel with a knowing nod. "I noticed that, time I got in. And they say the train runs mostly below ground, or anyways in a deep cutting. That way it can't be seen, see? It's a secret train."

"How often does it run?" asked Is.

"Once a month, Susie told me," said Mary-Ann. "The night afore new moon. I reckon she was right. So, when owd Ma Walters give me the stick for crumpling the pink sarsnet last night, I reckoned I'd up and hop it, fust chance I got. An' she sent me out today on an errand, to get some more pink worsted, so I jist prigged the fourpence and scarpered." She giggled. "If this train was to be searched by the rozzers, I bet they'd find a deal of prigged stuff aboard."

The boys nodded.

"I run off from a candle factory," said Abel. He exhibited a bag of fat wax candles.

"Who'll want *them* in Playland?" said Mary-Ann scornfully.

"Oh, you never can tell. They must have dark there, same as everywhere else."

"Oh, you! Think you're mighty clever, don't you!" said Mary-Ann. She and the boys began to exchange a great many jokes, which meant little to Is, unused to this kind of talk. She found them boring, and moved across the aisle to a vacant seat on the other side. Mary-Ann, she could see, would not miss her in the least; in fact she was already beckoning to Abel to come and sit beside her.

Opposite Is now were two girls, younger than herself; one might have been eight, the other nine. They puzzled her because their faces were identical, with pointed chins, triangular mouths, and neat little noses, but their coloring was completely different: the bigger one had thick, dark hair and brown eyes, the smaller was red-haired and blue-eyed.

"You two sisters?" asked Is. They nodded, shyly.

"How come you're so different, then?"

"We got the same mom," said the elder one, "but we got different dads. My dad took and died, and Mom married again. I'm Tess, she's Ciss."

"And my dad is allus horrible to her," explained the younger sister. "He clobbers her all the time, and won't let Mom give her enough grub, and said he was going to send her to the 'formatory. So we reckoned we'd run off."

"Mom'll cry, though," said Tess, looking rather miserable about it. "We was a help to her, lookin' arter the little 'uns."

"We'll write her a letter from Playland," said Ciss consolingly. "She 'on't grieve so when she knows what a real prime time we're having there."

The two girls hugged each other in joy at the prospect.

Now the train was sliding along soundlessly at what seemed a very rapid rate; Is could feel its gentle vibration as it carried them farther and farther north. After a while the passengers began to grow restless—they laughed and shrieked and chattered and bounced in and out of their seats —but the red-coated attendants worked extremely hard at keeping the noise level down by dashing to and fro every few minutes with trays of tidbits and sweets. This kept the children from larking about too much, in case they missed their turn for a treat. There was never anything very substantial, but always something to nibble, so nobody was ever satisfied, but always ready for more.

After a while the travelers began singing. This, too, seemed to have been prompted by the red coats, and had the effect of keeping people in their seats; it was plain that the train staff wished to discourage their charges from too much wandering up and down the aisle.

As they sang, Is recognized many of her father's old songs: "Calico Alley" and "Oh, How I'd Like to Be Queen," "Three Herrings for a Ha'penny," and "Hopsie Toe." Some of the songs had been given new words. To the tune of "Oh, How I'd Like to Be Queen," the children sang:

> "Carry me quickly to Play-land
> Let's start on that journey of joy!
> Off to the happy and gay land
> That welcomes each girl and each boy . . ."

Is, for her own reasons, had always specially detested "Oh, How I'd Like to Be Queen." Many of her father's tunes reminded her of her miserable childhood, but that one did so more than all the rest. It recalled days of beatings, being locked in the damp cellar, being obliged to run errands through snow and rain in ragged, thin clothes and wretched, old broken shoes.

When the passengers began singing that song, she got up, dodging a red-coated steward who was offering small fried potatoes on sticks with a pale yellow sauce to dip them in. (Is had tried one already and found it very sickly and nasty).

"Where you off to, missy?" the man asked. "We don't like the young 'uns shifting about too much."

"See a friend, farther back," said Is, nipping quickly past him.

She worked her way along the coach, past singing, laughing, talking, eating, sleeping children of all ages.

"How come you're going to Playland?" she asked a boy as they both waited for a red coat to serve small sponge fingers and move on down the aisle.

"Had enough o' being a chimney boy," he answered shortly. She saw that his skin was all grimy, pitted, and scarred, as sweeps' boys became after a few years of climbing up hot, sooty chimneys.

"Don't they have chimneys in Playland, then? Wonder who climbs 'em there?"

"Whoever does, it won't be me," said the boy flatly.

"You ever come across a boy called Arun Twite? Or a feller called Davie?"

"Nope," snapped the boy, and slid back into his seat.

Unsurprised, Is made her way into the baggage car. She had feared that it might be locked, and was greatly relieved to find that the door to it opened when she turned the handle, and that nobody appeared to notice her going through.

This car was piled high—almost to the roof—with bales, boxes, and sacks. Only a narrow gangway had been left along one side, giving access, she guessed, to the engine and coal tender.

Is, an expert tree climber, had no trouble in clambering up on top of all the packages. Having edged her way to the back, between baskets of clinking china and what smelled like coffee and spices, she burrowed herself a comfortable nook among bales of muslin and folded carpets.

I wonder if these are all smuggled goods? she thought sleepily. Wally's dad said the frontier was all closed off between the south country and the north. So this must be a smugglers' train, besides carrying the kids.

She lay in comfort, lulled by the rocking motion of the train, listening to the distant voices of the children, now beginning to grow peevish and quarrelsome. Glad I'm here and not there, thought Is; hope nobody else'll have the bright idea of coming to this car.

"I want my mom!" she heard somebody cry. "I wanna go home! Stop the train, I wanna get off. I feel sick!"

Is thought sadly of the big airy barn where, at night, she and Penny could hear no sound but the wind, the hoot of an owl, the distant cry of wolves.

I'd rather be there than here, she thought. It's pretty stuffy in this baggage car. Hope Penny and Figgin are looking after one another. I wish I was in our barn, listening to some of Penny's stories.

Since there was no point in such a wish, Is sensibly went to sleep.

How much later she woke up, she could not be certain; a good many hours, she thought. The train, at one point, had stopped for quite a considerable period; through her dreams she had been vaguely aware of this. Now it was going again, and she could hear the wheels rattle with a hollow note beneath her, as if they were crossing over a wide bridge, maybe above an estuary or tidal river.

But what had woken Is was neither sound nor light; though it felt like a mixture of both, and with an extra unknown something added. She felt as if she had been touched by some thrilling flash—or wave, or wind—making immediate contact with an unused, inside part of herself that had been waiting for a long, long time, ready for such a moment.

It was like being pierced by a needle, or a long, cold finger.

"What is it, what's up?" mumbled Is, jerking bolt upright and banging her head quite hard on the roof. At first she thought some person must have called her name; but no, here she crouched, amid smells of straw and coffee and carpet wool, and the train was steadily, speedily thudding on its way northward.

Next moment she heard another kind of sound as a cat, which had been comfortably sleeping on her stomach, shifted itself to a new spot and started up a hasty, polite purr.

"And what the dickens are *you* doing here, kitty?" Is asked it, recognizing, from its thick fur and small size, that it must be the redheaded engine driver's friend.

Indeed, not long after, she heard his voice calling, "Ginge? Ginger? Where the plague have you got to?"

"Here he be!" called Is, wriggled herself and cat to the edge of the stack of bales, and looked over.

"And what the pest might *you* be doing there?" said the red-haired driver sharply. "You're s'posed to be in the parlor car along with all the other little devils."

"I couldn't sleep there. They was all yelling songs, and some was sick. A body couldn't get no peace or quiet."

"Well, what the pize did you expect? And it'll be a sight worse than that where you're bound for," he muttered under his breath, reaching up for Ginger, who jumped on to his shoulder.

"Where *are* we bound for, then?"

"The Hotel Joyous Gard, they call it. And *that's* summat to take with a pinch of salt," he muttered in the same gloomy undertone.

"Why? Ain't it joyous?"

"Listen here, young 'un," he told her, in a different voice. "Dunno why, but I've took a fancy to you; saving Ginge like you done. I sure to goodness wouldn't want you on this train if you was one of *my* fambly—which, thank Providence, I got none. Listen: If you puts a value on your skin, you won't go along wi' the rest of 'em when they gets off."

"Why?"

"Never mind why. It ain't healthy, that's all."

"What had I best do, then?"

"When we stops (you'll know just before, acos we crosses another big river), when we stops, the kids'll all pile out and scamper for the exits. And there'll be folk there waiting to pack them into wagons to take 'em to Joyous Gard. See? So what *you* best do is drop down t'other side o' the train, where no one won't see you. It'll be dark, time we gets there. And you better go back acrost the bridge—you'll hafta dodge the guards—and make the best of your way back to Lunnon. It'll take you a week or ten days I reckon, chancy goin'—but that's healthier than where you're bound for. Where you're goin' ain't no ways wholesome for kids."

"But," argued Is, "I don't want to go back to Lunnon. I came here to hunt for somebody—a boy. For two boys."

"*You came here to look for two boys?* Young 'un," he said heavily, "you won't find no boys here. Boys in Playland comes and goes faster than raindrops."

An icy chill crept down her spine at the words, and at the way in which he said them.

But she answered stubbornly, "I *gotta* look for them. I said I would."

"Then I hope you got as many lives as Ginge here," he snapped. "And I washes my hands of you."

He was turning to go back to the engine when one of the red-coated stewards came through the door from the parlor car and said sharply, "Who are you talking to? Is one of the brats in here?"

The driver said, "I was talking to Ginge, here. Can't a man talk to his own cat?"

Is lay flat as a mat, and held her breath. Apparently the red coat had not spotted her, for he said, "That's as well. You know it's against the rules to talk to the cargo. As you're here you can take the grub through for you and Stritch. And remember the rules: No kids in the baggage car. You know that."

He gave another unsatisfied glance around, but missed Is.

"Certingly I knows that. But there's no rule agin cats that I knows on."

The red coat was still suspicious; he hoisted himself up and peered about over the top of the piled goods. Luckily by this time Is had squeezed down behind a barrel of shrimps, or something that smelled like shrimps. He failed to spot her.

"You know the penalty for talking to passengers!" he called out menacingly; but Ginge's owner had already made his way forward toward the engine.

Is went on holding her breath, and after a while heard the steward go back the way he had come; after a longer time she felt the train slow down, then clank its way over a wide bridge, then reduce speed even more.

Then she heard voices crying, *"Play*land! *Play*land! *Play*land!"

4

There was an old man, and he lived in Middle Row . . .

NOW WHAT'LL I DO? THOUGHT IS. I CAN'T STOP HERE, FOR they'll come to unload the freight car. Most likely, though, they'll get all the kids out of the way afore they does that. So I've a few minutes.

From outside, she heard a gale of sound—shrieks, footsteps, yells, and laughter—as the train doors opened and the children cascaded out.

She could also hear the voices of the attendants.

"This way! *This* way, if you please! Keep in line there. One at a time. *This* way!"

I'm right hungry, thought Is. Wonder when they'll give 'em breakfast. Wonder *if* they'll give 'em breakfast?

She remembered the driver's words: *Boys in Playland comes*

and goes faster than raindrops. The same chill ran down her back now as when he had said it.

Very quietly indeed, she crept down from the stack of wrapped bundles and stole into the parlor car. It was empty, silent, and stank horribly of greasy food, unwashed children, vomit, and worse.

At that moment, Is heard voices. Two men entered the car at the opposite end, carrying brooms and pails.

"By gar!" said one. "What a hogo. It's worse than cages in the zoo."

"Tha's reet," said the other. "Filthy little tykes. It gets worse every trip."

Is had ducked down behind a bank of seats when they entered, and was about to beat a retreat to the freight car. But now she heard more voices coming from behind her. It seemed that any minute she must be spotted.

Suddenly there was a commotion outside.

Whistles were blown, long and loud. Sirens sounded. There were shouts, apparently of warning.

"One's missing. *One's missing!* They're one short from the cars. Where's number two hundred and three? Search the train!"

Is, meanwhile, had crawled under a seat. It was all she could do. But, at the far end of the car, the two cleaners had begun pulling the seats from their sockets in the floor and rolling up the filthy carpet as they moved along.

"Dag it, if it ain't one thing it's another," said one at the sound of the whistles. "How could there be a kid missing? Sure there's noon in here."

"In among baggage, mebbe. Joost as well they counts 'em in and oot so careful."

They went on with their work, pulling out seats and rolling up carpet. Two minutes more, thought Is, and they are bound to find me.

But just then there came another outburst of shouts outside, and a man's frantic scream.

"Ah, ye black-hearted devils, don't *do* that! I never! I never! I said naught to *no* one!"

"Bowen says he heard ye talking to a passenger."

"I never! I was talking to my cat!"

The scream came again, and the furious yell of a cat. Under her seat, Is clenched her hands. The two cleaners walked back to the far entrance and looked out.

As soon as they did so, Is, with inspiration born of sheer terror, rolled out from under the seat and dived headfirst into the roll of Turkey carpet that lay halfway along the compartment.

She had just time to draw her legs out of sight before the two men came back to their job. One was saying doubtfully, "Well, I dunno. It's a bit hard, I think. Poor devil. After all, they don't knaw naught for sure . . ."

"There's a kid missing, ain't there?" said the other. "And they gotta make examples."

They hoisted out two more seats and rolled up another section of carpet, with Is inside. It was dreadful in the roll; pitch-dark and fetid. She lay and shivered, thinking of the redheaded man. That had certainly been his voice outside. What had they been *doing* to him? And his cat?

When the cleaners had worked their way right along the compartment, uprooting all the seats and rolling up the whole length of dirty carpet, they carried it out of the train.

"By gar, it's heavy," said one.

"All the moock that's on it," said the other. "They'll have a rare job washing it, this time."

Is imagined them dropping the roll into a tank of soapy water with herself still inside. She gulped. However, this did not happen straightaway. The carpet was dumped on a hard stone surface and left, presumably while they went back to give the same treatment to the other cars on the train.

Is dared not move, for she could hear people walking and talking close by. Miserably, she thought about the redheaded driver—and his cat—and wondered how long she could stand this imprisonment in the filthy roll of carpet. Each time the men had rolled it over, the layers around her had grown bulkier and heavier, more and more stifling.

"How many, then?" shouted a voice close at hand.

"Three—and this one. T'others'll pass."

"Fetch oop t'bogey, Dan."

While Is was still wondering what a bogey might be, she felt the roll lifted with her inside it and dropped onto a different surface. There were thuds as more rolls, several more, were dumped alongside hers, and one on top.

"Tie a cord over t'lot," somebody ordered. "Reet, that doos it. G'ddap, then."

A horse's hooves clattered, iron wheels grated on stone. The motion that followed next was particularly sickening, as the bogey swayed and jolted violently over what felt like large cobbles. Fortunately the journey did not last very long. After about ten minutes—quite long enough—the cart came to a stop.

"Heave 'em off here, will tha," said a new voice. "It's too late to set aboot 'em tonight. A bit o' snaw'll not hurt. They'll be fettled oop in t'morning."

"Time enow," somebody agreed.

Is it night again already? wondered Is. Did we spend a whole day on that train? It was possible, she supposed.

The rolls of carpet, including hers, were unroped once more and dropped on the ground. As the horse and cart clopped and rattled away into the distance, a man said, "We mid as well shoot oop shop for t'night," and a door slammed. Five minutes of complete silence followed.

Now's my chance, thought Is. And I'd best make the most of it before somebody comes back.

She began trying to wriggle out of the rolled carpet. But the very first thing she discovered was that she could not move at all. She had been wedged in so tightly by the successive layers wound over her, that her arms were pressed into her sides and she seemed to be jammed as firmly as a cork in a bottle.

At least it was possible to breathe. On the cart, the roll had been bent at right angles, which was nightmarish, for one fold had pressed right across her face, and she began to think she would suffocate. But whoever lifted the roll off the cart had unfolded it and left it lying straight so that, from the end of the roll, about an arm's length beyond her face, cold fresh air could reach her.

It sure *is* cold too, Is thought, urgently struggling to move her hands. If I lie here a few hours like this, without moving, I'll freeze up solid, and they won't hafta worry about their perishing missing number two hundred and three. They'll unroll the rug and out will tumble a frozen corpus.

The thought exasperated her so much that she began to struggle in good earnest. Giving up the battle with her arms and hands, she decided that she would have to lever herself along by means of her feet, alternately bending and straightening her ankle joints. This seemed to work, if slowly; she felt the greasy rug bend and give, a very little, as she dug in her toes.

Up—down. Up—down. Her calves and ankles began to ache. In places the carpet was so oily and slippery that her toes slid back on the surface. Would 'a been better off if I'd 'a been barefoot, Is reflected. But then, I'd be even colder.

She thought about Penny's stories. There was one about a man who had three wishes and married a swan. If I had three wishes, *I* know what *I'd* wish for, thought Is. I'd wish for those two boys to be found, and us all to be back on Blackheath Edge. She thought about Penny teaching her to read. "What's the point of reading?" Is had grumbled at first. "You can allus tell me stories, that's better than reading." "I'll not always be here," Penny had said shortly. "Besides, once you can read, you can learn somebody else. Folk should teach other folk what they know." "Why?" "If you don't learn anything, you don't grow. And someone's gotta learn you."

Well, thought Is, if I get outa here, I'll be able to learn some other person the best way to get free from a rolled-up rug.

Up—down. Up—down.

You might think, as you got closer to the edge, that the folds would be a mite looser. But that was not so. Twelve layers thick of stiff, rolled-up rug, all glued together with fried potatoes, formed a wrap that was solid as oakwood. And when at last her head did begin to emerge from its carpet collar, Is found that she had nothing much to be thankful for. Instead of being pressed against filthy carpet, her cheek now lay on stony, gritty, freezing ground. It was dark, with no moon or stars to give comfort; on the contrary, a fine, thick snow was falling, blowing like dust into the folds of the rug.

"Snow!" said Is in disgust. "Why, it ain't but November!"

But then she recalled how far north she had traveled, into a colder, darker part of the country. Humberland. The air smelled of snow, and had also a queer, thick, disagreeable tang—like badly burned milk, she thought.

After another ten minutes of hard toe-and-ankle work, she had her arms free as far as the elbows. And then, at last, she was able to drag one hand into freedom. The fingers were quite numb, from having been jammed against her thigh for so long, but she bent them up and down against her chest until they began to tingle. Then she hoisted out the other hand. Then, bracing both hands against the greasy mass of carpet, she managed to lever herself out into the snowy night.

"Well, that's better than a slap with a haddock!" said Is, and looked around her with pride. She almost wished there had been an audience to applaud her triumph.

Not too many coulda got themselves outa there, she thought. I bet that fat Mary-Ann couldn't, for one.

Still, perhaps it was as well there had been no audience.

Now, with eyes growing used to the dark, she was able to take stock of her surroundings. She seemed to be in a little cluttered yard with high walls round it, which lay beside a biggish one-story building. Where they cleans the carpets, guessed Is. The yard had a high gate of slats but this, when she tried it, she found to be locked—or, anyway, fastened on the far side. A sharp wind blew stinging snow into her face.

If I can get outa that rug, I can get outa this yard, Is thought firmly. She looked about for something to climb on and found an old washtub. That, tipped on end, would raise her enough to grapple her fingers over the top of the wall. With a wriggle and a struggle she was up, and kicked away the tub so that it would roll to a distance and not put ideas into anybody's head about how it had been used.

One thing about the snow, there won't be any footprints by morning.

She perched on top of the wall and looked down. The drop on the far side was greater—about twice her own height—because the ground sloped. With great care she slithered onto her stomach, hung by her fingers, and let go, landing on cobbles.

Now, where do we go from here? she wondered. And wondered, also, what had happened to those other children, all two hundred and two of them. Were they in the Joyous Gard Hotel? Where was *that*? And where was the red-haired man, what had happened to him?

I don't like Humberland, thought Is. I reckon it's right spooky. There ain't a good feel about it, not one bit. *Playland,* my aunt Fanny! I don't reckon as much playing gets done here.

She looked about her.

She was standing in what seemed to be a narrow, cobbled lane, running downhill. The buildings on either side were not dwelling houses, but might be stables, or sheds, or store-houses, and most of them looked dark and derelict. There were no lights to be seen anywhere at all. Farther off in the distance, a lumpy skyline suggested that the land hereabouts was both hilly and covered with buildings, but more than that she could not guess; the snow veiled everything and blew into her eyes, making her blink.

"Wish I could find a haybarn," Is muttered. "I wonder where the bogey driver took his rig?"

The night was quite silent. Where's all the fun and dancing and frolicking? she wondered. I don't hear much of *that*.

She started slowly down the hill. A massive stone building loomed up on her right. There was a bulky tower, not very high, with spikes and a steeple on top. A church. Is had never been inside a church; none stood near where she and Penny lived in the woods, and during her earlier life in London nobody in her household ever had any dealings with churches.

But somewhere she had once heard that church doors are always open.

It's worth a try, I've naught to lose, she thought.

The first door she approached had a white paper on it, just visible, and writing on the paper: PLEASE ENTER BY SOUTH DOOR.

There! she could hear Penny's triumphant voice: Now do you see how handy it is to be able to read? Yus, and which way is south? Is retorted, but she acknowledged that if she kept walking around the church she must, in the end, find the south door.

In fact it was on the next side she came to, a big arched wooden door with a heavy iron latch that turned obediently in her grasp. She slipped inside, closing the door softly behind her.

The air inside the church was not especially warm, but it certainly was a much more comfortable temperature than the snowy blast outside. And there was a faint radiance from one dim candle burning on a table somewhere a long way off. Is did not approach it. Close at hand she found rows of wooden benches with upright backs. There were no cushions, but she was in no mood to find fault. She stretched herself out luxuriously, had time for one longing thought of Figgin, then fell asleep.

When she woke next, a kind of gray dawn-twilight was beginning to filter through high-up rows of pointed, greenish windows.

What the blue blazes am I doing here? Is thought, lying on her back.

Then her memory came back with a rush, and she sat up. She saw what had doubtless been responsible for waking her —an old gentleman in a black gown who was pottering gently about in the distance, kneeling and standing and talking to himself. Or at least, he was not talking to Is.

She waited patiently until he had finished his business and was coming slowly toward her along a gap between the benches. He was, she noticed, entirely bald, which gave him a somewhat startled expression, since his forehead seemed to go up and up, over the back of his head. He had large round eyes and a large mouth, and reminded her of Humpty-Dumpty.

But still, he looked quite sensible.

She greeted him. "Hey, mister!"

He was so startled at the sight of her that he almost dropped the lamp he carried. But he recovered himself in a moment and replied to her kindly enough. "My child! How in the world did you arrive here in St. Bridget's?" He added after a moment, rather hesitantly, "Are you—are you attempting to take sanctuary?"

Sometime during the night Is found that she had decided on a course of action. This is a real havey-cavey place, she had concluded; I get a strong notion that kids is not treated right up here. I better find me a friend who isn't a kid, who'll maybe stand by me if there's trouble. What good is family if they don't look out for you, after all? I gotta find my uncle Twite. And then, if things comes up rough, maybe he can help out.

So, to the old gentleman's question, she replied, "No, mister, I ain't taking anything. I jist stopped in here to get a bit o' shut-eye and wait till day. Now it's light, can you help me? I'm looking for a cove called Twite, Mister Twite."

Again the old gentleman seemed greatly amazed. He studied Is long and doubtfully, then muttered to himself, "Well! I can do no more than accede to her request. In fact I can do no *less*. —My child, I am in a most favorable position to grant your wish, since I myself live in the same building as the gentleman you mention, Number Two, Wasteland Cottages."

"You do? Now, ain't that fortunate!" said Is. "Can we go there now, mister? Is it far from here?"

For she thought, firstly, that the sooner she was off the streets the better, in case the men who ran the Playland Express were still searching for their lost passenger, number two hundred and three; and second, she felt very hollow and rather hoped that her uncle Twite might be inclined to offer her breakfast.

"No, not far," replied her companion. "You may, by the way, address me as Father Lancelot. We will go there directly."

He led the way out into an icy-cold and foggy morning.

Is glanced about her with curiosity as they made their way down the hill. Through the fog and the snow, which continued to fall thinly, she could see glimpses of what looked to be a mournful, derelict, and battered landscape. Everything that could be done to it had been done. It had been dug up, piled into heaps, covered with machinery and buildings—

including hundreds of immensely tall, thin factory chimneys —and then it had all been allowed to go to ruin.

It's like a birthday cake someone jumped on and forgot to light the candles, thought Is, looking at all the spidery chimneys.

"Is this place Playland?" she asked the old gentleman.

"I believe by some people it has been so designated," he told her. "Its proper name is Blastburn."

Blastburn! Aha! thought Is, but she said no more, for the old gentleman walked at such a swinging pace that she almost had to trot to keep up with him.

The place was all slopes, uphill and downhill, steep ridges with narrow valleys between, and odd rows of little two-story houses set here and there in what seemed a very random manner. They were built mostly of gray stone, with roofs of gray slate, but some were of brown freckled bricks. All seemed unoccupied.

After going up and down several short, cobbled roads, Father Lancelot came to a stop outside a row of houses that, apparently because of being crammed into a particularly narrow gap between two steep ridges, were taller than the rest, four or five stories high. They looked unnaturally tall and narrow, like books in a half-filled bookshelf. One, at least, was inhabited; smoke trickled from its chimneys. A sign at the end of the small row said WASTELAND COTTAGES.

"Here we are," announced Father Lancelot, and picked his way across a small, untidy snow-covered garden patch, littered with half bricks and broken pots.

He opened the front door, which gave onto a steep flight of stairs and a passage leading through to the back.

"Mr. Twite?" he called. "Mr. Twite, are you there? Are you awake?" Taking a step or two along the passage, then turning to Is, he explained, "My chamber is upstairs, on the second floor. Mr. Twite lives here on the ground level. His daughter occupies the third floor upstairs. *She,* of course, might be a more proper person to receive you," he added doubtfully, "but I fancy that she is away at present on a mission."

"His daughter? On a mission?" Is gaped at the clergyman in astonishment. It was news to her that her uncle Twite had a daughter—but quite welcome news.

At this moment shuffling footsteps could be heard, and a man carrying a candle made his appearance, coming slowly along the passage.

The hand holding the candle trembled so much that melted wax flew all over the flagged floor. That was the first thing Is noticed.

"You don't require that candle, sir. It is day," said Father Lancelot kindly, and stepping forward, blew it out.

"Eh? Day? Oh. No doubt you are right." Mr. Twite laid the candle carefully down on the floor. Then, slowly straightening himself, he stared at Is. She stared back, quite silent with surprise.

He can't be my *uncle,* she thought. He certainly can't be Hosiah Twite's brother. Or my dad's. That just couldn't be possible. Compared to him, Father Lance is a choirboy.

Mr. Twite looked unbelievably old. His skin was grayish-brown, netted finely all over with wrinkles, but shiny, like weathered wood; in fact he resembled some aged tool that has been used by the same family for hundreds of years, bent, seamed, shaped, and polished with constant use. His eyes were blue—like mine, thought Is—but very faded. His hands were knotted like roots, and shook gently all the time. He wore a kind of dressing gown, which seemed to have been made out of a thick gray blanket; his skinny legs were bare; and on his feet he had red-and-green slippers, quite new and clean, with red bobbles on them. Somebody looks arter him right well, thought Is.

And his voice, when he spoke again, was clear and collected.

"Who is this young person? How does she come to be here? How is it that the constables or the wardens have not taken her up?"

"I found her in my church, not ten minutes since," explained Father Lancelot, "and she was asking for you."

Is recovered her voice.

"I'm a-searching for my cousin—Arun Twite," she explained. "His dad—that's my uncle Hose—he ast me to see if I could find the boy. I'm from down south, I ain't never been in these parts before. But my uncle Hose, *he* said that we got another uncle what lives hereabouts, and he'd a notion the boy might 'a run this-away. That's why I come."

She stared hopefully at the aged Mr. Twite, and he stared back at her, slowly taking this in.

"Your name, my child?"

"Is."

Old Mr. Twite thoughtfully nodded his head up and down several times.

"Is. Indeed that name brings back memories. Is. Isabett. You were named after your great-grandmother, then. A Breton name. Isabett was from Brittany. My cousin, in fact. Yes, indeed . . ."

"But," said Is, thunderstruck, "then—who the plague are *you,* mister? You surely ain't my uncle Twite?"

"No, child; I am your great-grandfather. At least, I con-

clude that you are the daughter of my grandson Abednego—
a gifted but worthless fellow. Where, by the way, is *he*?"

"He's dead," said Is shortly.

"And his brother Hosiah?"

"Dead too. The wolves got 'em."

"An ill-fated pair," commented their grandfather calmly.

He seemed prepared to stand discussing the affairs of the
Twite family indefinitely in the passageway, but Father
Lancelot suggested, "Shall we remove to the kitchen, sir? I
daresay your great-grandchild would not be averse to a warm
drink." His tone was hopeful, as if he would not be averse to
one himself.

Old Mr. Twite slowly nodded his head again.

"The kitchen. Yes, indeed . . ." He turned and led the
way back along the passage. Is and Father Lancelot followed.

The room he ushered them into plainly combined various
functions. A fire burned in one corner, and shelves around
the fireplace held pots and plates. A desk, littered with pa-
pers, occupied another corner. An easel supported a half-
finished painting; a fantastic map, with figures and buildings
in it. An untidy unmade bed was heaped with books, which
had also spilled onto the floor. Strings of onions hung from a
hook in the ceiling. A saucer of milk near the fire suggested
the presence of a cat somewhere. The room was L-shaped,
with two windows commanding an extensive view down a
snowy valley full of derelict buildings.

Mr. Twite gestured vaguely toward a chair which was
loaded with books; removing these to the bed, Father
Lancelot sat down. Is squatted on the floor, which was covered by a thin, torn rug; this made her grin, recalling last
night's escape. She watched her great-grandfather, who
moved slowly to a shelf from which he took a saucepan; then

he reached up for a jar that stood on a higher shelf. As he did so, he trod on the edge of the milk saucer on the floor, which tipped up and splashed its contents over his foot. This startled him so that his hand, reaching for the jar, struck a basket hanging on the wall and knocked it down; the falling basket dislodged a pile of tin plates balanced on a shelf below, which fell, and in their turn toppled over a colander full of walnuts, which, together with the plates, all cascaded onto Mr. Twite's foot.

He gazed at them mildly, seeming neither perturbed nor surprised. Is helped him pick up the plates and the walnuts, then she wiped away the spilled milk with a hideous old rag which she found hanging from a nail, while Mr. Twite poured more milk from a can into his saucepan, mixed it with gray powder from the jar, and set the mixture on the hob to heat. As he did this, he murmured to himself:

"Is, yes. The name of a drowned city. Off Finisterre; which, of course, means World's End. Can this be a portent? And Twite, too, is a Breton name; origin obscure. *Thouet,* possibly some kind of bird? Or a tow line? We have kinsfolk, of course, in the region of Finisterre, and it is undoubtedly from the Breton line that your aunt derives her weather wisdom, but I am not personally acquainted with that side of the family."

"You come from Brittany, Great-grandpa?"

"No, child; my great-grandfather did."

Is could not contain her next question any longer. "Great-grandfather, *how old* are you?"

"A hundred and two, my child."

"A hundred and two?"

He smiled a little, privately, to himself, pouring the hot beverage from the saucepan into three not very clean mugs.

"There, child; you must be chilled."

Is tasted her drink. It was rather strange; slightly sweet, with an earthy, peppery flavor, at first not disagreeable. "What is it?" she asked.

"Saloop; an old recipe, made from orchid roots. Your aunt Ishie finds them for me."

"My aunt Ishie—"

"She is out, just at present."

"On a mission, Father Lancelot said?"

"Let us hope that she will be back shortly." It seemed that Grandfather Twite preferred not to discuss the mission. Father Lancelot, looking slightly ill at ease, now rose, placing his empty mug on a corner of the desk.

"That was most excellent, sir. Ah—I will leave you to your family affairs." He turned in the doorway to say, "And I shall not—of course—mention this . . . arrival . . . to anybody . . . anybody at all . . ."

"I am obliged to you, Lancelot," Grandfather Twite answered. "It will, I daresay, be advisable not to. At present."

"Great-grandpa," burst out Is, when the door had closed, "what happens to kids in this place? Where did they take all them ones from the train I come on? What's the Joyous Gard Hotel? Where am I a-goin' to find my cousin Arun—if he's here? Or the other—" She checked herself and gazed urgently at the old man.

He, like Father Lancelot, looked uncomfortable and depressed.

"It is a disagreeable topic, child. I think I should prefer to leave it to your aunt Ishie to explain . . ."

He rummaged about and found a loaf of brown bread wrapped in a moldy old towel; having broken off a piece with some difficulty he gave it to Is, saying, "Eat, my child."

She chewed gratefully. It was the first food that had come her way for over twelve hours and, though hard as a brick, tasted delicious.

"You arrived on the—on the train, then, child?" She nodded, munching. "How was it, then, that you—that you became separated from the others?"

"A cove—the engine driver—he warned me. Told me I best get out o' there, if I valued my skin. So I cut and run."

"Most resourceful," he murmured to himself.

"Great-grandpa—how in the world do you get to be so old? If you don't mind me askin'? I mean—how come you didn't die years ago?" demanded Is bluntly.

Again he smiled to himself—a rather teasing smile—looking down at his empty mug.

He's a funny old cove, but he ain't a bad 'un, decided Is. I like him—I think. He's better than Dad, at least.

A random ray of sunshine filtered through the window onto the spot where she sat, and toasted her comfortably. The stale brown bread and warm, rather disgusting saloop had put new confidence into her. Maybe, arter all, I'll be able to find those boys, she thought.

"You wish to know the secret of my long life?" said Mr. Twite. "You are not the first to ask me that question, my dear, and you will not be the last. Your uncle Roy, for one, would dearly like to know the answer. Riddle me ree, riddle me Roy." He grinned to himself.

"My uncle Roy? So I do have an uncle in these parts, then?"

"Oh, my word, yes! You do indeed. Your uncle resides," her great-grandfather explained in a tone of distaste, "he chooses to reside in the new part of Blastburn, which, for heaven knows what fanciful reason, he and his colleagues have decided to rechristen Holdernesse."

"Is Holdernesse the same as Playland?"   •

"Oh—Playland. Playland is just a figment."

"What's a figment?"

"A nothing. A zero. A cipher. A duck's egg."

"Just as I figgered!" said Is in triumph. "Just a Banbury story to fetch the kids in."

"I suppose you could say that." Again her great-grandfather wore his look of unease. But it cleared when he cocked his head and said in relief, "Ah, now I hear the footfall of your aunt Ishie. What a comfort that she has come home. She, without doubt, will be able to explain everything you wish to know. And will be able to decide what it is best for you to do."

Hurrying as fast as he could in his loose slippers along the passage, he called, "Ishie! Ishie! Can you come in here a moment, if you please? We have here a most unexpected visitor—your great-niece from the south country, Desmond's daughter." And he gave a mumbled explanation.

To Is, the first sight of her great-aunt Ishie was a severe disappointment. The person who now hobbled into the kitchen was very odd-looking indeed: quite short, hardly as tall as Is herself, and dreadfully lame, so that she was obliged to hoist herself along with a sideways, crablike motion. She dragged behind her a kind of sled, or box on wheels, which it seemed she used when she went out for transporting either herself or her belongings. She was quite remarkably plain, with a backward-sloping forehead, no chin to speak of, and large bulging eyes like those of a hare. She was also amazingly filthy—covered in gray dust from head to foot, all her long, trailing gray clothes furred with greasy slate-color powder, as was the kerchief over her head.

But her voice gave Is another surprise, for it was warm, clear, and sensible.

"My niece from the south country. What an unexpected pleasure! But here I am, as you see, quite unfit to receive company. Give me ten minutes to step up and make myself presentable—or, better still—" as she seemed to pick up some inaudible plea for help from old Mr. Twite, "or better still, my dear, why do you not accompany me upstairs. For you will be needing somewhere to sleep, and can be settling *your*self in your own quarters while I tidy *my*self."

Is therefore followed Aunt Ishie up three remarkably steep flights of stairs, necessarily at a very slow pace.

"The rooms on the first floor are let to Dr. Lemman," explained Aunt Ishie, somewhat breathlessly, as they passed two closed doors. "He is a very clever medical gentleman, quiet in his habits, and out a great deal of the time on his rounds, which suits your great-grandfather very well. Father Lancelot is on the second floor, and you, my child, may have the attics all to yourself. I am afraid it may be rather *dangerous* for you in this part of the country—has your great-grandfather gone into that at all?"

"No, missus. He said you'd explain *everything*."

"Oh dear, did he? (Call me Aunt Ishie, my love, do. I am, I suppose, your great-aunt, but we will waive the great.) Now, this is *my* little territory"—opening a door on the third floor—"and I will just step in and make myself fit to be seen. You may continue on upward and take possession of your own quarters. Come down again as soon as you choose, my love, when you are quite established." And she vanished behind the door.

Is climbed the last flight—which was very steep indeed, almost a ladder—and found two tiny rooms with sloping ceilings, facing each other across a narrow strip of landing. She looked out through each window in turn. One faced into a rocky, heathery hillside, the other commanded a wide prospect, down across the network of valleys so confusingly jumbled with ruined houses, mills, warehouses, viaducts, and skyward-pointing chimneys and dyehouse towers. Far in the distance high, snow-covered mountains reared up like sharks' teeth against the dark gray sky. And down to the left, beyond the massed chimneys, lay a faint dark horizontal that might perhaps, Is thought, be the sea.

But where in all this cold, deserted, mutilated landscape were David and Arun? And the two hundred and two children from the Playland Express?

Is very soon ran down the stairs again, and tapped on Aunt Ishie's open door.

"Come in, my love," called a voice from behind a screen. "Sit down and make yourself at home."

From the splashing behind the screen, Is concluded that her aunt was taking a bath. In a moment or two she appeared, wrapped in a garment made from a gray blanket like that of Mr. Twite.

"Axcuse my asking, Aunt Ishie, but I'm still not quite straight: Is the old gent your father or your grandpa?"

"He is my father, love; and an excellent parent he has always been, I am glad to say. Now: Did you find all well upstairs? Shall you be comfortable up there?"

"Some kind of bed 'ud be nice," said Is. (There had been no furniture of any kind.)

"A bed. Oh dear me, yes. Yes, if you are to sleep in this

house, you should certainly have a bed. Dr. Lemman may have something suitable; we must see about that."

"Any old folded rug would do," said Is. "I ain't particklar."

"And you are the daughter of my nephew Abednego," said Aunt Ishie reflectively. "Are you fond of him?"

"Couldn't stand him," said Is briefly. "But he's dead."

"A most teasing, unreliable boy," recalled Aunt Ishie. "But he was able to compose, as I well remember, tunes that found their way into one's head and stayed there forever. So he is dead. Ah, then; where are his tunes now?"

"All over everywhere," said Is, thinking of the children singing on the train. "Aunt Ishie—*please* tell me, I gotta *know*—what happens to all the kids hereabouts? And where are all the folks? This is like a dead town. In Lunnon there ain't any kinchins—here there ain't no one at all. Looking outa the window up there, I couldn't see a single soul—not one! Nor even a thread o' smoke. All the houses ruined— where *is* everybody? Is there some monster what eats them all?"

Aunt Ishie, after inviting her niece inside, had vanished again behind the screen; from time to time the sight of a hand or a foot protruding and waving about suggested that she was putting on her clothes; but at this moment her entire head came out from the side of the screen. She looked, thought Is, who was now getting used to her, not unlike an otter. Particularly now with her damp gray hair slicked back; her flat-topped gray head and large, friendly wide-set eyes quite powerfully suggested that gentle, timid creature.

"Monster!" said Aunt Ishie. "Yes! There is a monster. But not the sort you have in mind. This monster's name is Greed."

Next minute she emerged entirely, robed in another long gray cotton gown, which fell about her in folds and was tied around the waist with a cord.

She sat down on the bed. (Aunt Ishie's room was furnished very sparsely, with a narrow cot, a box, the stool on which Is was sitting, the screen—behind which presumably there stood a tub—and some hooks on the wall from which clothes hung.)

"You have not yet met your uncle Roy?"

"No, ma'am—Aunt Ishie. I did wonder if he'd help me find Arun."

"Most unlikely. Your uncle Roy," said Aunt Ishie, "is a very rich man. When he was young he made money selling old iron off a barrow. He did well, bought the iron foundry, then the pottery, next he bought the coal mine, and by now he owns the whole region. First he was made mayor, then president, and now he is moderator of the Regional Council."

"Fancy!" said Is. "But if he's so grand, surely he oughta know if his own nevvy's about the place."

"I would not depend on that. Not at all," said Aunt Ishie. "Were you aware that New Blastburn—or Holdernesse, as they call it—is an underground town?"

"*Underground?* Save us! Why?"

"While digging out and enlarging the first coal mine, they discovered a huge natural cavern under Holdernesse Hill and so—at your uncle's command—the city has been entirely rebuilt inside it."

"Well, I'll *be*! A whole town inside of a cave! I suppose that way," said Is, thinking about it, "they don't get no rain or snow. It would be jist prime for the street kids. No crossings to sweep, though, no mud. Is *that* where all the kids are?"

"No," said Aunt Ishie. "They are in the mines. Or the foundries. Or the potteries."

"In the mines?"

"All children here," said Aunt Ishie, "are set to work. From age five. In the coal mines, in the foundries, in the breweries, in the potteries. The mines are far from the town, now, under the sea; they are very, very extensive. The children work and sleep there." Her voice sounded flat with exhaustion and depression. "I send them comforts when I can get hold of a messenger. And I visit the ones who are closer at hand."

"Is *that* where you jist come back from?" exclaimed Is, suddenly illuminated. "The old cove—Father Lancelot— said you was on a mission."

"Yes. Those poor wretches spend their lives working. They have no free time. I talk to them—tell them what I can. A little history. A few tales or poems—something to put into their minds, to lighten so many hours of drudgery."

"Their minds . . ." said Is slowly.

And suddenly—like a signal, like a summons—the same tingling shock exploded in her own mind as had roused her when she lay asleep in the freight car. It felt exactly as if somebody had reached out a cold, vibrating tuning fork and touched her on her most sensitive point.

"What is it, child?" said Aunt Ishie. "You have turned white. Are you faint?"

"N-n-no," said Is slowly. "It's naught. Do you think my cousin might have been sent to work in the mines? If he traveled up here on that kids' train?"

"Almost certainly—either the mines or the foundries.

That's where boys go. They—the workers in those occupations—have to be replaced most frequently; there is a continual need for new hands. That is why—"

"That's why they gotta fetch in new ones from the south all the time—*now* I see. What happens to the old ones? No," said Is, "you don't hatta tell me, I can guess."

Aunt Ishie crossed her arms over her thin chest and bent her head.

"Your great-grandfather and I—when your uncle became so rich he offered us a fine, large house in the new city. Underground. He greatly dislikes our continuing to live here. But we do not—we could not—no, we could not. My father, indeed, would be happy to remove entirely—go to some other region. Or at least so he sometimes says. But I . . . but I . . . no, I could not do that. Little though my efforts achieve, I would rather stay and do what I can. And your uncle . . . has a reason of his own for wishing to keep your great-grandfather here. But he strongly disapproves of us—of our habits. It makes him angry. He feels," Aunt Ishie finished with a wintry smile, "that we bring disgrace to the name of Twite."

"Disgrace to the name of Twite," repeated Is slowly. *"Blimey!"*

A step was heard on the stair, and a tap on the door.

"That will be Dr. Lemman," said Aunt Ishie. "He is always very obliging about disposing of my bathwater."

And indeed a head poked round the door and said, "Shall I take the tub now, Isabetta?"

"Yes, thank you, Chester. And here is my great-niece, my nephew Abednego's daughter, Is. She and I share the same name. She has come to us from the south."

"Good gad, dearie!" said Dr. Lemman, stepping completely into the room. "Don't she know what a plaguey dangerous spot she's come to?"

Is had no ready-made notion as to what a doctor should look like. She had not seen many. Doc Spiddle at Lewisham was fat and red-faced. But certainly Dr. Lemman was far, far from anybody's vision of a regular doctor. He was thin and wiry, with bristly rusty-brown whiskers that seemed to sprout all over his head and face at random, rather scantily, so that he looked like a teasel or a sea urchin. His eyes were bright brown and very shrewd.

He wore a suit of greenish old velveteen, more suited to a gamekeeper than a man of medicine.

"What'll you *do* with the chick?" he said to Aunt Ishie, striding behind the screen and returning with a large zinc bathtub of very dirty water cradled easily in his arms, and an empty white enamel pitcher inverted on the top of his head. "You can't keep her mewed up in this house all day. She'd be bored to death. But if she steps out-of-doors, she'll be snapped up by the wardens before you can say ipecacuanha. And then she'll be whipped off to the mines, and that's the last you'll see of her. Precious little good you did yourself traveling to these parts, dearie!" he said to Is.

"I was wondering," offered Aunt Ishie timidly, "whether, Chester, you could take her with you on your rounds—to grind your powders and mix your ointments? Whether you could tell people that she is your apprentice? I am sure she is a remarkably capable and sensible girl—five minutes with her and you'll see that. Well, she must be resourceful, when you consider that she got herself all the way from the south, as far as here! Without being taken up!"

"Humph!" said Dr. Lemman. And he went off down the stairs with his load.

When he returned—this time carrying the empty wash-tub, with a full jug of clean water standing inside it—he said, "All rug, dearie! And don't say I never do anything for you! But if G.K. cuts up rough, don't blame me! We'll give it a try, at all events. You," he told Is, "will have to get up devilish early."

"I don't mind that, mister."

"Good—very well. Six o'clock tomorrow morning. We'll see how it goes. Adiós!" And he ran off down the stairs again, whistling loudly.

Aunt Ishie drew a long breath of relief.

"Oh, I *am* so glad that he agreed. It will make such a difference. Dr. Lemman is a man of standing in the community, you see, my dear. I know that he looks a little odd, but everyone accepts his way, and he is an *excellent* doctor; he has the confidence of your uncle Roy, and everyone of importance. So long as you are with him you will be perfectly safe."

"But will I have a chance to ask people about Cousin Arun?"

"As good a chance as any other," said Aunt Ishie, sighing. "But—I must warn you not to let your hopes climb too high."

Is nodded glumly.

Aunt Ishie sighed again, and then limped out of the room. Is could hear her slow and painful progress down the stairs.

Real rum sorta ken I got myself into here, Is thought. Great-grandpa . . . Aunt Ishie . . . the old reverend gentleman . . . that Doc Lemman—put 'em all together, you got a freak show in a circus. Still, I reckon I was uncommon lucky to land here.

Just the same, her heart was dreadfully heavy. The thought

of the two boys, and their probable whereabouts, lay inside her like a freezing pain. And one of them the king's own son! What *would* that poor white-haired gentleman think if he knew? Either in the mines under the sea, or in the iron foundries. *Boys in Playland comes and goes faster than raindrops.* And what about Tess and Ciss? And that poor silly yellow-headed Mary-Ann?

I'm awful hungry, Is thought. She had been reminded of this fact by the smell of cookery coming from downstairs. Aunt Ishie must be making a meal; I'd better go down and help her, poor old duck. She's got enough troubles of her own, obliged to drag herself about like that. Yet she goes into the foundries and the potteries and tells the kids history . . .

As she stood up, Is felt again that freezing tingle somewhere inside her head, and a voice—not her own, yet present inside her—seemed to call: "Listen! Listen! *Can you hear me?*"

What the plague is the matter with me? Is wondered. Am I sick? Or am I going cuckoo?

5

Doctor Foster is a good man
He teaches children all he can . . .

AUNT ISHIE PROVED TO BE AN EXCELLENT COOK. OVER A FIRE OF wood fragments she had prepared a kind of mutton hash, with cut-up potatoes in it.

"Where do you get your meat and 'taters, Aunt?" Is wanted to know. "There's no market around here, nor nothing; you must have to go a precious long way."

Aunt Ishie smiled her gentle inward smile and said, "Well, my dear, we have secret neighbors. But I will tell you about the Warren some other time."

Grandfather Twite was now properly dressed in a black jacket, shiny with age, a waistcoat, open over a workman's shirt of ample cut and coarse cotton, but perfectly clean, and a woolen cravat around his aged neck. He still wore the red-

and-green slippers. Noticing the direction of her gaze, he
said to Is:

> "Two slaves carry me all day
> For not a penny of pay
> I make them work as I think best
> They stand empty while I rest."

As Aunt Ishie handed him a plate of hash, he smiled
fondly at her; it was plain that the pair were deeply attached.

"After the meal I will show you my press," he told Is.

"Press, Grandpa?"

"Your great-grandfather is a printer by profession, my
love," explained Aunt Ishie. "He prints programs, broadsheets, journals, music, ballads—anything, in fact, that people want printed. Did—can you read books, my child?"

"Yus," said Is. "I can read. But we didn't have much *to*
read. When I lived with my sister Penny we had *The Horse
Doctor's Handbook*—that was real interesting, but tough—and
Robinson Crusoe and *Gulliver's Travels* and some rhymes we
bought off a peddler. But arter we read them about a hundred times, Penny used to tell me stories."

"Indeed?" said Grandfather Twite. "Tales she invented
herself? Did you enjoy them?"

"Yus! They was prime! Penny used to tell 'em while we
made the dolls—that's how she gets a living, you see, she's in
the toy-making line—"

"I have sometimes thought," murmured Grandfather
Twite, "that small books of tales—something to engage and
occupy their thoughts—might be of solace to the children
working in the mines."

"But you do not recollect, Papa," said Aunt Ishie mournfully, "so many of them live and work entirely in the dark."

"Ah yes," he answered after a moment. "Yes, I had forgotten. In the dark. I had not reflected . . ."

"Aunt Ishie, you said—" put in Is, who had been thinking about the miners, "you said that they never comes out at *all*?"

"It would take too long to bring them out, the overseers say. And it is not worth the expense of transporting them to and from their place of labor. And—and"— Aunt Ishie's voice wavered—"it would only make them dissatisfied."

"But they could have a light at night, when they're not working, to read by?"

"Many are working at night—on shifts, you know. And the more lights they have, the more danger of fire. So— except when it is absolutely necessary—they have no light."

"Always in the dark—*Jay*!" said Is, and ate in silence for a while.

After the meal Grandfather Twite showed her his printing press. It was in the cellar, down a flight of stone steps, under the kitchen: a massive piece of machinery on a stone table, with an upright frame like a house over it, and a long iron handle, and a great screw on top.

"That's the bar that pulls the press down with the paper in it onto the bed of type. Weighs a hundred and forty pounds, it does," said old Mr. Twite. "Excellent for the muscles!" And he held out a stringy old arm like a steel cable.

Bales of clean paper lay on the floor; newly printed sheets hung from clothespegs, drying on the walls. Dozens of boxes held little metal letters, all back to front.

"Grandpa," said Is, "don't you ever plan to stop workin'?"

"Why should I, my duck? If work is what I enjoy?

> Black and white and red all over
> Truth and lies in me discover
> A hundred characters under one cover.

Guess what I am."

"A book," said Is, after some thought.

"Right. You and I'll get on if you can guess riddles. I'm always putting them to Roy—your uncle—and he can't guess a riddle to save his life. Makes him mad as a weaver—poor old Gold Kingy."

Old Mr. Twite grinned, pulling down the heavy bar of the press. He was engaged in printing a poster. "It's to pin up on the doors of inns," he told Is.

WANTED! it said in large letters. VOLUNTEERS FOR THE HOLDERNESSE MILITIA! DEFEND YOUR NATIVE LAND! STRONG BRAVE YOUNG MEN REQUIRED. NOW IS THE MOMENT TO APPLY! SIGN UP WITHOUT DELAY! SIGN TODAY!

And there was a picture of a strong, brave young man waving a bayonet.

"What's militia?" asked Is.

"An armed troop, an army. Your uncle Roy is afraid that King Richard may send troops from the south to try and recapture the lands up here that have been lost to him. Indeed it seems quite likely that he may do so."

"How did it happen?" asked Is. "*Why* did the country split up?"

"It all began over soccer."

"*Soccer?*"

"There were two Soccer Unions—one northern, one southern. And they couldn't agree which should be the superior one."

"Did it matter?"

"To them it did. And your uncle Roy—who is quite a clever fellow in his way, it must be said—egged them on to dispute because he could see that if the north broke loose, he could assume the leadership in this region. And the north is the richer part of the land—with the coal, and the mills, and the foundries. But now your uncle Roy wants the south too."

"Why? If the north is richer?"

"He needs more customers to buy his goods. So he is telling everybody that King Richard will invade us, and that we must stop him by invading the south first."

"Well, I don't think he will; that ain't a bit likely," said Is slowly, recalling the tired, sad-faced man in Mr. Greenaway's warehouse. "The poor cove has too many other troubles. His queen died, you know, and there was the Chinese wars . . . and his boy run off—"

Then she bit her lip, wondering if it had been unwise to let fall that piece of information. But, after all, Grandfather Twite was a decent, sensible old boy, and kind, too . . .

"The king's son ran off? Was that a recent occurrence? How old is the boy?"

"I dunno. It's best not to talk about it," said Is. "Don't tell anybody, please, Grandpa."

"Whom should I tell, my child?"

He flung a scrumpled bundle of ink-smeared sheets into a large waste-hamper that stood by the wall. The unsteady basket fell over on its side, disgorging a whole mass of rubbish and a skinny, molting, black-and-white cat with battle-scarred ears, who growled loudly at having his rest disturbed and, ignoring Is, went sulkily off upstairs. ·

"That's Montrose," said old Mr. Twite, packing the rubbish back into the basket. "It's no use, he won't speak to you. He barely speaks to me. But then, he is almost as old as I am, in cat years.

> My first is in coat, but not in fur
> My second in claw, but not in rib
> My third in grunt, but not in purr
> My whole will come to the call of Tib.

Not that Montrose *ever* comes when he is called. Where were we, now? Ah yes, you were going to tell me some of your sister Penelope's tales."

"Was I?"

"Certainly you were."

And he listened attentively while Is related the one about the queen whose hair screamed at her, and the mystery of the rocking donkey, and the curious affair of the leg full of rubies.

"Hmnn. I see that my grandson Abednego or Desmond— scoundrel though he undoubtedly was—at least passed on an inventive faculty to his progeny," he murmured as he absently initiated Is into the skill of picking up the back-to-front letters with a pair of tweezers, and packing them into a case that he called a stick. He showed her how to ram the press handle down in order to press the message onto the prepared paper.

"Croopus, Grandpa, you really could print a book of stories on this!"

"No reason why not," he answered somberly, "but, as

Ishie says, who would read them? Now, riddles!" He picked up his candle, declaiming, "In a white petticoat, with a red nose, the longer she stands, the shorter she grows!" and moved to the far end of the cellar. Here stood a quantity of large earthenware vats, stone jars, wooden kegs, firkins, and puncheons, which appeared to be full of liquor in various stages of preparation. Some of them bubbled gently; thick, oily liquids trickled at a slow pace down through glass tubes, bubbles rushed upward through other pipes, and then, cooling again, dripped down to be collected in stoppered flasks.

There was a warm, yeasty smell of brewing, much more welcome than the sharp odor of burned milk which hung over the whole of Blastburn and even crept into every corner of the rooms upstairs.

"What a deal o' toddy!" said Is, looking around.

"Distilling is my hobby," explained Grandpa Twite. "Alcoholic drink is *very* bad for you, and I hardly *ever* touch it myself; but, it is my hobby to make it."

"So who drinks it? Aunt Ishie? The Reverend?"

"Bless me, no! Various people, at various times," he answered vaguely, and repeated for the third time, "Making it is just a little hobby of mine."

"My dad used to get flaming drunk," said Is. "And then he'd clobber me."

"Disgraceful," said old Mr. Twite. "It is as well he—"

Aunt Ishie called down the cellar stairs. Her voice was raised, as if in stress or annoyance.

"Father! Your grandson Roy is here to see you!"

"Oh, perdition it. I wish my grandson Roy were at the bottom of the Red Sea!" muttered the old man, beginning to climb the cellar stair.

Is could hear her uncle Roy's loud voice, and his loud,

rattling laugh, long before she saw him—it seemed to fill the whole kitchen, thundering and booming, echoing from one wall to the other. She was quite startled when she came in sight of Roy: He hardly seemed big enough to account for such a row. Though short, he was thick and stocky, gray-haired and whiskered. His face, round and red, had a blob of nose in the middle. Two pale, close-set blue eyes fastened at once on Is and studied her sharply. The eyes had a bright, suspicious stare, like that of a scarlet-faced baby grasping and sucking at its bottle, sure that the whole world intends to snatch it away. He wore a suit of reddish plush—to match his face, Is thought—and a tall hat of the same fretful color. The hatband was a broad gold ribbon, sparkling with colored stones. A kind of crown, in fact. So *he's* Gold Kingy, she pondered; he's the one in charge of this whole shindig. He owns the mines and the foundries; it was his notion to split off this land from the south. He's the enemy of poor old King Richard.

And he looks like an enemy, sure enough.

"Gad's teeth! I don't know how you can stand to live in this kennel," Uncle Roy was declaring irritably. He flung his hat down on the table. " 'Pon my soul, I don't indeed! It's a disgrace, a downright disgrace to *me*! I'm more ashamed and mortified each time I come here."

"Then it is odd, Roy, that you come so often," remarked Aunt Ishie tranquilly.

She sat by the table with a bale of coarse canvas, and was cutting squares from it with a pair of sharp scissors. Glancing up as she completed a square, she went on in the same tone, "And here is your brother Desmond's daughter Is, come to visit us."

"How do, Uncle Roy?" said Is.

"*Desmond*'s brat? How can she be that?" he demanded. "I thought he had only the two, Penelope and Dido. Come to think, though, I suppose she does have a look of Desmond." Is scowled at this suggestion. Uncle Roy went on, "Well, my girl, you'd best get right back where you came from—unless you want to work in the mines. Up here in Humberland, children don't just loll around and play—they have to earn their bread, same as adults. Do you know what a *doul* is, niece?"

"A slave."

"And that's the status children have here—*douls*—until they are twenty. They have to make their contribution to society. And so will you, if you stay." He gave her a glance of dislike.

"Don't worry, Roy, she's already 'prenticed to Chester Lemman," said Aunt Ishie placidly, rethreading her needle.

At that moment Dr. Lemman himself walked into the room.

"Hilloo, dearie," he said coolly to Uncle Roy. "Saw your rig outside. How's the liver—eh? Giving us a bit of a twinge —eh? I can see that, from the color of your cornea. Let's have a look at the tongue. Open wider . . ." And he peered thoughtfully into the huge red cavity of Uncle Roy's open mouth. "Hmnnn, *not* very pretty; no, by Joshua! You'd best lay off rich food, pastry, and stimulants for the next few weeks. No more Early Purl. Stick to broth and rice pudding —that's my advice."

Uncle Roy looked glum, but seemed prepared to pay heed to the doctor's counsel.

"Follow the example of the gaffer, here," went on Lemman, patting Mr. Twite's bony shoulder and darting a bright-brown, needle-sharp malicious glance at each man in turn. "You want to live to a hundred and two like him—eh? Then moderate your way of life, my dear fellow!"

The malicious smile moved, like a sunbeam, to Grandpa Twite's face.

He said, "Roy hasn't my constitution, more's the pity! Here's a conundrum for you, Roy:

> My first is a vessel, my second revered
> First's round as a penny, second wears a beard
> And my first holds my whole, neither wine nor wealth,
> Which keeps my second in good health.

Well? What's the answer, my dear grandson?"

"You know perfectly well that I've no time for your cursed nursery-rhyme balderdash!" said Roy angrily. He seemed ready to burst with exasperation, but restrained himself and, after a moment, went on, "I came to invite you to a review. But what welcome do I ever get here? Can't think why I trouble to come, no I can't, damme!"

"A review of what, Roy dear?" mildly inquired Aunt Ishie, stitching two of her canvas squares together.

"Of the militia, what else? Are those broadsheets ready, by the by? We have got a tolerable troop now, but we should have double the number."

"Yes, yes, they are done."

Old Mr. Twite returned to the cellar and reappeared with an armful of posters. The cat Montrose came in through the back door, let out a kind of subdued, angry caterwaul at sight of Uncle Roy, and made a beeline for the cellar. Grandfather Twite tripped over him and he lashed out with a forepaw, drawing blood from the old man's leg, but this seemed a routine occurrence; nobody expressed surprise.

Except Uncle Roy, who muttered, "Why you keep that ill-conditioned, mangy beast—"

Aunt Ishie broke in, as she selected another pair of squares, "How can you expect to recruit a sizeable troop of young men, nephew, when most of the lads do not survive into their twenties?"

"Oh, there's always a new supply from the south," he returned carelessly. "So—how about the review? You wish to attend? You may sit in my box, provided you arrive at least two hours beforehand. It is at three tomorrow."

Aunt Ishie shook her head. "Thank you, Roy, I am far too busy." At which he hardly tried to conceal his relief. "Papa may wish to come, perhaps."

"I doubt it, I doubt it," said old Mr. Twite. "Perhaps if I finish my pamphlet for the Nautical Union.

> I can break and mend again
> I wear a crest and a snowy mane
> I can whisper, I can roar
> And I shall last forevermore."

He grinned broadly at Roy, who scowled. "How about Is, here? She'd like to see the review, Roy. All your gallant young fighters."

"Certainly not! The moderator's family are one thing, children another," said Roy sharply. "That would be a shocking example for the lower orders."

"Anyway, reckon I'll be out with the doc here," said Is. *"Working."*

She had taken a strong dislike to her uncle Roy, and thought it a pity that he had not met the same fate as his brothers. Not enough wolves in these parts, she thought; reckon they stay south, where it's warmer.

A sallow-faced man with straight black hair falling to his shoulders now stepped into the room and said to Roy, "Your Worship, we shall be late for the managers' conference if we don't leave here directly." He sent a supercilious glance over the shabby room and the people in it.

"Oh, very well. Very well. Though it won't hurt those fellows to wait for me. Take those posters, Dagly. Here—*you*—" said Roy to Is. "Step out-of-doors with me a minute, will you?"—beckoning her with a stubby, short-fingered hand.

Is caught Aunt Ishie's eye. It was full of warning.

Slightly mystified, Is followed Roy, who had stumped ahead out into the little, untidy, snowy front garden. In the road beyond waited a handsome carriage, drawn by four fat, glossy horses.

"Listen you—what's-your-name," said Uncle Roy. "*Lord* knows how you found your way here, and you're *devilish* lucky not to be down the mines this very minute. And I want you to keep that in mind! *I'm* the moderator of this region, and if I choose to send you down the mine, that's where you'll go. Understand?"

Is nodded.

"Well, then! Remember that! I don't object to your working for Dr. Lemman—he's a clever doctor, and he could use some help—so long as you work hard and pay heed and learn all he can teach you. That way you can make yourself useful. But you'll be doing it on *my* sufferance. And there's something I want you to do for me in return. Understand?"

"What, Uncle Roy?"

"You're staying here with your great-grandfather and aunt?"

She nodded again.

"Good. That is, it *ain't* good, it's devilish annoying, to have my own family practically squatting in such filthy, beggarly conditions. Lord knows, I've tried—but that ain't to the purpose. You may have noticed that your great-grandpa is . . . is a strapping, likely old fellow for his age—eh?"

"Yus," said Is.

"You may have wondered how he *got* to such an age—you may even have asked?"

"Yus."

"*Did* you ask?"

"Yus."

"And did he—by any chance—let fall the cause . . . er, that's to say, the regimen, nostrum, jorum, physic, diet, whatever it is he does or takes—to which he *attributes* his great number of years?"

"No," said Is stolidly. "He didn't."

"Oh." Roy's face fell. He fiddled with his hatband. "Well —see here! You seem to me like a gal with good sense. Like your old man, eh? He was a one-er, if ever there was!" Uncle Roy grinned, a most unpleasant grin. "Had it over *me,* Desmond did, when we were boys, many a time! Anyway, that ain't to the purpose either. What I want *you* to do is keep your eyes peeled—comprenny? Just you keep an eye on your grandpa, see what he does or takes. For it'd be a shocking pity if one of these days he were to topple off the twig—as he must in the end, you know; none of us can expect to go on for ever, damme—and carry off his secret with him. Wouldn't it, now?"

"Dunno as *I'd* want to live to a hundred and two," said Is thoughtfully.

"You stupid child! Who cares what you want? That ain't the point!"

"What is the point?" asked Is, wondering if the strong liquors brewing in Mr. Twite's cellar had anything to do with his great age.

"The point is that you are in a very, very good position to watch him and see what he does every day to keep himself alive. If you find out and tell me—damme, I'll see you get a handsome reward! Yes, I will!"

"What kind of reward?" inquired Is, her mind on the lost boys.

"Cash!" he said impressively. "Maybe as much as twenty pounds. But it'd have to be the true duff, mind. You can't pull the wool over me."

"Can't promise," said Is.

"Well—you'd better do your best," he said, suddenly losing patience. "Or I may decide to have you sent off to the foundries anyway. So be warned. Remember you are nothing but a *doul*. —Oh, very well, Dagly, here I come—" And he sprang into the carriage, the door of which had all this time been held by the black-haired man, evidently his secretary, who looked despisingly at Is as he followed his master.

Is returned to the kitchen.

"My love, I hope you didn't *tell* your uncle anything?" said Aunt Ishie quickly and anxiously. "About—about where you came from, you know—or anything of that kind? I should have warned you that it is a great, great mistake ever to tell your uncle anything at all. He makes use of every scrap of information to his own advantage, and everybody else's *dis*advantage."

"That's all betsy, Auntie. I didn't tell him a thing," Is assured her.

"Why did he want to speak to you?"

"A horse to a hen I know!" said Dr. Lemman, grinning. "He wants you to try and find out what keeps your great-grandpa ticking over, ain't that so?"

Is nodded.

"And you couldn't tell him, for you don't know. Right?" She nodded again.

"I bet he told you that the welfare of the whole human race depends on finding out the old boy's secret?"

"No. He didn't," said Is.

"Well, he will next time! Depend on it, he'll keep on at you. He can't stay away from this house. He's around here morning, noon, and night."

"Poor Roy," said Aunt Ishie, rather as she might refer to some toad or small, ugly beetle, "he envies us so."

"And he's frightened of you, Isabetta," said Lemman affectionately.

"Frightened of Aunt Ishie? Uncle Roy is? Why?" Is wanted to know.

"Frightened of her and her friends. Because they can tell about the weather beforehand, and he doesn't know what else they may be able to do."

Aunt Ishie sighed and said, "He is so stupid."

"At least it means he lets you stay here in peace. In relative peace."

"Now, my love," said Aunt Ishie briskly, "are you going to help me with these pockets for the children, or are you going on his rounds with Dr. Lemman?"

"I'll go out with the doc now, and help you when I get back."

Grandfather Twite had long since retired to the cellar, from which thumps and clangs could be heard, as he operated his press.

Dr. Lemman made his rounds in an unimpressive pony trap, drawn by an elderly and docile mare.

"Now listen, dearie," he said as they rattled downhill. "You are going to see a deuce of a lot of things here that you won't like at all. Things that'll maybe put you in a passion and make you low-spirited. None of us back in that house are happy with the way matters go on in Blastburn. But there ain't a deuce of a lot we can do. Roy 'ud have us clapped under hatches if we tried to interfere. Your aunt takes comforts to the kids—those she can get to—and reads to 'em. Your grandpa, he makes up riddles for 'em. Maybe it don't help, maybe it does. Who can say? Father Lance— well, he prays. Only Father Lance knows if that helps or not. At least it can't do harm. And I—I do what I can. I look after the rich folk to make ends meet, and the others—at other times. See? So you keep a quiet tongue in your head. Your aunt tells me you are hunting for some boy?"

"There are two," said Is. "You see—"

"Don't tell me any names, dearie," he said quickly. "Mum's the word. No title, no treadmill. What I don't know, I can't tell. You never *can* tell here, if you follow me."

"You don't surely mean—" began Is, horrified—and then, yet again, she suffered from the queer visitation that had come three times before, as if the very focus of her being were suddenly pounced on and pierced by some outside force.

"Let me alone!" she gasped in a kind of childish rage. "Leave me be! Get away!"

Dr. Lemman pulled the mare in to the side of the road and looked hard at Is.

"What's up, dearie? Are you all right? You're white as lint!"

"*I* dunno!" gulped Is. "It feels like I'm a-going mad. Every now and again I can hear a voice, kind o' calling. Did *you* hear a voice, Doc? Jist now? A voice calling help?"

"No," he said slowly, staring at her even harder. "But that's not to say it didn't call. You say you have heard it before?"

"Once on the train, and again twice in Aunt Ishie's house. And each time louder. It's the sort of call," she said, hunting for words, "that you can't *stand* not to do summat for 'em, it sounds so broken-hearted—but where *is* it?"

"You heard it on the train? And then again in Ishie's room? And now here? Was it the same each time?"

"No. It gets louder. If it gets *much* louder, I shan't be able to stand it!"

"Have you tried answering?" he suggested, giving her a thoughtful, observant look.

"Answering? How d'you mean?"

"In the same way that it comes to you. Try to think a message and send it back—that you are a friend, that you'd like to help if you can—something of that kind."

"No," said Is, "reckon I hadn't thought of that. But I will try, next time. If there is a next time. It comes on me so sudden, it's like a sickness. I'm not a-going mad, am I?" She shivered violently.

Dr. Lemman flicked at the mare to start her again.

"Let me know, if you are able, another time when it

happens. —No, I am quite sure you are not going mad. When human misery reaches a certain peak," he said thoughtfully, half to himself, "I think it may distill into another form . . ."

"Like Grandpa's brew in them bottles?"

"Could be. And some people are able to pick up those echoes more acutely than others. You, it seems, are of that kind. Your aunt, and some of her friends, have another kind of extra sight. You will find how to use it."

"Maybe," said Is. She did not wholly understand his explanation but it made her feel a good deal more comfortable. At least he seemed to recognize and respect her plight.

"Why did you choose to conduct your search in this part of the country?" he asked after a while.

"I made a promise to a cove." She explained about Uncle Hose and his dying wish, and mention of an uncle in the north. "But I didn't know about Grandpa."

Dr. Lemman nodded thoughtfully. Then he said, "By the way. About old Mr. Twite. I think I should warn you—"

A maidservant in cap and apron came running toward them along the cobbled street.

"Doctor, oh, Doctor! I'm so thankful to have caught you! Can you come directly? Missus is having *such* a screaming fit —she's got the histricks summat shocking. No one can't do nothing with her, not the housekeeper nor any of the footmen—"

"Yes, I'll come," said Lemman, sighing. "Jump in the trap and I'll drive you back." And he added to Is, "Now, dearie, you'll get to see where old Blastburn ends and new Holdernesse begins."

The pony trap rattled on through some derelict streets composed of what had once been handsome buildings:

banks, chambers of commerce, churches, and large stores—
all empty now and ruinous. Then, where a steep hill rose
ahead, the street ran in under a wide archway and through a
tunnel, which was lit by brilliant white lights. The road was
well paved and wide enough to take three carriages abreast,
but there was no other traffic on it. On the curved white
walls were written up slogans in huge letters: NEW IS BETTER
THAN OLD! UNDER IS BETTER THAN OVER!

"Not far to go, fortunately," said Lemman. "Mr. Gower
lives in the main square of Holdernesse. He is the keeper of
the exchequer—one of your uncle's most important aides."

After about five minutes in the tunnel they came out into
what, Is could see, must be a huge cavern, with a roof so
high that it was hardly visible, for lights hung below it sus-
pended on cables. (They were, Lemman told Is, electric discs
fed by currents from electromagnetic machines.) They flung
brilliant light into every corner.

"Don't they never let them out?"

"At night they reduce the power."

The main square of Holdernesse town seemed to Is about
the same size as the new Trafalgar Square in London, and
resembled it in having a large central statue on a column,
surrounded by four granite lions. The figure here, Is recognized when they passed nearby, was that of her uncle Roy:
squat, stubby, and scowling.

Two sides of the square were occupied by grand public
buildings with pillars and porticoes; the other two appeared
to be handsome private houses. Dr. Lemman halted his pony
trap outside one of these. "Hold the mare, will you?" he
asked Is. "I'll not be more than a minute or two. Here—"
and he tore a prescription form from a small block, having

first scribbled on it, "The girl, Is Twite, is my official assistant. Chester Lemman."

Then, with the maid, he vanished inside the house, from which loud, jerky, hysterical screams could be heard issuing.

It was lucky that Lemman had given Is the paper, for almost at once after he had left her, a dour-looking man in dark green uniform strode up to her and said, "What's a doul your age doing on the street? Why ain't you at work?"

She silently handed him her credentials and he read the paper with slow, laborious care, moving his lips as he battled with each word.

"Is Twite. B'goom, are ye any kin o' Gold Kingy, then?"

"Yes," said Is coldly. "He's my uncle."

"Ye're a loocky lass for sure. N'wonder ye bain't in the foundaries." But just the same, the look he gave her was hostile rather than respectful.

Dr. Lemman soon reappeared.

"Hysterical fits are very common here," he explained, taking the reins. "I fancy it is the result of living entirely in artificial light."

"What did you do for her?"

"Dashed her with cold water, then gave her a soothing draft. She'll sleep for hours."

"Don't folk *want* to go outside sometimes?" pondered Is. "For a bit of air and sun?"

"Why would they want to? Out there is nothing but snow and ruins. All the shops and entertainments are in here. You'll see."

She did see. They drove out of the huge main square (Twite Square) and into Twite Avenue, a glossy, well-paved street of stores, galleries, and amusement arcades. Everything was new, smart, and sizzling with color. Small electric tramcars ran slowly on rails up and down the middle of the thoroughfare; passengers could climb in and out of them at any point. Here there were quite a few people to be seen, strolling and gazing into opulent shop windows. No children, though.

"Don't they have no kids—these rich folk?" Is asked, studying a woman wrapped in white fur, sparkling with diamonds, who was absorbed in a study of some porcelain in a shop window.

"If they do, they send the children away to be brought up elsewhere. The risks here are too high. Any unattended child over five will be arrested. Many people choose to remain childless. Humberland is a place where—" Lemman hunted for words, at last said bluntly, "where children are not in favor."

"Why?"

"Well—I believe many adults naturally dislike children. Don't you agree? Because children have so much energy . . . imagination . . . hope . . . enjoyment. Their life lies all ahead of them. An untapped reservoir. Envy fills some people with hate—don't you reckon?"

"Dunno," said Is. It had never occurred to her to envy another person.

He said, "I fear you are not likely to find the boys you are after among my well-to-do patients. But later, perhaps, among the others . . ."

For a couple of hours he drove to and fro along the streets of new Blastburn, or Holdernesse town, and Is, though disappointed at not seeing a single child whom she might interrogate, was nevertheless much interested by this queer underground city.

But I couldn't never live in it, she thought. No, *never*.

The barn on Blackheath Edge seemed a haven in comparison with this rich, gaudy, silent, unnatural metropolis. It ain't a proper town at all, Is thought; proper towns grow up over hundreds of years, and have crummy little old parts with junk shops and cobblers and tenements and bits of waste ground. Proper towns have street markets and kids riding hobbyhorses and sweeping crossings and bowling hoops and dropping cherrystones. And the goods in the shop windows here are by *far* too fancy—the kind o' stuff a body would buy only if they had got everything else already, and had no way to pass the time but only to buy more things. Gilt dishes! Marble apples! Pink sofies! Who wants 'em? thought Is scornfully. This is a *nothing* place.

Dr. Lemman took considerable trouble, as he drove her on his rounds, to describe the symptoms of the people he treated, and explain what he had done for them. It was real obliging of him to take such pains, thought Is; she did her best to repay him by giving her full attention to all he said, and asking questions when she did not understand. Besides, it was interesting, what he told her; quite a lot of it seemed to connect with what she had memorized in *The Horse Doctor's Handbook*. I guess folk ain't so very different from horses, when you get down to it, thought Is.

"I daresay you will feel that most of these people's troubles are very trifling—headaches, palpitations, backache, bad dreams—and that I am making money from them for very slight services," Lemman remarked after a while.

"None o' my business," said Is, who had thought this.

He glanced at her with respect.

"I try to strike a balance, you see. Now we have finished with the paying patients, and go to the infirmary. Nobody pays there. And there you *may* find a few children, though not many. It is not thought worthwhile—" He broke off, and guided the mare carefully over a set of crisscrossing tramlines.

The streets hereabouts were darker and narrower. At one point the pony trap traversed another large square with an equestrian statue in the middle. One side of this space was dark—simply a wall of cliff, divided in the center by a massive pair of iron gates reaching halfway up to the cave roof. Sentry boxes guarded the gates, and half a dozen men in uniform marched back and forth in front of them. Great beams of white light played down upon them from the roof.

"What's those gates?" asked Is.

"The main entrance to the mine. We are very close to the shoreline here. The mines extend under the sea, you know that? For more than five miles. Your aunt is grieved that she is not allowed in with her comforts for the children—but it would be much too far for her to walk, in any case. The gates are kept locked, as you see; only mine officials may go through them. And, of course, the wagons full of workers when they first arrive off the train."

"Ain't there no other way in?"

"Well—" Dr. Lemman began, then checked himself. He said, "Certainly none that your aunt could use. Though she does not let her lameness deter her from visiting the foundries and the potteries. And she has a—" He broke off again and said, "Now, this is the Strand Gate," as they passed under an arch into daylight, of a sort.

Holdernesse town, it seemed, was scooped out of a bulging hillside, rather as the pith is scooped out of a Halloween pumpkin; it had several different exits to the outside world. The one through which they had just come led to the docks, and not far from it stood the infirmary, which took care of injured sailors, besides accident cases from the nearby iron foundries.

"It's the best place for the foundries, for coal comes straight from the mine and the iron ore is fetched by boat," Lemman explained, "either by sea or by canal."

The infirmary was a gaunt old building, left over from the days before Blastburn's transformation. The wards were cavernous and dark, each one holding about fifty beds. The nurses were weathered, elderly women who took no nonsense from anybody, neither patients nor doctors, though they seemed kindly enough disposed to Dr. Lemman, who addressed them all as dearie. Is, whom he introduced as "my new helper," they regarded with scorn.

"Is Twite? Mind she don't faint on you, that's all. Not exactly what *she's* used to, I'll be bound."

Afterward, Is rather wondered at herself, that she had not fainted. Some of the sights there were so awful that she had to drive her fingernails into the palms of her hands before she could bear to stand looking at them and pay attention to what Dr. Lemman was saying.

But if *they* can put up with what's happened to 'em, then *I'd* better be able to, she told herself fiercely, over and over.

Strangely enough, as she stood at one terrible bedside, dizzy and nauseated, listening to Dr. Lemman's quiet explanation, she felt again what she now described to herself as "the Touch": the powerful, alien jolt, coming from who knew where, grazing the exact center of her mind—and this time it came as a welcome relief.

"Yes! I can hear you!" she found herself able to call back. "I hear you! I need help just as badly as you! Can you help me? Can you hear me?"

"Yes. Yes!" came the strong answer.

"Who are you?"

There followed a pause of a second or two, for consideration, it seemed. Then the reply came like a waterfall: "TomJimNanMarySuePhilPatEllenDickCharlie—"

On, on and on.

"But who are you? What does that mean?"

Another pause. Then: "We are the Bottom Layer. That's who we are!"

Suddenly the connection failed. It broke. Is found herself alone—terribly alone, sick and hollow—by the bedside of a man who had had both his legs cut off. Although the ward was full of noise—clangs and rattles, groans and shouts—she felt, for a moment, as if she were deaf.

Dr. Lemman gave her an encouraging nod, and they moved on to the next bed . . .

The patients in this place were all adults, she noticed. There was not a single child in the infirmary.

But still I gotta learn, she thought. It's the least I can do. Clenching her fists, she set herself to pay attention to what Lemman was telling her. Sometimes, when treating an accident or burn victim, the first part of his method was all talk. Is found this very puzzling.

"Listen to me; look at this," he would say, holding up a candle or his little silver pencil. "Imagine that you are not here in the hospital; think that you are walking down a grassy path to a cool, fast-flowing river. Now you are *in* the river—in the cool water. You feel very cool and light, your pain has all drifted away . . ."

A few of the patients looked at him blankly, without comprehension, and seemed unable to imagine themselves anywhere else, but they were not the worst sufferers. Many of these appeared to obtain great relief, right away, from being told that they were in a cool, swift-running river. Often they would fall asleep, which made it easier for Lemman to do what was needed for them. And when they woke later, Lemman told Is, they were often a good deal better than might have been expected.

After he had finished his rounds in the infirmary—which took a long time, several hours—and they were outside again in the fresh air, Lemman said to Is, "You did well, dearie. To tell the truth, I was surprised at how well you did."

Is said, "Axcuse me, Doc—I gotta go off a minute and lob me groats—"

She fled away from him, around to the far side of a huge heap of coal dust. When she returned she was pale, damp, and shivering, but composed.

They climbed into the pony trap and started for home.

After the doctor had driven a short way, Is asked him, "Doc, how the blazes do you do it? That game of telling folk they are in a river—what in the name of wonder put such a fix-up into your head?"

"Why, dearie," he said, "the notion wasn't mine. A doctor called Braid, in Manchester, he first had the idea, not long ago; I worked with him for a short time and studied his methods. It's called *Braidism* or hypnotic suggestion. You've seen how it works. If you persuade someone that they aren't so bad as they think—well, as you see, it often has a good effect. They fall asleep, and when they wake, the symptoms are relieved."

"Suppose you suggested summat bad—that they might get worse, or die?"

"No doctor would do such a thing!" he told her severely. "A doctor swears an oath, at the start of his training, that he will work only to relieve suffering."

Is pondered. After a while she said, "Could *I* do that to folk, d'you think? That Braid job?"

He took a moment to answer, then said, "I think it quite possible that you could. You're a pretty strong-minded lass, dearie! You might be an ornament to the medical profession —only, of course, women aren't permitted. You'd not be allowed to qualify. But just you watch what I do, as we go the rounds, and you will soon be a great help to me. Furthermore you'll find that folk put a lot of trust in you, once you've Braided them a few times." He whipped up the mare.

"You ever do it to Aunt Ishie? For her lameness?"

"Couldn't," he said cheerfully. "Your aunt Ishie has all her—"

"Oh, look, Doc! There's someone a-calling to you."

They were crossing the dock and passing a ship, the *Dark Diamond,* that was being loaded with coal. A bearded man leaning over the rail called, "Hey, Doc! Doc Lemman!"

"Captain Podmore! How are you, man?"

"All the better for seeing you, Doc!"

"And the leg?"

"I'm walking on it, bean't I? Come aboard for a noggin, and I'll show you—and while you're here you can look at one of my men who has the Spanish quinsy."

"We must not stay above five minutes," Lemman said, with a quick look about him. Dusk was thickening, and the dock seemed deserted. The mare once tethered to a bollard, they climbed up the companionway onto a deck that was black and gritty with coal dust.

"We sail on the night tide," explained Captain Podmore. "That way it's easy to run the blockade—bless you, I know all the ways around the sandbanks like the palm of me own hand! Now, just you take a look at this leg, Doc; ain't that enough to make your heart swell with pride? When you think it was lying separate in the scuppers?"

He pulled up his bell-bottomed trouser leg to exhibit a complete ring of stitches around the knee, then executed a few steps of a hornpipe. "He sewed it right back on, missy, like you might sew the leg on a doll," he explained to Is, while Dr. Lemman quickly examined the crewman with quinsy, "and now I reckon it walks faster than the other!"

"Captain Podmore," said Is, who had suddenly been visited by an excellent notion, "where do you take your coal?"

He laid a finger alongside his nose and winked. "Ah, now, my lass, mum's the word on that course! I know Humberland is at war with the south, but there's folk down to Lunnon town as wants their sea coal, war or no war! And Isiah Podmore's not the man to fly in the face of turning a few honest guineas just because of two-three pesky gunboats— no, stap my vitals, he isn't!"

"You go to the Port of London? Captain Podmore, did you ever run across a chap called Greenaway—a big, blind cove, lives in a ware-us, Shadwell Dock way?"

"Know him?" cried Captain Podmore, pouring out a mug of grog for Lemman. "Know Sam Greenaway? Why, bless you, him an' me's just like that!" And he set down the bottle in order to slam one fist into the other palm.

"Could you take a letter to him, Captain Podmore?"

The captain glanced about warily, as Lemman had done, and said to the doctor, who joined them at that moment, "Hearken to the lass! She just wants me to lose my ears and my charter, that's all! But . . ."—to Is, as her face fell—"I don't say but what I might manage it, to oblige a friend of the doc's, here. Let's have it, then."

On another sheet from Lemman's prescription pad, Is wrote: DERE WAL IM AT GRANDPA TWITES IN BLASTBURN. THINGS HERE IS DICEY. HAINT SEEN U NO WHO BUT ERLY DAYS YET. CAN YOU PASS WORD AN LOVE TO PEN. ILL BE HERE LONGER THAN A MUNTH I REKON.

"I'm reel obliged to you, mister," said Is, handing him the note, which he slid into his tobacco pouch. ("That way, no one's like to come across it.")

"We'd best be on our way, dearie," said Lemman, "or your aunt Ishie will be in a fret."

When they were driving home, Lemman asked Is, "If you saw a leg like that, one that had been severed, what would you do?"

She thought. "Fust, I'd shove down hard on the spot what stops the blood coming out—here"—she demonstrated—"then I'd put on a whatyoucallem, the thing where you winds a kerchief around a kindling stick—don't tell me the name, *don't*—a turney-key. Then I'd sew the leg on again, quick as be-damned."

Laughing, he patted her shoulder.

"Yes, I do believe you've the makings! Too bad females can't train."

"Ho! Can't they?" said Is. She stuck out her jaw. "Ask me, a whole lot o' things wants changing."

"Did you have another of your hearkening experiences back in the hospital?" he asked. "You were pretty quiet in there."

"Wouldn't a person *be*? Yes, I did, though," she said. "And you were right. I found out how to talk back a bit."

"You did? But, dearie, that's exciting! Who is he? Who is it?"

"It ain't a him. It's a *them*—a whole lot of 'em. They say they are the Bottom Layer."

Journal of Is

So much as bin goin on I ardly knows were to start. Had luk getn off trane an fund G.P. Twites place more luk. Ant Isshie is Prime. Kids in Play Land is slaves. Lord nos if Ill ever find Arn or tother Cove it dont seem likly. But Doc Lems goin to tak me in the mines an fundris he sez. Hes Prime too. Sez hell lurn me doctrin. Fancy me a doc. Pennl be rit pleezed. Uncle Roys a nogood. GP Twite a bit Queer. Rit a note wich Capt P sez hell tak thats more luk. Summat reel spooky is makin me here Voicis its scary. I feel reel sad about pore King Dick wot lost is Boy.

6

DURING THE NEXT TWO WEEKS IS WORKED EXCEEDINGLY HARD, going out with Dr. Lemman on his rounds by day, helping Aunt Ishie make pockets by night. And when she went to bed, sleeping on a little frame cot Lemman had rigged up for her, she had terribly strange dreams. She dreamed that she was all alone in a stone forest, in the dark, trying to find her way; sometimes she could hear whispers and murmurs, as if other people were there, but she could never find them. She woke up from these dreams very anxious and perplexed.

"What do you think they mean?" she asked Aunt Ishie, who said, "I think you will find out quite soon. My dreams always come through to me in some real-life happening quite quickly."

The pockets they were making, Is learned, were for the children who worked in the mines.

"They have none, otherwise," Ishie told Is. "The gals wear naught but a short skirt, or breeks like the boys. They have no shirts, for they work mostly on all fours, hacking the coal or pulling the trucks along, and clothes would only hinder them—some are naked. So they've no place to tuck in a handkerchief, or a bit of bread or cold potato. That's why I make the pockets, you see, with a flap and a button, pockets they can tie around their necks."

For once, Is had nothing to say. She just nodded and went on helping.

"I am not permitted to take the pockets to the miners myself," Ishie went on. "I have asked Roy repeatedly, but he will not allow it. And," with a sigh, "even if I were allowed through the mine gate, I fear the distance would be too great. Some of the galleries are five miles from the entrance."

"Five miles under the sea?"

Aunt Ishie nodded. "As I told you, that is why the workers are never allowed out. They live in the mine. Mercifully I am lucky enough to have a—an associate who undertakes that part of the task, delivering the pockets to the colliers and hurriers—"

"What's a hurrier?"

"They bring the coal in trucks from the rockface to the loading area."

"Who takes the pockets for you?"

"Well, my love, I think I had better not tell you his name. He is a simple fellow, slightly crazed, but it is a dangerous mission; and what the ear does not hear, the tongue cannot divulge. Even your grandfather does not know him—"

"It's not Arn Twite—nor Davie?" Is asked anxiously.
Aunt Ishie shook her head and laid her finger on her lips.

> "I tell the truth, but never speak
> French or English, Latin or Greek
> My face never smiles, my hands never hold
> Though they may be made of silver or gold"

chanted Grandfather Twite, passing through the kitchen
with a bale of paper.

"Easy, Grandpa! A clock!" Is shouted after him down the
stairs to the cellar. The sound of her voice made him trip
and drop the paper; she ran down after him and helped
gather it together again.

From her rides with the doctor, Is quite soon began to
have a fair knowledge of the underground city of Holdernesse, not only its grander main squares and avenues, but also
the smaller, darker streets near the sides of the great cave,
close to the mine entrance. Here the less prosperous citizens
lived, some of whom had already begun to wish they were
back living out-of-doors again; they found that the benefit
of never having wet or snowy weather outside the front door
was quite outweighed by the stuffy atmosphere, and the low-
ering effect on their spirits of never being able to see sky
through the windows, or feel the wind.

"Even if 'tis gray and bitter and blowing marlin spikes,"
one old man said, "at least 'tis *there*! I'd dearly like a sight of
the old moon, or a star or two. I reckon 'Im Above sent us
the weather to keep us 'opping on our pins; 'tain't natural to
live without, 'tis like vittles wi' no salt."

There were a great many rats in Holdernesse too. But they
were not mentioned by polite people.

At the end of the second week there was an explosion at the iron foundry; one of the blast furnaces had blown out. Dr. Lemman was sent for urgently.

The ironworks lay close to the docks. As they approached, Is could see lines of rail cars and great piles of iron ore—rusty purplish-brown powder, rough and dirty as it had been dug out of the ground—waiting to be cleaned of its impurities, melted down, and made into pots and tools and machines. Like brown sugar, she thought, waiting to be melted into candy.

Ahead of them lay the blast furnaces, rearing up like giant brick beehives.

"What do they burn in them?" asked Is, while the old mare picked her way among piles of scrap metal and files of trucks.

"Coke; that's coal with the gas baked out of it. They do that here first, in those kilns on the left."

"Why not use coal?"

"Coke heats up hotter. Also, coal's full of gas, likely to explode."

"Well they got an explosion now anyway, don't they?" said Is.

"That's because they never take enough care. There's always a bit of gas left in the coke."

Dr. Lemman, followed by Is, walked into a huge place like a frightful satanic cathedral, with a high roof supported by pillars of iron; a place that echoed all the time with the clang of machines and the roar of furnaces and other unidentifiable noises—wrenching, hissing, grinding—as well as human screams and shouts. The humans were there, but could only be seen dimly among jets of flame and clouds of smoke, among heaps of coal or slag, among pipes and machinery, and the sudden awful glow of red-hot metal.

People were running about frantically. Lemman was wanted everywhere at once.

"Doctor! Doctor! Here for God's sake, come here!"

At first Is helped him, handing remedies and bandages as fast as she could; then, since there were so many waiting for attention, she began dealing with the less serious cases herself. They were mostly terrible burns, which Lemman treated with wet cloths dipped in bicarbonate of soda, or with a mixture of olive oil and lime water. And, over and over, with his quiet, soothing, potent suggestion that the sufferers were walking into a river of cool, buoyant water that would help to heal their hurts. Some of the cases, not so serious, were simply anointed with lard; Lemman had stopped at a butcher's shop on the way and picked up several large tubs of it.

One boy had lost his hand in an overflow of molten metal. He lay on a pile of sacks, moaning.

"No sense treating *him*, he won't be much use after," said one of the overseers, passing near.

Is caught the boy's eye. He was conscious; he had heard what the man said.

Blazing with fury, she determined to save him if it could be done.

"Doc. Doc! Could you come and see to this feller? I'll do the gal with the burned back, I can manage that. *Please*, Doc!" as he hesitated.

He gave a sudden grin and a nod, changing places with her; she heard him say to the boy, "We'll fix you up, dearie, don't fret."

Kneeling on the muddy, puddly, coaly ground, Is carefully poured oil over the girl's back.

The girl, who had been whimpering faintly, caught her breath and said, "*That* helps. Thanks, love!"

"You been here long?" Is asked, carefully laying on court plaster (which was silk treated with isinglass and balsam of Peru; she had helped Lemman prepare a quantity of it earlier in the week).

"Nope—only a coupla weeks—came on the perishing train—wish to blazes now I'd stayed at the lacemaker's in Shoreditch—" gasped the girl.

No use asking her about the boys, then, thought Is.

She moved on to the next patient, and the next . . .

Meanwhile the rest of the workers in the foundry went about their business; furnaces roared, white-hot dazzling metal was poured like liquid sunshine into great sluices, cooled to a dull red glow; was beaten, puddled, sliced, hammered, reheated, and slung into water, where it hissed and gave out clouds of scalding steam. The hurt workers were forgotten, the work went on.

After four hours of nonstop labor, all the possible cases had been treated. Since there was room in the infirmary for only about half of them, the rest were taken to a shed near the river, where they lay on canvas cots or piles of sacking.

"There's a boy over here wants a word with you," said Lemman as—filthy, grimed, greasy, and bloodstained—he and Is were preparing to leave.

Is went where he pointed: It was the boy who had lost his hand.

"Reckon I owe you," he said hoarsely. He could only just speak.

"No odds, cully," said Is. "You'd do as much for me. When you mend, you could get work doing folks' gardens."

"No gardens in this place," he muttered. "But I'll find summat—"

"You ever come across a boy called Arn Twite?" Is asked him in a low tone. "Or David Stuart?"

"Never met no Arn. Davie I knew well enough—he was with me on Number Four furnace . . ." His voice trailed off.

"When? How long ago?"

"I—I—" His eyes closed.

"I'll come back tomorrow," Is muttered quickly.

But when they came back next day the boy was no longer there. The overseer in charge of the accident cases told them he had died in the night and already been buried.

"And it's as well," he said shortly. "What use would he 'a been? Nowt but wasted time, treating ones like that."

Is found one or two other people among the injured who had at one time or another worked on Number Four furnace, but none could remember David Stuart.

Grandfather Twite had decided to print some of Penny's stories, and asked Is to recall as many of them as she could.

"Ishie can write them down for us—she writes a neat hand—and then I will print them and make a little booklet, and perhaps she will find some means of distributing it to the workers. Such as can read, or have any chance of reading."

"Shouldn't think as how many can," said Is doubtfully. "If they start work at five, how'd they ever have time?"

But still, she liked the idea. And at least the workers in the foundries, breweries, or potteries worked in daylight, and lived together in lodgings aboveground; perhaps they might be able to snatch a chance to read occasionally. Penny would be pleased, too, Is thought. So at pocket-making time, while she stitched, she told Aunt Ishie the stories about the harp of fishbones, and the crocodile who swallowed the dark, and the glass dragon, and the girl who talked to the dead king, and Aunt Ishie wrote them down in her neat, clear handwriting.

"Aunt Ishie?" said Is one evening, when they were putting away their work.

"Well, my love?"

"When you foretell the weather that's coming—how do you do it?"

"I begin to have a kind of prickle, or a tingle, and then I can *feel* the cold—or the heat, or the wind, whatever is coming. Sometimes I can see sky or snow, or clouds—"

"See them? How?"

"In my mind's eye," said Ishie, and Is nodded. She was beginning to see faces in her mind's eye. But the Touch had not visited her for some time.

Not long after the foundry explosion, Is and the doctor had just returned from a long round of mixed patients when Lemman was called out again. A ship had been sunk by a southern gunboat, and hurt survivors were coming ashore on the beaches beyond Holdernesse Hill.

"I'll come too!" said Is at once, but he told her, "No, dearie, you've done plenty for today."

"I don't mind. Honest!"

"No," he said again firmly, "I've another errand I want you to do for me, dearie, and that's to take some pills to Mrs. Gower."

"Mrs. Gower!" Her voice showed her scorn.

"She has her troubles too. Run along, like a kind crea-ture."

"Oh, very well!" snapped Is.

It was no more than a twenty-minute walk down through the ruined streets to the arched entrance into Holdernesse town and the tunnel leading to Twite Square; but it was just as well that Dr. Lemman had obtained an official pass, coun-tersigned and sealed by the district supervisor, for Is was stopped three times by wardens or constables, demanding to know what an unaccompanied child of her age was doing out in the street.

It'd be like *prison* living in this town, she thought as she rapped the knocker, and the handsome door of the Gower mansion was opened by a parlormaid in cap and apron.

"Who is it? Is that the doctor?" came an anxious call from upstairs.

"No ma'am—'tis only the young lass, his 'prentice," the maid called back.

"Oh dear—I had *so* hoped for Dr. Lemman himself!"

"He had to go to a shipwreck!" Is shouted crossly up the stairs.

Mrs. Gower came out and leaned over the banister. Her face was pale and disappointed.

"Will you come up, please," she said, glancing warily at the maid. "That will do, Maria . . . I wished to ask Dr. Lemman *so* many questions—about taking the tablets—"

"Every two hours, he said, till the pain gets better," said Is, dying to get back to pocket-making and storytelling.

"But I also wanted to ask him about little Coppy."

Reluctantly, Is climbed the stairs. She felt certain that all Mrs. Gower's alarms would turn out to be needless fuss

about nothing. Dr. Lemman seemed to have unlimited patience with such people; Is found this hard to comprehend.

She followed Mrs. Gower into a large, handsome first-
floor parlor. Its bow windows looked out across the brightly
lit square. The waxed floor shone like a frozen lake; spindly
pieces of furniture stood elegantly about with wide spaces in
between; there were china ornaments in glass-fronted cabi-
nets and silk curtains and crystal lusters. It was very different
from Grandpa Twite's kitchen.

In the middle of the floor, on a Persian rug, a small curly-
headed boy was playing with a wooden train.

"Chuff, chuff," he murmured busily. "Chuff-chuff-
chuff."

Another woman sat on a slender settee watching him intently. She, like Mrs. Gower, was thin, pale, dark-haired, and
wore an exquisitely frilled and embroidered gown. There
was a look of infinite sadness on her face.

"My sister, Mrs. Macclesfield," said Mrs. Gower vaguely,
"er, Dr. Lemman's assistant . . ." She made no attempt to
discover Dr. Lemman's assistant's name.

Now they could study Is close to, both ladies gazed at her
in evident dismay. And she could easily read their thoughts.
What possible help would she be able to give them?

"Look—Doc Lemman tells me everything he can about
the folk he sees, and what he does to cure 'em," Is explained
to the sisters. "I'm beginning to be able to guess what he'll
do, as often as not. So, what's fretting you? If I can't be any
use I'll tell you straight enough; I wouldn't fool you. Honest!
Is it summat ails the kid?"

She glanced at Coppy. He looked well enough—pale, as
everybody was in the town of Holdernesse, but quite stocky
and robust in his little blue velvet sailor suit and frilled collar.

Mrs. Gower burst into racking sobs.

"No—no—no—he is well enough," she wept. "That's the trouble! He is very well-grown, he looks already like a boy of five. But he is only four! I'm afraid—I am so afraid. We ought to send him away. I know it. My husband says so. Mr. Gower says Coppy ought to be sent off to boarding school in Scotland—there is an accredited school at Grantown for the children of government officials—but oh, but oh, he is so *young* to be sent so far away from his home!"

"You're feared he'll get nabbled if he stays here?"

"He *looks* like a five-year-old!" wept Mrs. Gower. "And they are growing less and less scrupulous—my husband says there is an acute shortage of pit-hands."

Her sister put a protective arm round her shoulders; she turned and hugged the other woman convulsively. "Oh, Susan! Whatever shall I do?"

"But—croopus! If your husband—if Mr. Gower is a government official—can't he see that don't happen? To his own *son*?"

"Even he would not dare. People have vanished away—nobody knows what becomes of them. My own sister's husband—"

"Can't you jist leave, both of you, with the kid? Go to live somewhere else, where they *don't* swipe the kids off the streets?"

"Leave our beautiful house? And Mr. Gower is a very important man—deputy moderator—he does not enter into my feelings about this—he says it is *best* that we send Coppy to Scotland. I cannot argue with him. But I had hoped that Dr. Lemman—"

"Indeed, my dear, I believe you must send the boy," said

Mrs. Macclesfield earnestly. "Better that, than what—" She stopped and bit her lip.

"My sister's Helen was taken," Mrs. Gower gulped out. "She was eight—they thought they had managed to keep her presence in the house a total secret—she was never, never allowed out. But somebody—one of the servants—must have laid information. The wardens came at night and seized her—the parents had to pay a heavy fine—Helen has never been seen since. And my brother-in-law—when he protested—he, too—"

Is took a long, slow breath. She looked at the two unhappy ladies. Then she squatted down on the floor beside Coppy, still busily pushing his train between two lines of the pattern on the rug.

"Hey, Coppy! Would you like to go to school in Scotland? And learn lessons out of books? And play with other kids?"

"Iss!" he said cheerfully.

She experienced a warm, jolting shock in her mind, as if some ray of communication had shot between them on a level that he, surely, was far too young to understand. But—understanding or not—he was aware of it, all right. He grinned up at Is, patted her cheek, and said, "Go to Scotland with *you!*"

"Heavens above!" breathed Mrs. Gower in astonishment. "He *never* did so before. Usually he is shy with strangers—afraid of them."

Is rose to her feet. "I reckon you'd do best to send him to Scotland, ma'am," she said. "He's got plenty of grit in him. He'll make his way. Not but it ain't right hard on you, having to let him go; but I reckon Doc Lemman'd say the same."

"Thank you," whispered Mrs. Gower. "I—I daresay you are right. Since Coppy . . . has taken such a liking to you—" Her throat closed, she could say no more, but turned and hid her face on her sister's shoulder.

Is, embarrassed, nodded awkwardly at the other woman, then turned and took her way down the stairs. The unsmiling maid was ready at the foot to let her out, and she started on the walk home.

Poor devils, she thought, stirred and saddened by what she had seen and heard. *Nothing* about this hateful place is any good. Nobody is happy. Not even the rich ones.

And while she walked, in her mind again she felt the Touch, as she had done just now when kneeling by Coppy— but this time it was immeasurably magnified: a chorus, a host of voices all calling to her at once: Help us, help us, we are so lost and lonely and separated, talk to us, tell us there is hope somewhere, help us, help us, help us.

I will. I will try to help you, she promised; only tell me where you are, *who* you are, tell me how to find you, where you are, tell me?

But, as before, the connection faded and failed, and she was left to finish her walk home in dark and solitude. I sure miss Blackheath Wood and the smell of leaves, she thought, and my old Figgin-cat. But at least there's plenty to do here, and plenty to think about.

When she reached Wasteland Cottages she was surprised to find that Number Two still had lights showing downstairs. Normally by this time the elderly inmates would have retired to bed. But perhaps Dr. Lemman had come back unexpectedly soon from his errand to the shipwrecked sailors and was sharing Mr. Twite's nightly mug of saloop.

Is pushed open the door and walked along the passage to

the kitchen. A candle guttered low, but no one was in the room. Even Montrose was missing from the box where he normally slept at night. A note on the table in Aunt Ishie's small, neat writing said: "Called out to deathbed in Warren. Cannot say when will return. Soup in brown bowl. Remind your great-g to take his warm drink. I.T."

Since Grandfather Twite was neither painting at his easel, nor reading, nor in bed, Is guessed that he must still be working in the cellar. The stair door was shut, but a crack of light showed under it. Taking the candle, she went to the door and was about to open it when she heard somebody coming up from below. The step seemed queerly heavy; it was slow, powerful, and uneven, like a large beast blundering its way through a thicket, ready to pounce.

Is opened the stair door.

"Grandpa?" she said, "Is that you?" peering past the candle into the dimness below. "Aunt Ishie said—"

No answer came, save a loud grunt. Startled, somewhat discomposed, she raised her candle higher.

If the man coming up the stair had not been wearing Grandfather Twite's clothes, Is would not have recognized him. Even as it was, she doubted her own eyes.

He seemed to have increased hugely in height and bulk. His pale-brown skin was shiny and swelled, darkened to a crimson, almost black color. His mouth was wide open. His eyes were so inflamed that they seemed twice their normal size, and they blazed at her with the expressionless luminosity of wild-cats' eyes. Runnels of sweat ran down his forehead and cheeks; his scanty white hair was soaked, as if someone had poured a jug of water over his head. In one shaking hand he held a mug of liquor, in the other the long iron handle that was used for dragging down the printing press. He panted heavily.

"Grandpa?" said Is doubtfully. "Grandpa, are you—are you sick?"

The brilliant eyes flared and fixed on her like those of a stalking tiger. He lifted up the iron handle and yelled, "Fiend! Devil! Begone, accursht shpirit!"

To see her familiar great-grandfather so monstrously transformed was such a shock—so totally, bewilderingly unexpected—that, for a second, Is hesitated. If she had waited another second, she would have been done for. She leapt back, the iron bar came smashing down on the top step of the stair, and bent into a U with the force of the blow. A large chip of stone flew up.

"Grandfather!" yelled Is. "It's me—Is! Don't! *Don't*!"

For he was coming at her again with the bent handle.

"Fiensh!" he growled. "Shor—shor—shorshereshesh! Shplit their shkulls!"

His mug of toddy had fallen and broken on the stair, but a tremendous fume of spirits came from him. Is, recalling her father, could now recognize that he was drunk—but she had never encountered drunkenness like this. It was hair-raising.

She fled through the front door and hid behind a holly bush.

The fearsome figure came out of the house and blundered down the path.

"Shlay 'em all!" he was shouting. "Shlaughter 'em all—shplit and shtab and shtifle 'em!"

He vanished, swaying and staggering, into the snowy lane.

Is thought of Aunt Ishie, who might return at any time—of Dr. Lemman, who might also appear. But she needed help; she could not tackle this transformed grandfather on her own.

She hurled herself back through the front door and up the stairs, up and up again, afraid that at any moment she might hear Mr. Twite's step behind her. A gleam of light showed under Father Lancelot's door.

She banged on the panel and shouted, "Help me, *please*! Grandfather's on the rampage!"

The door opened at once. "I was afraid of that," said Father Lancelot, and pulled her inside. "Montrose has been in my room these last two hours."

The cat was crouched nervously and angrily on Father Lancelot's table. He greeted Is with a snarling mew and a hiss.

"Gold Kingy called while you were out," said Father Lancelot. "The wretched man always seems to know, as if by telepathy, when your grandfather is on his own. He comes here and encourages him to drink . . ."

"But what'll happen when they come back—Aunt Ishie and the doc? Grandfather nearly done for me just now, with the press handle—what'll he do to them?"

"Oh, he won't hurt them—he knows them too well. He never does, even when he's like this. Very soon he will fall down and sleep. Stay there, child, while I investigate."

Is was glad to drop limply onto a stool. Her opinion of Father Lancelot shot up as, apparently quite unafraid, he ran briskly down the stairs. She heard his voice:

"Mr. Twite? Mr. Twite, are you there?"

Feeling almost light-headed from shock, Is turned to the cat. "Why didn't you warn me Grandfather could be like that?" But he only growled in answer.

If Grandfather can change so, suppose the others can too?

thought Is in sudden terror. She tried to imagine Aunt Ishie with a meat ax in her hand, Dr. Lemman coming at her with one of his scalpels, Father Lancelot wielding the poker. But no, no; they were safe, they were sensible and reliable. And it was not Grandfather's fault, poor old sausage. It was Gold Kingy she really had to thank for this.

Father Lancelot was calling from below: "He has fallen in a fit—or swooned. Can you help me lift him?"

Shakily, but scolding herself for a faintheart, Is crept down the stairs and went out to Father Lancelot, who stood in the lane, where old Mr. Twite lay snoring under a thornbush.

"We daren't leave him here, he would freeze. If you take his arms and I his legs . . ."

"Ain't he a weight, though!" panted Is, as they struggled. "I wish we had Aunt Ishie's sled."

"Solid muscle," grunted Father Lancelot. "All that ramming down of the press handle."

Luckily, while they were still only halfway to the door, Dr. Lemman arrived home.

"Oh, devil take it!" he said, at once grasping the situation. "Gold Kingy's been here."

"No prizes," growled Father Lancelot.

"Here—give us a leg. That bastard always gets him drunk; it's his notion of a good joke."

The two men carried Grandpa Twite inside; Is ran ahead and cleared the books off the bed so they could lay him in it.

"Now he'll sleep for twenty-four hours," said Lemman. "We can do nothing more for him. Very likely when he wakes he'll remember nothing. —Were you scared, dearie?" to Is.

"Scared? I was *scarified*! Look: He went for me with this." She found the buckled press handle. "If he'd a' hit me with that, I'd 'a bin in two halves. A body takes their life in their hands, staying in this house."

"Poor old boy. I suppose we should have warned you. It does not happen very often—only when Roy finds him alone. He always hopes, you see, while your great-grandfather is the worse for drink, to extract the secret of his longevity from him."

"What a rotten game! I reckon Grandpa's one too many for Uncle Roy."

"Well—so far he has been. But his tongue does become loosened when he is half-seas-over. That is why it's best not to tell him anything that . . . that you would not wish to reach the ears of your uncle."

Dr. Lemman glanced about him and went on in a low tone, "As a matter of fact, dearie, I have something of that kind to tell you now. So it's as well the old fellow is off his hinge."

"I'm away to bed," said Father Lancelot hastily. "*I* don't want to hear anything of that kind."

"What's up, then?" asked Is, when she and Lemman were alone.

"The ship that went down was Captain Podmore's *Dark Diamond;* but he and his crew were all rescued, luckily. I saw him and he gave me a message for you. Your letter was safely delivered. He had an answer for you, but it was lost in the wreck. But he told me to tell you that the matter is very urgent, for somebody referred to as *him with the hatband* is getting queerer and queerer."

"With the hatband?" Oh, Lordy, thought Is, I reckon that must mean Dick, poor old King Dick. Getting sicker and sicker. Croopus, there ain't any time to lose.

Is went slowly up the stairs, rubbing her forehead. Dunno

as I can go on staying at Wasteland Cottages, she thought. Lemman's a good cove, I wisht I could go on learning from him. And I purely love Aunt Ishie. But . . .

Journal of Is

Seems every now & then Grandpa has a lush-out & then Hes a Holy Teror. Im sory now I let out to im about Prince Dave. But hope he wont remimber. Rekn I gotta leev here & go in the foundriz, rekn thats were those boys may be. Can't keep a jurnel there, so Ill havta stop.

Aunt Ishie was deeply distressed, next day, when she came home from her charitable errand to find Grandpa Twite flat out on his bed and reeking of spirits.

"Oh, how I wish he would give up these terrible drinking bouts. Indeed, I quite thought he had; he has not indulged like this for many months."

She looked regretfully at the old man, who was snoring like a traction engine.

"He will be so sorry when he wakes. He always is."

"Couldn't you throw out all his liquor while he's swiped off?" suggested Is.

"No, we tried that once. But he would only brew up some more. He cannot endure to think that there is none ready at hand, although he touches it so rarely."

"But when he *does*—croopus!"

Is and Dr. Lemman had come back for the noon meal. While they were swallowing their soup, a black Maria, drawn by two black cobs, drew up in the lane outside.

A crease appeared in Ishie's back-sloping brow. "*Now* what is Roy up to?" she wondered.

To the pair of officials who came to the door she said, "If you want my father, it is no use at all. You are wasting your time. He is asleep and will be for hours yet. Tell my nephew —tell the moderator that."

"It ain't the old cove we want," said one of the constables. "It's the young lass."

"For pity's sake—what for?"

They shrugged. "None of our business. 'Bring her,' he said."

"Me?" said Is. "You mean me?"

One of the men pulled out a requisition form. "See? Is Twite. His Nibs wishes to parley with you."

"Don't let him fuss you, that's all, dearie," advised Lemman. "You stand up for yourself." His tone was calm, but his eyes were anxious.

Is rather wished, as the black cab approached Gold Kingy's residence, that her clothes were in better condition. The fur jacket that Penny had made her (what a long time ago that seemed!) was now very worn and greasy. And the grandeur of Uncle Roy's palace was daunting, with its row of pink granite pillars all along one side of Twite Square.

However, she jumped out of the carriage, displaying what she hoped was a bold and carefree countenance.

Two more men, dressed as ushers in dark green with white gloves and stocks, were waiting to lead her inside and down a long hall.

All these big strapping coves just idling around, thought Is; they could use 'em better in the foundries.

"His Grace will receive her in the audience chamber," somebody said.

The audience chamber was on the ground floor and was

modeled (so Lemman told Is later) on the palace of a Mogul prince.

Gold Kingy sat perched in a seat on top of a pillar in the center of the chamber. The pillar (about the height of two men) was connected by four arched stone bridges with a gallery that ran around the sides of the room. And the throne on which Roy sat was made to revolve so that, when the hall down below was full of people, he could rotate himself and speak to anybody below, wherever he chose.

At present the hall was empty, apart from Is and her escort. But another man came quietly in from a different door and stood listening not far away in the shadows. Is did not look at him. Her attention was all on Gold Kingy.

Today he wore a white ruff around his neck, a prune-color velvet jacket and bulgy breeches with slashed satin insets. Is recognized the costume; it was like one that Penny had used for an old-fashioned King of England doll. But her uncle, she thought, looked right silly in the fancy dress.

"Come here, girl!" he ordered. "Down below, there, where I can see you."

The ushers nudged her forward.

"Hey-day, Uncle Roy," she said coolly. "But ain't it Doc Lemman you oughta be seeing? Is it your liver that's a-fretting you? Doc told me to advise you to drink a lot o' cold water—gills and gills of it—with a teaspoonful of bicarb to every gill. That's if you drank as much as poor old Grandpa did last night—"

"Quiet, girl! If I wished to consult Lemman, I would have sent for him."

He scowled down at Is.

"Yes, you do have a decided look of your father—that scheming devil," he muttered to himself. "That cheating swindling robbing lying underhanded mealy-mouthed false black-hearted brother of mine! Many a dirty trick he served me. —I suppose you were very fond of him?" he suddenly demanded of Is.

"Who, me? Of my dad? No. Not on your oliphant. Why should you reckon that? I couldn't stand 'im," retorted Is. "He never did *me* any good turn that I can recollect—except dying before he gave King Dick the trouble of hanging 'im."

"Ah: That's what I want to talk to you about. I had a law passed that anybody who comes into the principality of Humberland must report all important news that they bring with them from abroad."

"How the pize should I know about any such law?" demanded Is.

"Well—well, your great-grandfather should have told you. Or your great-aunt. They know very well that all important foreign intelligence must be brought to me directly."

"Such as what?" inquired Is. "I was living in the woods on Blackheath Edge. What d'ye expect me to know? The price of hazelnuts?"

"Do not chop words with me, girl! You know what I mean. You told your great-grandfather that the king's son was lost—run away. Why did you not bring that information to me?"

Oh, Crispin, thought Is. I knew I shouldn't have let that out to Grandpa; the minute the words left my mouth I knew it was a bad mistake. Poor old Grandad; he can't help hisself, but now what a peck o'trouble he's let us in for.

"It was a Banbury story," she said. "No one knows if it's so or not. Very like he ain't lost at all. No one in Lunnon spoke of it. Or not as I knows of."

"Oh? And how do you know what the people in London

know—or don't know—if you lived in a wood on Blackheath Edge?"

"Tales that peddlers tell," said Is vaguely.

"So you have never seen the king himself? You have never been to St. James's Palace?"

"Why the blue blazes should King Richard want to see *me*? Or ask me to his palace?"

"Then *why* have you been asking questions about a boy called David Stuart?" suddenly thundered Uncle Roy. Taking advantage of her startled silence, he jumped from his throne, nipped across one of the bridges to the gallery, and ran down a flight of steps to ground level.

He walked up to Is, stared her in the face (his eyes were very bloodshot, she noticed, and he smelled of rum and peppermint), then roared at her: "I think you know more than you say. What can you tell me about King Richard? What is his state of health?"

"I can't tell you a tuppenny thing, Uncle Roy," answered Is calmly.

"Why are you searching for his son?"

"I'm a-looking for my cousin Arn Twite, Uncle. Son of my uncle Hose, you remember him? Uncle Hose lost his boy Arn and he was real cut up about it, missed him something crool (goodness knows why, for he said himself he never spoke to him when he was at home). Anyway, with his last dying breath he ast me to look out for Arn. Which I am a-doing, as best I can. Arn had a friend called Davie and—with luck—if I can find one, I kin find t'other."

Heaven help me, she added inwardly.

"Davie Stuart is not the son of King Richard?"

"How the dickens should I know that?" asked Is. "Stuart's a common enough name—specially up here in these parts."

Uncle Roy looked at her long and hard.

"You had better not lie to me," he said. "For if you do, I can—I can send you to a place you won't like at all."

Well, and if you send me to the foundries, thought Is, if that's what you mean, you nasty bully, maybe that'd suit me down to the ground.

She did not utter this thought aloud, but it almost seemed as if some inkling of it had penetrated into her uncle's mind, for he went on, very menacingly, "You think yourself mighty clever, don't you, riding about with Lemman on his visits, doling out drops and drams to his patients, asking questions about lost boys. Well—you take a look at this!"

Out of his bulging breeches' pocket he dragged, with some difficulty, a kind of small sledgehammer. It had a short handle and a massively heavy head. "You see this hammer?"

"Can't hardly help it, can I, Uncle Roy?"

"I could get one of my wardens to strap your hand to a bench, and another one to bring this hammer down on it— hard! Yes"—as she flinched—"you were asking questions of a boy without a hand the other day in the foundry; asking him about Davie Stuart. Weren't you? So you know what it would be like to lose a hand. You'd not be so handy then at helping the doctor, would you?" He laughed, most unpleasantly. "Now"—as her mouth opened to answer—"I don't want to hear any more from you. Not at present. You go home and think over what I've said. Maybe there's some more information you can give me about King Richard. Information that would be useful to me. Or about the boy. Go home and give my regards to your great-grandfather and your great-aunt. You're fond of them—eh? You wouldn't want any harm to come to *them*?"

"*Grandfather*—and Aunt *Ishie*? You *wouldn't*—"

"You don't think I got to be Moderator of Humberland by fooling around being kind to my aunts and cousins, do you?" he yelled at her.

No, I certainly don't think that, Uncle Roy, she silently responded. But still, you got a *use* for Grandfather—you don't want to lose him. Or do you?

As the thought struck her, she came out with it.

"Did Grandpa *tell* you, then? When he was plastered—ginnified?"

"Tell me what?"

"About what keeps him ticking over; why he's lived for such a tarnal long time."

One glance at his face assured her that this information was still Mr. Twite's own secret.

So, she thought thankfully, Gold Kingy's got plenty of reason for wanting to keep Grandpa alive and kicking.

"Gower! Take the girl away!" yelled Uncle Roy.

The man who had silently appeared during the interview and stood behind Is now gestured to her with a jerk of his head to follow him.

So he must be the husband of that poor worried lady, thought Is—she said he was an important government official, the deputy moderator. He's the dad of little Coppy.

"I seen your little boy, your little Coppy the other day, Mr. Gower," she told him chattily as she turned to leave the audience chamber. "He's a real nice, bright little fellow. Too bad you gotta send him off to school, all the way to Scotland!" She received a look of fury in return from Mr. Gower: a tall, thin, black-haired man with a closed, shut-in face and such a small, sour mouth that, thought Is, he'd have a precious awkward job opening it far enough to swallow a cherry.

"*You* have a boy, Gower?" demanded Gold Kingy sharply. "Why was I not told? Do I know your boy?"

"Oh, I am quite certain that I have told you about him, sir —at one time or another. He is young as yet—barely three I understand—still wholly in the nursery, sir."

Gold Kingy nodded, then suddenly flung the hammer onto the floor so that it cracked a pink marble paving stone.

"We need them smaller in the mines *every day,* remember!" he said ominously. "He could be a trapper—he could be an opener!" And, turning, marched off to the back of the chamber.

Does Uncle Roy have a wife—children? wondered Is, as he vanished through a door. It seemed unlikely. Where could he be going now? What to do? Practice the flute? Read? Play cards with somebody?

Mr. Gower angrily escorted Is to the street.

"You go home and behave yourself, as the Leader said," he snapped. "And I advise you to behave much more respectfully toward your uncle from now on, or you will find yourself in very bad trouble."

"Yus. I can see that," said Is. And then she thought, I'm sorry I gabbed about little Coppy. I done it to tease that prune-faced Gower, but I shouldn't have spoke out about him in front of Gold Kingy. He seemed a real decent little nipper. That was a stupid thing to do.

7

Sieve my lady's oatmeal
Grind my lady's flour . . .

IF I EVER LET GOLD KINGY GUESS THAT HE FRIGHTENS ME, thought Is, I'll never get anywhere.

She could see that his whole power was built on fear—everybody who worked for him was afraid of somebody else, so nobody dared make any protest, even when terrible things were done. And people had grown accustomed to the terrible things.

"We need them smaller in the mines every day!" Gold Kingy had shouted at Mr. Gower; that had put Gower in a cold sweat, because he was terrified for little Coppy. Was Uncle Roy planning to pass a law that four-year-olds might be taken for work in the mines?

The best thing I can do, thought Is, will be to disobey Uncle Roy; *not* go home, like he told me, but nip straight to the foundries and ask some more questions. That'll show him I don't care for him and his threats.

The shortest way to the foundries from Gold Kingy's royal residence was through the smaller, darker streets that lay to the rear of the palace, and past the entrance to the mine. The mine gates were, as usual, locked and heavily guarded, and the approach to them illuminated by a blaze of white light shining down from the rock roof overhead.

Opposite the gate was another statue of Uncle Roy, mounted on a horse, wielding a pickax, and much larger than life-size. The horse, in particular, was enormous; big as a small elephant, thought Is, who had once seen an elephant trundling along in a circus procession. The horse was rearing up on its hind legs and Uncle Roy sat in the saddle with a nonchalance that made Is chuckle each time she passed the statue, for she felt sure that he had never ridden a real horse in his whole life. The statues of horse and rider, and the big rocky base on which they balanced, cast black shadows over the ground, and as she walked nearby Is thought she saw something—some*one*?—scurry into the shadow and vanish in the patch of inky black. What—who—could it be? Holdernesse swarmed with rats and mice, but it was too big for one of those; big enough for a dog, or a small person. A child? The guards, yawning at their posts, had observed nothing. They pounced on Is and made her show her pass; now she wondered why Gold Kingy had not confiscated this. You'd think he'd do that right away, she pondered, walking quickly and lightly along the road that led to the town's dockside entrance. The lights here were scanty; between them lay long patches of shadow. Now and then Is thought she heard footsteps behind—but that might have been the echo from the tunnel roof.

Still, it was a relief to come out of the cave into daylight—
even if only the gray light of a murky December afternoon
—among the slag heaps of the dock, the drums of tar, piles
of firebricks, rail cars filled with coke, coal, or ingots.

It's all so ugly here, Is thought sorrowfully, and a great
wave of longing nearly choked her—longing for the frosty
silence of Blackheath Wood, for the mist rising, the drowsy
bedtime whispers of the birds, the glisten of toadstools in wet
grass among layers of dead leaves—for her cat Figgin,
bounding ahead toward the gleam of light that would be
Penny simmering a kettle on the hob.

I dunno how folk can *stand* it here, thought Is, taking a
long, resentful breath of the sharp, thick air that always
smelled so strongly of burned milk. And she stood still for a
moment, trying to squeeze her homesickness into a manage-
able size, collecting it into a kind of solid lump inside her
chest, so that she could bear it and go on. If *I* feel so, what
about all them poor devils on the train, who believed—the
silly nuddikins—that they were due for a lifetime of larks in
sugar candyland; now they're slaves in the mines or mills, and
no way to get out. At least I'm free, and can go where I like.

But oh—don't I jist wish I were in Blackheath Wood this
very minute!

The Touch came to her again: the long, cold piercing
finger of contact. We share it, the voices told her. We feel
that, too, all of us. And it is not so terrible if it is shared.

Is looked around her in bewilderment, almost expecting
to see a huge host of companions marshaled over the waste
spaces of the dock; but the spaces were empty, except for
herself. In the distance, the foundries roared and glimmered.
Sudden gusts of flame spurted upward as fuel was tipped into
the furnaces; the clang and thud of the steam hammers re-

called Gold Kingy saying, *"You know what it's like to lose a hand."*

"I've come to see the ones that were burned in the blowout," Is announced boldly, stepping into the flaring, gastainted, dusky confusion of the main area. And she showed her pass to the overseer.

"Most of 'em's back at work now. There's only two left out in the butteker—and I reckon they're past crying for," he told her indifferently. "You can go and look at 'em if you've a mind to."

She made her way to the storage shed where the hurt workers had been taken, and found that the last two were indeed past crying for; both were cold and dead, and had probably been so for a day at least. A little snow had fallen on them, through gaps in the roof, and had frozen. One of the two—a girl with badly burned hands and arms—still seemed to clutch something in one of those burned hands.

What can she have set such store by? wondered Is. Something that might give a name to her—be sent back to her family? Or a bit of bread?

Hating the task, she pried at the stiff, frozen fingers.

"There's naught now," said a voice behind her. At the overseer's orders, two boys had followed her. "Tha'll find naught, luv."

The second boy said, "T'gaffer gave orders to drop 'em in t'river if they're done for. T'lass did have like a keepsake i' her hand, but one of t'others took it."

"What kind of keepsake?"

"Kind of a bootten, like," he said indifferently.

"Did it once belong to a boy called David Stuart?"

"I'd not knaw that. Ann used to keep it i' her mouth."

The second boy said, "T'lass as took it off Ann is called

Nettie. A red-haired lass. Reckon she's still aboot—she was workin' as a sampler, last time Ah see 'er."

"Where?"

"In t'main building. Can't stop now, luv, or t'gaffer'll have our hides."

Without more ado, they dropped the two frozen bodies in the river, which was tidal here, frothy and swift flowing.

Is went back to the main building.

The samplers were equipped with long-handled ladles. It was their job, Dr. Lemman had told Is, every time a load of molten ore was discharged down the trough, to dip out a sample, allow it to cool a bit, and take it to the engineers' office to be tested for impurities. The task was fairly dangerous, because of the heat of the white-hot metal running down the trough and the sparks that cascaded out from it, but the work was not heavy, so it was mostly done by girls.

Red-haired Nettie was there, neatly dipping out a ladleful of white-gold ore. Like giants' jewelry, thought Is.

While she stood waiting for it to be cool enough to carry, Is asked her, "Did you take a token off a dead girl called Ann?"

Nettie glared at her suspiciously, then recognized the doctor's helper and nodded.

"Ah, I did. But it weren't for mysen. A gal called Tilda wanted it, but she couldn't no way get there; she's on the bellows, see, at the blast furnace, working all the time."

"Why did she want it? Was it like this?"

Is showed a corner of her own token, through a gap in her jacket seam.

"Ah! That it were! Tilda wanted it 'cos she'd been friends with a lad who'd been friends wi' the cove as had it."

"Davie?"

"Ah dinna knaw."

"Is Tilda still here?"

"Look, lass, I must flit, or he'll toss me in t'runner."

She tipped her red-hot ingot into a metal pan with a wooden handle and ran off with it.

Is felt a hand on her shoulder. The overseer was glaring at her with black disapproval.

"I never gave thee leave to come in here, young 'un, interferin' wi' the workers—that I dunna. Be off with thee —right away—or I'll call the constables."

And what would the constables do with me? Is wondered, reluctantly obeying; in fact she had no choice, as, with his heavy hand on her shoulder, he practically shoved her out of the melting shop. Would they send me to prison? Is there a prison in Holdernesse? That's one word I've never heard. Maybe they don't need a prison here—everywhere else is just as bad.

Is made a detour on her way home to visit a couple of Dr. Lemman's older patients. These were among what he and Ishie called "the Warren"—various of Aunt Ishie's friends who had either secretly disobeyed the order to move into new accommodation in Holdernesse, or had stealthily and inconspicuously left that new accommodation again, once the general move was over and the authorities were no longer paying heed to them.

There were twenty or so of them scattered over the dismantled landscape of Old Blastburn, making what use they could of its ruined amenities. Mostly they were old people, living like rabbits in concealed burrows: small, half-ruined houses in out-of-the-way glens or dells where they could grow a few cabbages, keep a hen or two, and kindle a morsel of fire at twilight without being observed.

Miss Sibley and Mrs. Crockett were among these: two elderly sisters, one of them a widow. They lived on the western side of Holdernesse Hill in what had once been a flour mill, surrounded by a few scrub fir trees that had managed to survive the poisonous fumes from the blast furnaces. The roadway to Corso Mill ran up to a bridge that was half broken. A young and agile caller might just be able to cross the gap by taking a tremendous leap over the millrace that ran below, but the two elderly owners preferred to follow a more circuitous route, crossing the stream lower down by a natural bridge formed from fallen ash trees webbed together by creeper. Dr. Lemman also used this approach, tethering the mare to a tree on the near side.

"What'll you do when the trunks rot through?" Is had asked on her first visit.

"My dear, by that time our aged bones will be long scattered. And this rustic gangway provides a useful defense against persons of a superstitious habit. There are plenty in Blastburn—yes, I assure you!—who, already half suspecting us of witchcraft, are afraid to cross a bridge composed of mountain-ash trunks."

What the sisters lived on, nobody knew. Mrs. Crockett suffered severely from rheumatism (very possibly because their hideout in the ruined mill building was so close to the millstream); she was obliged to go about almost on all fours, bent double, and helped by a short stick. Dr. Lemman called on her as often as he could, treated her with aconite and bryony and applied arnica to her joints with a camel-hair brush.

The sisters had been schoolteachers in the days when there had been schools. Now they were certainly thought to be witches, if anybody thought about them at all.

Is, carefully manipulating Mrs. Crockett's stiff joints, told them about Grandpa Twite's plan to print storybooks for the workers.

"There's a fine library still in Blastburn, did ye know?" said Mrs. Crockett. ("Ah, that does me a power of good; thank you, my dear.")

"A library? In the new town?"

"No, no, no. In the old town, in one of those ruined buildings. Nobody sets foot in there now, it has been declared unsafe. Books in Holdernesse? Nobody wants them, nobody reads. They play that game instead, with dice and counters."

"Yes, I've seen them," said Is, who had noticed the guards, overseers, and constables playing this game when otherwise unoccupied.

"It is called *Steal a March*—Gold Kingy invented it, so he makes a profit on every set sold."

"Now the other side, missus, if you'll turn over," said Is. "Does Gold Kingy have any family?"

"No, my dear. He did have a wife, but she ran off and left him. (Can't blame her, can you?) Went off in a ship to Holland, ship got wrecked, that was the end of her. Some said Gold Kingy got word beforehand, had the ship scuttled. Wouldn't put it past him. Stayed single after that. Out for number one. He always was that, Roy Twite. I knew him from my evening class at the Workers' Institute—always stealing ideas and textbooks from his next neighbor."

There came a loud, plangent, angry caterwauling from the entrance.

"See to him, my love, would you," said Mrs. Crockett to her sister, "while this dear child just finishes my back."

"Sounds like a mighty big cat you got out there, missus," said Is.

"Oh, it's not a cat at all, my love, it's a poor mad boy who thinks he's a cat. He worked in the foundries and then in the mines, and the things that happened to him unhinged his brain. Now he just scampers over the hills; he's harmless so he is left alone, even by the authorities. After all they can't employ a boy who thinks he's a cat. My sister and I give him a bit of fish when he comes this way; there is always fish in the millstream."

"What's his name?" Is asked alertly.

"Bobbert. Bobbert Ginster."

"Oh."

"There, my dear, thank you a thousand times, you have loosened me up remarkably. Now I may even be able to walk upright for a couple of days."

Miss Sibley came back, brushing fish scales off her hands.

"Would he not come in?" said Mrs. Crockett, disappointed.

"He heard the strange voice and that always scares him off. He was very wild tonight. He ran off up the hill."

"When it is very cold he is prepared to spend a night by our fire," Mrs. Crockett explained. "Poor boy—it is rather sad."

Better than being in the foundries, Is thought, and Miss Sibley echoed her thought.

"He is far happier running wild, Caroline, than in one of those atrocious places. Good night, my dear child, and thank you for your care. Our best regards to your great-aunt."

"I'll come again as soon as I kin," said Is, stepping out into the windy dark. She wondered if from some bush or whin or ruined building the mad boy who thought he was a cat might be watching her.

When she got back to Wasteland Cottages she found Grandfather Twite in a desperately dejected and penitent state of mind. Aunt Ishie was hovering over him with a wet cloth for his head and a dose of soda for his stomach. Her eyes were full of pity, although she scolded him.

"Look at that handle! Look at what you nearly did to your great-granddaughter."

He could not believe in the handle. "How could *I* have done that! Somebody else must have done it. I shall have to get the blacksmith to straighten it. My own handle! I would never do such a thing. Besides not having the strength."

"Well—you did," said Is bluntly. "I was there, so I can tell you that if I hadn't nipped back pretty smartly, you'd be out in the snow a-digging my grave this minute. I'll not hold it agin you, Grandpa, but I wish you'd smash up all those crocks full of grog in the cellar."

"Oh, I couldn't do that," said old Mr. Twite instantly. "I need them, you know—not for myself, but for the requirements of hospitality. However, I swear and declare that I will, myself, never touch spirits again—" He paused, looked sorrowful and added, "Just the same, you had better not trust me. And . . . and do not tell me anything that I might divulge to . . . to unsuitable persons when under the influence."

"Oh, Grandfather!" said Is. "It ain't only that. It's that— when you're bosky—I can't trust you not to beat my brains out!"

"I know, I know it!" he lamented. "It is perfectly true!

But what can we do about it? I fear, my child, that you must take to carrying arms." And he chanted:

> "I have a barrel
> But no bung
> I have a muzzle
> But never a tongue
> I have a stock
> That cannot tie
> And when I speak
> Some man will die."

"Oh, Grandpa, are you crazy? Me carry a barking iron? Firstways I wouldn't know where to get one, secondways if I had it I might shoot *you*! No, no, that ain't the answer."

"Then what is, my child?"

"The answer's for you to stop brewing that wicked tipple and kicking up shindigs with Uncle Roy."

"Out of the question."

"Why, *why*?"

While they were staring at one another, with no questions answered, Dr. Lemman walked in. On his face, usually so alive with cheerful cynicism, there was a look of consternation.

"I'm afraid something terrible has happened," he told Mr. Twite. "I hardly know how best to break it to you. It is about Montrose . . ."

"A wolf got him? So early in the winter?"

"No, sir, worse than that, I fear."

Grandfather and Ishie hurried outside, she carrying a lamp. There on the path lay Montrose, or what had once been Montrose; now he looked like a flat two-dimensional drawing of a cat, done by some savage.

Aunt Ishie burst into tears.

"I never liked that cat!" she sobbed. "He was always bad-tempered and disagreeable. He bit me every time I fed him! But that someone should use him *so*!"

"That was done by a steam hammer," pronounced Grandpa Twite, closely inspecting his flattened pet. "Well—at least he won't need a deep grave."

Is said nothing at all. I gotta get out of here, she thought, aghast. That was a message—to me. From that human rat. That murderer. That monster.

"Poor old Montrose," Grandfather Twite was saying. "But at least it must have been a quick end. And he has been very surly for the last few years."

"Surly? He was the worst-tempered cat in Humberland."

"It's my fault," said Is. "Oh, Grandpa, it's my fault."

"Why?"

"Come back in the kitchen," said Aunt Ishie.

They left Montrose leaning against the house like a piece of board.

"Why your fault?" repeated Mr. Twite.

"Because I wouldn't tell Gold Kingy anything about King Richard. And he said if I didn't he'd hammer me, and I was to go home and think, and then tell him some more. But I haven't *got* anything to tell him. And I reckon he had Montrose hammered for a warning."

"He is really quite lacking in moral sense," said old Mr. Twite.

"My child, I think you had best go home to the south country," said Aunt Ishie.

"How, though?" said Dr. Lemman.

"Any case I can't," said Is. "Not till I found what I come for."

"Your sense of duty is going to land you in trouble, dearie," said Lemman.

"But I *gotta* do what a dying person asks," argued Is. "And never mind about anyone else."

The three elders looked at her, frowning with worry.

Journal of Is

This'l be my larst. I gotta leev here afore G.K. thinx up sum more nasty trix on the old uns. Ive a Noshn I kin find more abut D.S. in the foundriz. But I misdowt hes ded an whats that news agoin to do to his dad? Still I gotta tell im if its so. You cant tell whoppers to kings.

After writing these lines, Is hid the little red notebook (which Penny had given her) behind a loose brick in the attic wall. For I'm sure to come back here sometime, she thought . . .

Next morning Grandfather Twite was feverishly at work in the cellar long before daylight.

"The foundry blacksmith straightened out the handle for him," Aunt Ishie told Is, "and he is printing quick sheets of riddles for me to take to the children."

Indeed he could be heard chanting:

"When I'm black they seek me
When I'm red they beat me
When I'm old and white
They fling me out of sight."

"Aunt Ishie, I'm going to go and live with the old 'uns at the mill," said Is. "And I'm a-going to work in the foundries. I reckon that's the only way I'll ever get to find out for sure about . . . about what I want to know—" as Aunt Ishie laid a finger on her lips.

Grandfather Twite was climbing the stairs, mumbling to himself:

> "A brook or a boy, I hold them tight
> I run forever out of sight
> I'm made each morn, unmade at night."

"I guess it's a bed, Grandpa," Is told him kindly as he came into the kitchen for his morning drink of saloop. He looked sad and drawn, aged by what had happened.

"Is tells me that she is going to live with Jane Sibley and Caroline Crockett," Ishie informed her father, handing him the mug of warm drink. "She wants to work in the foundries, and that way she will be closer to her place of employment."

Grandfather Twite sighed, a sigh that began in his stringy chest and went right down to his bony feet in the red-and-green slippers.

"I fear you are right to do so, child. We shall miss you sorely, sorely; but I fear you are right. Your continuing presence in this house . . . might lead to trouble."

Trouble, thought Is; that's putting it flea-size.

Aunt Ishie's huge otter-eyes were full of sorrow. She hugged Is.

"I shall come and visit you, my love, in the foundries; that way I shall not lose you entirely, I—I hope."

"I'll be right happy to see you, Auntie, anytime," Is said, hugging back.

Dr. Lemman came running downstairs, munching a crust. "Ready to go, dearie?"

"Only as far as the dock. I'll explain while we ride," she told him, embraced old Mr. Twite (he still smelled of spirits, mixed with saloop) and left Number Two, Wasteland Cottages, with deep regret.

"I'll miss you as a helper, Is," Lemman said when she had explained her plan. "But I reckon you are doing the right thing. For the sake of Ishie and the old boy, certainly. Gold Kingy won't come around so often when you are gone. When he does come, Mr. Twite can't resist teasing him and that's bound, sooner or later, to lead to ructions. I hope you soon find what you are looking for; when you do, my best advice is to get back to the south and warn your friends that there may be trouble coming from here."

"How'd I ever get back?"

"I think Captain Podmore would take you."

"But his ship was wrecked."

"He has already been appointed to another. He is a very fine skipper. You could always send him a message by your aunt."

"*If* I find what I'm looking for," sighed Is. "It's like looking for a pin in Piccadilly."

He clapped her on the shoulder. "But you've got the grit for it, dearie! I'll lay odds you do find it! And I'm sad to lose your help. But you'll be better in the south."

"Doc—why does *anybody* stay in this hateful place?"

"Most can't get away, dearie," he said soberly. "And a few—like your aunt—stay because in some way, however small, they can help the others."

"But why don't nobody *do* nothing?"

"What's needed," he said, "is a leader. And one hasn't turned up as yet. Now—good luck, dearie! I'll keep in touch—" as the old mare reached the docks, and Is jumped down to run off toward the smoke and gusts of flame coming from the blast furnaces.

Davey, Davey Dumpling
Boil him in the pot . . .

PROCURING WORK AT THE FOUNDRIES PRESENTED NO PROBLEM.
The manager was, indeed, so amazed that somebody should
actually volunteer instead of being dragged, confused and
protesting, off a wagon, that he offered Is a fairly safe job
shoveling coke, but she said she'd rather work on the bellows
that blew the blast furnaces to maximum heat.

"Why?"

"I've a mate there."

"No talk or fooling, mind! That's the rule. If you talk,
you get the strap. See this?" He held up a thick leather strap,
heavy as a horse whip.

"Yus," said Is.

"Right. Remember that. You get five minutes for your
dinner and five for your supper. Got your grub with you?"

"No," said Is.

"Go without, then. You'll know to bring it tomorrow. Jem! Take this one to the bellows team on Number Two furnace."

It would be no use, Is could see, asking to go to Number Four furnace; she must simply watch for her chance and take one, if it offered, to change over or to talk to the Number Four team.

The bellows were kept in action by a team of seven or eight pulling on a rope. The work went on continuously, all around the clock; when one team took over from another, each member in turn passed his or her section of the rope (half of them were girls) to somebody who stood waiting at their shoulder, ready to jump in and grab. The work was hard, but not intolerable. The smell of sulphur was very bad until you got used to it; so was the boredom. The worst times were when you wanted to scratch an itch, or to relieve yourself. (There was an unspoken working agreement, in the latter event, that one member of the team at a time could run off to a dark corner while the others pulled harder—but not, of course, if the overseer was anywhere in view.)

For the first two days, Is did not try to ask any questions. It took her that time to get used to the noise. There was a terrific continuous blasting roar from the furnace itself, besides the shriek of the bellows and the grating rattle of the hoist that fed coke into the top of the furnace, a hundred feet above. It might have been thought impossible for people to talk and hear each other in such conditions. But Is observed that the other members of the gang were able to talk and understand one another with as much ease as if they had been in a peaceful meadow. Also they had a system of talking without moving their faces, to avoid being spotted by the overseer.

At noon a whistle blew. The bellows had to go on working, so each member of the team had a few minutes off in turn to bolt down whatever food they had brought.

On the first day Is, having none, shook her head when it came to her turn.

"You got no crib?" shouted the boy behind her in the line. "Here—" and he offered her half of a cold potato. But she shook her head again.

"Thanks, cully. You keep it. I ain't that hungry."

He didn't wait for her to change her mind but bolted it down in one gulp. He was as thin as a rasher of wind, Is noticed; she wondered if that was all the food he had to eat in the twenty-four hours.

After a twelve-hour shift they were relieved by the next team. The other members of the gang did not stop to chat—they raced off as if the militia were after them.

"Where d'you live?" panted Is, running beside the boy who had offered her the potato.

"Ma Cobb's lodging. Most o' the gang lives there. It's by the infirmary—reckon she'd take you too—" He nodded at a dingy building that looked like a storehouse.

Is decided that she would go in there and ask some questions, but not tonight. She was very tired—her arms and back felt as if she had been pulled in half. And she still had to arrange about her own accommodation.

But when she reached Corso Mill she found herself expected. Aunt Ishie had called there during the day, and the two sisters gave her a kind welcome. As soon as she had bolted down a big bowl of fish and carrot soup, Miss Sibley rubbed her aching back with poppyheads.

"A fair exchange for all the rubbing you have given my sister."

While being massaged, Is heard again the howling of the cat-boy.

"Perhaps he will consent to come in this time," said Mrs. Crockett, hobbling hopefully to the door with a plate of fish. But she came back shaking her head.

"Still too shy. But he is sure to grow accustomed in time to Is, now she is living here. Indeed we are delighted to have some young company, my dear!"

Is found that she had been provided with a comfortable bed made from a pile of old sacks on the upper floor, in what had been the grain store of the mill. "But no need to worry about rats," said Miss Sibley cheerfully, "as they have all departed to the new town, where there are choicer pickings. And you will have no trouble in waking for your shift, my dear, since you may easily hear the factory hooter from here."

This was so; at four-thirty a fearsome yelling whistle sounded on the dock, a quarter of a mile away, to rouse the workers who began their duties at five A.M. Is scrambled into such of her clothes as she had taken off, and ran down the ladder.

To her dismay, both sisters were up and had a breakfast of porridge and a roast turnip waiting for her.

"You shouldn't, ma'am—you shouldn't, missus. It ain't fair you should havta get up early for me—"

"Nonsense, child. In any case, my sister is very strongly affected by changes in the weather, and just lately she has been having some terrible twinges, which wake her very early—there must be a shocking climatic disturbance over the Atlantic moving this way. Run along now, dear child, and here is a noonpiece for you. Make haste . . ."

Is gulped her thanks and was off down the hill.

Running past the gate guard she caught up with the potato boy.

"What's your name?" she panted.

"Col. Got some grub today?"

She nodded. There was no chance to say more, as they took their places on the bellows rope· with the overseer watching. But later in the day Is seized a moment to ask the girl ahead of her, as she returned from bolting down her noonpiece, "You ever come across a boy called David Stuart?"

"Ah, I done! He were a real decent feller!"

The overseer, stepping close, caught each of them a stinging slash with his strap, putting all the weight of his arm behind the blow. "No talking!" he growled.

At the end of the day Is followed this girl and asked her name.

"Fanny. What's yours?"

"Is. What happened to David Stuart?"

"He switched to Number Four. Then I didn't see him no more. Ted, over yonder, might tell you more."

Ted, hurrying home to supper at Mrs. Cobb's lodging, was a surly-looking, towheaded boy who might have been about fifteen.

"Whadya want to know for?"

"A pal of his was asking for him."

"Promise me your tomorrow's noonpiece and I'll tell."

"No!" said Fanny. "Don't promise him that. You *tell* her, jist," she said to Ted, "and don't be so pin-mannerly. That

Davie was a real sweet chap. Ted were there when it happened," she explained to Is.

"When what happened?" Is felt her heart sink horribly, though it was not hard to guess.

"Dave were working on the runner of Number Four, see?" Ted said, apparently deciding to cooperate. "And a feller, Danny Rowe, he were going over the gangway, and he slipped, and he were hanging on the rail, screaming for help."

Is knew by now that the *runner* referred to was a wide, deep trough of white-hot metal, and the gangway over it no more than a single plank.

"What happened?" she asked with a dry mouth.

"Dave turned to the chap next him—Bob, his name were —and give him a luck piece what he used to carry—kind of a button, like—said, 'See my dad gets this, wiltha, Sam Driver knows where 'e is'—and then he went to help t'other chap, but they both slipped and fell in, an' that were the end of 'em."

"What about the button? And Sam Driver?" Is felt for her own button, safely stitched inside her hem.

"Why—what Davie didn't know was that Sam his own self had been done for by a blowout o' gas that same week. So no one knew what to do wi' the button."

"What *did* they do with it?"

Fanny broke in.

"*Everybody* liked Davie—someway he were a cut above most o' the rest, but no swagger or brass about him, not a bit —and he used to say that all this, the way we gotta work, was wrong, and one day it'd be stopped, when his dad got to hear about it. We used to pull his leg a bit, ask who was his dad, did he mean God-a-mercy up above, but he says no."

"He were a right mystery-ous cove, Dave were, he useda say as he could hear voices," Ted ruminated, taking up the story, growing more involved as he remembered.

"Voices?" Is felt a queer leap of excitement.

"Yus. He come from Scotland, Dave did, his dad were a Scotty, he said. Up in those parts they have what he called Sight, they can hear things and see things what other folks can't. So Dave used to hear those voices, times. An' they told him—he said—that things wouldn't allus be like this here. Kids wouldn't allus be made to work without pay fourteen hours a stretch. Wouldn't allus be douls. He said—he said—"

"He said someone *else*'d come!" Fanny interrupted.

"Someone else?"

"Ah! And this other cove 'ud have another button, just like his'n. And when this other cove come—with the button —that'd be the start of things getting better."

"Where—what did they do with the button *he* had?"

"It still gets passed around, like. Just to have it and handle it for a day or two puts more gumption into folk. And they figure, sooner or later, someone'll find a way to get it to Davie's da."

"A girl called Tilda had it, I heard," Is said.

"Tilda Thatcher? She ain't got it now. I bleeve she passed it to Hattie Smith."

"Where'd I find Hattie?"

"She's a puddler. Dunno what shift, though—come and ask at Ma Cobb's if you've a mind."

It took Is two weeks in the foundries—asking, probing, and persuading—before she caught up with the button. Tilda had passed it to Hattie, who had passed it to Annis, who had passed it to Len, who had passed it to Jack . . .

Nobody seemed to feel the need to keep it for more than a day or two, but they all said it put new heart into them. One odd thing Is found out was that, with each person who had contact with the button, the story, the legend of Davie Stuart was enlarged and extended. He were a right decent chap, clever, too, with it, but no side or pride about him, not a bit, though his da was some big weight down Lunnon way; he had saved several people from accident or trouble before the unfortunate Danny, had done no end of kind deeds and good turns, he was a real nob, a nonesuch, a nonpareil. And was he really truly dead? asked Is over and over again. Could her informants be certain of that? Yes: Ted and another boy called Rodge had seen both him and Danny fall into the runner. And *nobody* could survive that. In fact there was nothing left of them, not so much as a buckle nor a bootlace.

With a heavy heart, when the token finally came into her possession—from a girl named Dorcas—Is took it back to Corso Mill, borrowed pen and paper from the sisters, who, as ex-teachers, still had a stock of such things, and wrote a note to Wally.

DERE WAL HERES TARBLE SAD NEWS. YOULL HAFTA TELL HIS NIBS THAT YOUNG DAVE AINT NEVER COMIN BAK NO MORE. HES DED, DYED TRIN TO SAVE ANUTHA FELLA. ALL THE FOLKS HERE SAY HE WERE A REEL GOOD COVE AN ALLUS TOLD EM BETTER TIMES WUZ CUMN. NO USE TRYIN TO KEEP THE NEWZ FROM HIS DAD HED HAFTA NO SUM TIME. THINGS UP HERE IZ RITE BAD THAT GOLD KINGY IS A DEVIL ON TOAST. TELL MY SIS PEN IM WELL AN SEND LUV. IM STILL LOKKN FER ARN TWITE. KIND REGARDS TO YOU AN YORE DA. IS.

Then she sewed letter and token together into one of Aunt Ishie's pockets, which she had brought with her from

Wasteland Cottages. Next morning she was lucky enough to encounter Aunt Ishie herself, off on a mission to deliver pockets and riddle sheets to the workers in the potteries, pulling her box on wheels behind her. Aunt Ishie readily undertook to transmit the pocket to Captain Podmore.

"I won't ask what's in it, for I think it better I do not know."

"No, and I'd better not tell. But it's dreadful sad news," Is said, hugging her aunt. "And now I gotta think hard what to do next. Mustn't stop, Auntie, or I'll be late for the buzzer."

And she ran on toward the foundries.

The main problem that puzzled her now was what to do with her own token. She had felt quite badly at removing Davie's from circulation in the foundry because, finding its way from hand to hand, from shoe to mouth, it seemed to have done so much good. Is was not at all certain of her own right to deprive the workers of its beneficial effect.

In the end the solution was simple. During her five-minute lunch break she nibbled through the stitches in the hem of her jacket, pulled out her own token, and passed it inconspicuously to Col.

"Here—reckon it's your turn for this."

"Josie!" he said. His whole aspect brightened, he almost capered, then removed his clog, tucked the token between his toes, and slipped the clog back on again.

Is felt the Touch, sparkling in the center of her mind.

"Are you near?" cried the voices. "Are you coming to us soon?"

"Why—why, yes!" she stammered in reply. "But aren't I here already? Aren't I with you now?"

"No, not yet. No, not quite. But near—soon—very soon—"

A group of constables strode into the furnace yard, trim in their dark-green uniforms, amid derisive yells from the workers and shouts of "Yah! Boo! Black beetles!"

"We're looking for Is Twite!" they told the overseer. He sourly pointed her out, and they came over and grabbed her.

"What's to do, what's up?" she demanded as they hustled her out of the yard and into their conveyance, deliberately dragging her through a pile of coal dust on the way.

"Y'uncle wants yer."

The carriage door slammed, the horses broke into a trot.

"Hey, driver! You're taking a right roundaboutaceous road to Gold Kingy's palace!" Is pointed out, after they had been driving for about ten minutes. Instead of turning through the tunnel entrance and into Holdernesse town, the carriage had threaded a way upward through the ruined streets of Old Blastburn and was now climbing steeply. Soon, in fact, Is recognized where they were: on the way to Wasteland Cottages.

The driver made no reply to her expostulation; merely whipped up his horses. And the two men on either side of her remained silent. But when they came round a corner, one of them said, "Y'uncle wanted ye to see this before he speaks to you."

This was the narrow, cobbled lane where Wasteland Cottages had stood. *Had* stood—for they were there no longer. All that remained of the gaunt little row of derelict dwellings, their sheds and clotheslines and patches of garden plot, was a ridge of shattered brick, earth, and slate, from which the dust still rose like smoke and fell again onto a sprinkling of new snow.

"*Lord a' mercy!*" whispered Is, after a moment of stunned silence. She could hardly believe what she saw. She worked her tongue against the roof of her mouth and swallowed. "What's come to the houses? What *happened*?"

"His Excellency had them blown up."

"Wh–where's Aunt Ishie? And Grandpa? And Father Lance?"

"Ask your uncle," said the man dryly.

Is felt herself shaken by such a storm of rage that she had to clench her teeth to stop herself from flying at the men, sobbing and bashing them and screaming out furious insults. In the midst of this inner whirlwind she was startled when the Touch passed through her mind like a shaft of ice and cooled her wild reactions.

"What is it, what troubles you so?" the voices were asking.

"That rat, that *garbage* has blown up my aunt and grandfather—"

"Wait, wait; keep calm, it may not be so . . ."

The black police cab was again steadily rolling on its way; Is twisted around for a last glance at the forlorn heap of rubble where Ishie, Grandpa Twite, Father Lance, and Dr. Lemman had lived their peaceful, harmless, and on the whole, useful lives.

Grandpa's printing press! And my little red book, behind a brick in the attic.

Some way soon I'm a-going to make sure that Uncle Roy gets his deuces, she thought. I'm a-going to see he goes where the devil's waiting for him.

Then she began to consider. Gold Kingy would never blow up Grandpa; not unless he got the true gaff out of him about what helps the old boy keep going, and *that* I'm certain he never did. So he jist blew up the houses out of pure meanness and cuss-mindedness, like he flattened poor old

Montrose. So, he musta shifted the old 'uns out somewhere else; and not to his palace, because firstways he'd be shamed to have 'em there, and secondways they wouldn't go.

These thoughts had begun to relieve her a little when she looked out to see where the carriage had got to. It was just rolling to a halt in James Street, which had once been Old Blastburn's grandest thoroughfare. Now grass and weeds were pushing up between the cobbles, and blackberry brambles had grown over the lions outside the main public library. The library itself was still a fine building, though most of the windows were broken, the bronze doors dangled crazily slantways on their hinges, and great slabs of stone had fallen off the façade.

"You fellows take the kid in," said the driver to the others. "I don't fancy that place above half. Somebody told me that a set of old hags and witch coves use it for a consort house." He shivered.

"They'll not overturn me," said one of the other two. "I live too near the woods to be frit by an owl. Come on, you!" He laid a forceful hand on her shoulder and shoved Is up the wide, shallow flight of steps that led to the main doors.

The entrance hall of the library was a deep and lofty space with a marble-paved floor and two flights of white marble stairs curving away from each other to meet again at the top. But the floor was now scattered with litter and broken stone; shoots of trees were pushing between the cracked paving stones, and earthy mildew covered the ground. The stairs, however, were still intact.

"And this place is a *library*?" marveled Is. "Jist to read books in?"

Her guides did not trouble to reply. She was led from the main lobby along a wide passageway, much obstructed with lumps of masonry and broken furniture, then down a flight of stone steps. The basement region that they now entered was dark, but a few lights gleamed ahead of them in the distance. Toward these they made their way.

"Where the pix are you taking me? And why in the name of wonder should Uncle Roy want to come down here, when he's got all of his pink palace to confabulate in?" Is demanded, but she did not expect an answer to her questions and she did not receive any. She had spoken to encourage herself by the sound of her own voice in this drear, dark, and somewhat menacing region, which was full of unexpected echoes.

The distant lights appeared to be in motion, and kept receding as they pursued. What a queer, huge place, thought Is; but I suppose libraries gotta have storerooms or cellars, just like people's houses.

It took a while for her eyes to become accustomed to the dim light; then she realized that the walls between which they passed were not solid at all, but consisted of what seemed like an endless series of high racks or shelves, built from some heavy dark wood and containing thousands, perhaps millions, of moldering volumes. What in the world could they all be about? The bygone history of Blastburn, and the older towns and villages that had stood in these hills and valleys before Blastburn was built? It's too bad they should all rot and crumble away, thought Is, but it sure is plain no one wants to read 'em anymore.

Next she noticed that the wooden shelves or stacks that held the volumes were not fixed in their places, but were set on rails so that they could be moved sideways; behind them were more rows of stacks, and yet more behind them; in fact they appeared to recede forever into the gloom. *Croopus,* thought Is in fright, almost in horror. What a lot o' books that no one's a-going to read; who in the name of milk can have written them all?

Sometimes a gap between the shelves would show a narrow alley where they had been pushed aside to let some bygone librarian pass through and gain access to the volumes kept farther back. And the passage along which Is was being escorted was not the only one; there were intersections and other passages branching to right and left, signposted by lettered cards: A1, B3, H14. It's like a maze, thought Is, a big, moldy, freezing maze.

At last the light ahead of them came to a stop, and they caught up with it. They had arrived at a kind of crossroads where six passages met in a space that was the size of a small room. Here several people were assembled around a little plain table, on which burned a lamp, and a chair, on which sat Gold Kingy. A group of guards clustered nearby and between them they held a person, a woman; she stood in the shadow at the edge of the opening, and her face could not be seen. Too tall for Aunt Ishie, thanks be! Is at once decided, with a kind of shamed relief. Whoever it was, she felt sorry for the poor devil, *mighty* sorry. Thinking this, she suddenly had a sharp flash of perception, of recognition. Although the woman's face could not be seen, a wordless message was pouring from her: I remember you, I know who you are; if you can, help me, help me!

And: I don't know *how* I can help you, but I'll try, I surely will try, Is launched back through the shadows. Yes, I do know you, I remember you.

The woman was Mrs. Gower's sister, the widowed Mrs. Macclesfield, the aunt of little Coppy; her head was covered by a hood, but Is felt quite sure of her identity.

Gold Kingy now began to speak in a very disagreeable voice: a mean, gloating voice.

"Have you men brought my niece along? Good, that's good." He laughed his loud, meaningless laugh. "Now, my girl, I want you to take a careful look at this female prisoner."

"How can I—" Is began, but he went on. "Bring her forward. Take off her hood."

Mrs. Macclesfield was thrust forward; the hood was dragged off. Is could see that her arms were bound tightly together behind her back. She stared at Gold Kingy with a look of profound loathing and scorn.

"You stupid, scheming woman!" he shouted at her. "You have been found guilty of illegal, malicious contact with the workers in the mines. Not only that, but you bribed a guard with a gold watch. You paid him to let you into the mine; you planned to carry contraband luxuries to the pit-workers and ask them unlawful questions."

He paused, waiting, apparently, for Mrs. Macclesfield to say something in her own defense or deny the charge, but she made no reply for a few moments. Then she asked in a dry, detached manner, "What happened to the guard?"

"He, very properly, reported the matter to his overseer and was rewarded."

"I see." Mrs. Macclesfield said no more.

Gold Kingy suddenly bawled at her, "You must have had accomplices! Tell me their names, and I might be prepared to remit part of your punishment."

Oh Lord-a-mercy, thought Is, now what do you bet she was Aunt Ishie's helper, taking the pockets to the kids? But if Mrs. Macclesfield had been Aunt Ishie's unknown accomplice, she was not betraying the connection. She stared silently at Gold Kingy, her face full of contempt. After a while she said, "You took my husband, you took my daughter. There's not a lot more you can do to me—choose how!"

Gold Kingy suddenly lost his temper. "Isn't there, by gar! You obstinate, spiteful hag! I can make an example of you— that's what I can do. And it's what I *shall* do! I can cage you up here alone in the library stacks to molder away, along with all those useless old books—and that's what I'll do with you, or my name's not Roy Twite. You won't look or sound so pert when you've been here a week or a month and the rats have been at you. —Take her farther in!" he ordered the guards. "Take her as far as you can go. Leave her in there, push the stacks to, and lock them around her. —As for you," he said to Is, "that may give you a taste of what I can do to folk when they work against me. You saw your grandpa's house? Did you like that? You see what's going to happen to this scheming fool of a woman—?"

Mrs. Macclesfield twitched herself out of the hands of her guards and took a step toward Gold Kingy.

"Listen!" she said. "You listen to me, Roy Twite! You have come a long way, haven't you, from the ragged boy who used to push a barrow of rusty iron through the streets of Blastburn. You've traveled a long road, but you are nearly at the end of that road. I can feel a wind, I can hear it beginning to blow, off there . . ."—she waved an arm to the northwest—"and I can hear the sound of voices. At present they only whisper, but soon they will shout, soon they will roar—and that roar will sweep you away, Gold Kingy, like a leaf in a torrent."

"Take the crazy fool away!" shrieked Gold Kingy, and Mrs. Macclesfield was hustled off into the darkness between the stacks, farther and farther, until she was completely lost to view.

Then, in the far distance, Is could hear the grinding sound of the stacks being trundled sideways along their runners and fastened, each to the next, with a loud clang. Clang! and a pause, and then the grinding, then another clang! and a pause. No sound came from Mrs. Macclesfield. After fifteen or sixteen such clangs, the guards reappeared and saluted.

"Right: she's fixed in there till the moon turns to cheese," said Gold Kingy with a grin. "She won't last long. Apart from the rats, those stacks are airtight. There's only enough in there to last her a few hours. —And I won't hesitate to serve you likewise, miss!" he added, fixing Is with a blood-shot, angry eye. "Unless I get a whole lot more cooperation from you. Understand? Now bring the girl along to the post office!" he barked at the guards. "I'll talk to her again. This place gives me the ague!"

And he bustled off along the passage, his escort only just able to keep pace with him. Is and her guard followed, she trying to fix in her mind the way they took and the number of turnings and crossings so that she might come back at the first chance and try to rescue Mrs. Macclesfield, whose pite-ous wordless message still came piercing through the dark: Save me if you can! I am helpless, tied up, imprisoned in this cave of books!

And Is, hard as she was able, sent back the message: I will try to come back as soon as they let me go. I will come as soon as I can.

She was bundled back into the cab and taken at a brisk trot along James Street. A five-minute drive brought them to the old post office, in a side street where the mail coaches had once drawn up in glittering dark-blue rows; now the skeletons of several horses lay moldering among rotten wheels and broken axles.

The post office was in a worse condition than the library, with half its roof open to the sky and, in the sorting office to which Is was taken, huge heaps of rotting, crumbled letters piled high as sand dunes all over the floor. Through these they picked and shuffled their way, and found Gold Kingy at the far end of the large room, perched—grinning like Mr. Punch—on the rostrum from which the postmaster must once have given orders to his staff.

It was plain that Uncle Roy enjoyed nothing better than inspecting the desolation that he had made of Old Blastburn —not just in contrast to Holdernesse and its brand-new glitter, but because devastation itself delighted him. "Look at all those letters nobody's going to read!" he called gloatingly to Is. "Ha, ha! How it makes me laugh to think of all that wasted trouble."

"Proper shame if you ask me!" snapped Is. "*Someone* musta paid postage on 'em."

"They are all to the south, or from the south," he retorted coldly. "We have no dealings with the south—not until the day when there is a glorious reunion and my troops are pasturing their horses in Hyde Park."

And that won't be till fish wear rollerskates, thought Is.

He was the stupidest boy in the class, she remembered Mrs. Crockett saying; the others used to laugh at him. Perhaps that's why he hates books and letters so.

Her guards pushed her close in front of Gold Kingy, who in the meantime had refreshed himself from a black-and-gold flask that must have held something very potent, for he suddenly yelled at Is in a loud, bullying voice, "Now, I want answers, girl! Don't try to fob me off, for I've had you followed; I know all you've done and every soul you've spoken to. I know you've been hunting for the Stuart lad, and I want to know where he is. If I can only get that boy in my pocket, I can tip a settler on King Dick. *I'll* call the shots; he'll have to swallow my terms."

"No he won't, Uncle Roy," said Is. "There bain't no way you'll ever have that boy in your pocket. 'Cos why? 'Cos he's dead. He's gone and diddled you."

The moment the words had left her mouth she wondered if it had been wise to disclose this news to Gold Kingy—but it had been too much of a temptation. For once he seemed really taken aback and gaped at her with furious, startled eyes, which were growing bloodshot again as he swigged down more and more from his flask.

"Dead? How do you know that?"

"Acos I took trouble to find out, that's why. He was killed in your foundry—like plenty of others. He fell into a trough of melted metal. He won't come back. So you got no hold at all over King Dick. He'll find himself some other heritor— he'll havta, won't he? Maybe he's got a nephew, or a cousin."

Gold Kingy took a long time considering this. Then he said, "Well, maybe that ain't bad news. King Dick'll surely be knocked endways when he hears his boy's a goner. He's sick already, I've heard tell. Maybe this'll knock him off his perch." Uncle Roy chuckled at the thought. "Then the gate'll be wide open for me to walk down and take over the Southland."

Is feared this might be only too likely; remembering the thin, sad, woebegone man she had met in Mr. Greenaway's warehouse.

"But what I want to know is," Gold Kingy now roared at

her, "what's *your* fiddle in all this? *Why* were you looking for Davie Stuart? What was he to you? And I want a true answer. Don't fool with me. You saw what came to your aunt's cat? You saw what I did to that grog-sodden, rat-infested ken where they lived?"

"Yes, I did see!" Is burst out, too furious to care about caution. "You flattened poor old Montrose and you smashed their home—*fine* doings! Two decent old bodies as never harmed anybody in all their days—unless Grandpa had a bit o' drink in him—not to mention Doc Lemman and old Father Lance. You did that! How do I know they ain't all dead in the ruins?"

"The doctor was out on his rounds; Father Lancelot had permission to leave—"

"And what about Grandpa? What about Aunt Ishie? Where are they?"

"Never you mind where they are—" Uncle Roy was beginning, when Aunt Ishie's voice interrupted him.

"We are safe and sound, dearie, don't you trouble your head about us. But no thanks to Roy."

Is looked up and, to her huge relief, saw her elderly relatives gazing down at her. A gallery ran around three sides of the room; its rails supported hooks from which hung quantities of rotting old dark-blue canvas mailbags. Aunt Ishie and Grandpa Twite had evidently managed to enter at a higher level, for outside an alley ran uphill beside the post office. Both of them looked dusty and untidy, Aunt Ishie even paler than usual, Grandpa ominously flushed; but at least, thank heaven, they were alive.

Roy, who had started violently at the sound of Aunt Ishie's voice, now bawled at the guards, "Get them down from there! Who let them in? How did they get up there?"

The guards hesitated.

"Get them down!" repeated Gold Kingy furiously.

"Y'r Honor—" one of the guards stammered, "Y'r Honor, everybody knows it's terrible bad luck to touch Y'r Honor's kin—specially Miss Twite . . ."

"It will be worse luck if you don't!"

But just the same, Is could see that Roy was not easy in his mind about having his elderly relatives manhandled. Do they think Aunt Ishie is a witch?

"Uncle Roy!" she suddenly addressed Gold Kingy boldly. "I had a dream about you last night."

This was true, she had; but she had forgotten all about it until this moment.

"Be quiet, girl! Why should I wish to hear your rubbish?"

Yet she could see that he was startled and his attention caught; the whites of his eyes seemed to enlarge.

"Shall I tell you about my dream, Uncle Roy?"

"Be quiet, girl!" His face was flushed; he banged on the rostrum with his fist.

"Yes, dearie, go on, you tell him your dream!" Aunt Ishie called encouragingly over the gallery rail. "The women in our family often have true dreams; my mother once had a dream foretelling the fire that burned down the Houses of Parliament."

Gold Kingy threw her an angry look, but he said to Is unwillingly, "Well—?"

Is chose her words with care.

"I dreamed that you was walking along this wide green track, Uncle Roy. It was as wide as a street, an' all grassy an' flat, very smooth and easy underfoot. Birds was singing in the hedges an' sun shining, all as happy as can be."

"Well?"

Now he was following her with close attention, his eyes almost glaring out of his head. Why? Did it tie in with a dream that he had dreamed himself? Is remembered how she and Penny had sometimes shared the same dream—mostly something quite simple. A dream about a tree or a fish.

Uncle Roy's face had grown even redder and he was sweating copiously.

"You was walking down the path, Uncle, very happy and jolly, laughing a lot, and the way started to slope downhill. That made the going even easier, you was regularly busting along, swinging your arms."

Gold Kingy looked down at his arms—his hands were clasped tight in front of him—as if he were slightly surprised to find them still attached to his shoulders.

"And then the way got narrower, Uncle Roy, just a single footway—like a sheep track—with hedges on each side— and then, bless me, if it didn't run plumb into a river!"

A dark slit showed where his mouth had opened; his lips and cheeks were now a uniform brick-red. His eyes were trained on Is like gun barrels.

"Well, it didn't matter a bit, Uncle Roy, that the path went into the water, 'cos, do you know what you *did*? You was able to walk on top of the water! Yus! Jist fancy! You walked along on top of that river, jist as if it was a pavement in a street!"

Gold Kingy leaned back with a huge breath of relief, an enormous sigh of satisfaction. He cast a triumphant look up at Aunt Ishie and Grandfather Twite.

But now old Mr. Twite leaned over the rail and addressed him.

"Do you want to hear my last riddle, Roy Twite? I made it up for you especial. Which was an act of charity, mind! for

I don't owe you any kindness. No, bless me, I don't! You killed my cat, you wrecked my home, and my printing press . . ." His voice shook a little and Aunt Ishie laid an anxious hand on his arm. But he smiled at her and said, "Never fret, my dear. You don't get to the age of a hundred and two without learning to keep your temper." Then, turning back to Gold Kingy, he announced, "Here's my last riddle, Roy, boy, and you'd best pay close attention:

> As backward you go, take a turn round the pond
> If your threescore-and-ten you would pass beyond!
> But is a long life worth all this trouble
> When even a short life is such a muddle?"

Grandfather Twite showed his yellow teeth in a malicious grin, studying Roy.

"Well, boy? D'you get it? D'you fathom it? You had best commit that one to memory, for you won't get a second chance to hear it. That's your last. And do you want to know why that is? Because I have come to a decision. I don't care for the kind of usage that Ishie and I have had from you lately; no, by hokey, I do not, and I don't intend to put up with it any longer. So, do you want to know what I have done? I learned to brew other things, you know, beside a long-life essence, down there in my cellar that you just demolished. As well as a long-life potion I brewed a *short*-life potion."

Uncle Roy looked up sharply at that.

Grandfather Twite grinned again. "Ah, that makes you twitch, doesn't it? Well it may! For, half an hour ago, I swallowed it down—hemlock. Yes, Ishie and I had a few odds and bobs stowed away with a friend in another refuge because we had a notion you might one day do something hasty and ill-advised—a few rags and bones and bottles—and we were right to do so, weren't we? Eh? So I have just ten minutes left now in which to tell you, Roy, that as well as being a stupid, greedy, callous ning-nang, you are left now with only a very short—"

Grandfather Twite came to a stop in this oration. A thoughtful expression came over his face. He said, "*Not* ten minutes." And collapsed slowly, sideways, against the rail of the gallery.

Aunt Ishie said, "Oh dear!" but her quiet exclamation was drowned in Uncle Roy's yell of rage.

"The old *devil*! The old *gullion*! He's done me, he's diddled me, he's—"

Gasping for breath, flapping his hands as if in a vain effort to pump more air into his lungs, Gold Kingy toppled forward off the rostrum onto the dusty floor.

The guards rushed forward to him.

"Is he dead?" Is asked hopefully.

"No, just a fainting fit. He gets taken like that when he's had a shock—it's nowt out o' the common," said one of the men, expertly loosening Gold Kingy's cravat. "He'll be right as rain in two shakes of a lamb's tail."

"What a pity."

In fact almost at once Gold Kingy opened a bloodshot eye, fixed it angrily on Is, and announced, "That was a lie! A goddamn lie. About the lad, Davie Stuart, being dead. I don't believe it's so. He's still alive. In the mines, very likely."

His eyes closed again.

"Suit yourself, Uncle Roy. Believe just what you fancy,"

said Is angrily, and then, since nobody was paying her any particular attention, she left the guards engaged in arranging a carrying litter for Gold Kingy made from mailbags, and ran up a flight of steps that led to the gallery.

9

I feed my cat by yonder tree
Cat goes fiddle-I-fee . . .

IN THE DUSTY GALLERY OF THE OLD BLASTBURN POST OFFICE, IS
was not particularly surprised to find Dr. Lemman with her
aunt, kneeling by the motionless, apparently lifeless body of
her great-grandfather.

"Is he really dead? Oh, *is* he?" she cried, clutching at
Aunt Ishie.

Lemman was feeling the old man's heart, testing his pulse.

"Well, we don't know yet," he said. "The first thing will
be to shift him to an airier spot than this grubby hole. If we
can get him along to my trap—"

A footway led from the gallery to the lane at the back
where Dr. Lemman's trap was tethered. They got the old
man out, with some difficulty, by means of Aunt Ishie's
wheeled sled.

"Stupid old clunch. I knew he'd go and overdo the dose if I was not there to supervise . . ." Lemman was muttering. "I knew he'd make a mull of it."

"Didn't he mean to do hisself in?" asked Is.

"Not to my knowledge . . ."

"Where were he and Aunt when Roy blew up the house?"

"Out. They'd had a warning from an associate of Kingy's —that fellow, Gower—don't know why *he* turned neighborly all of a sudden—surly, Friday-faced devil in the general way— Good, that's right, heave his feet in, and then we'll be off."

"Where to?"

"The library."

"The *library*?"

"Your aunt and great-grandpa have a notion to take up quarters there; not a bad plan, I daresay, it's in middling good repair. And I believe there's even an old printing press down in the basement, which your great-grandpa—*if* he survives this crazy freak . . ."

Aunt Ishie was already crouched in the back of the trap beside the huddled form of Grandpa Twite. Is clambered in beside her and clasped her hand. But Ishie looked resigned, even calm.

"If your great-grandfather dies, I shall take it as meant," she explained, "and shall consider that he brought it on himself, teasing poor Roy."

"*Poor* Roy?"

"Oh, such a hopeless, wretched, unlovable creature!" Aunt Ishie sighed. "I suppose it is almost always that kind who change the course of public events, because they have nothing better to do with themselves."

"D'you know what he did? He locked up Mrs. Maccles-field in the library basement, among all them books! Soon's we get there I'm a-going to let her out—"

"That's a good child; no, Mrs. Macclesfield should most certainly not be left in there . . . Ah, here we are. Now, Chester, if you can just help me up the stairs with Papa . . ."

There were two flights of stairs to be tackled: the impos-ing steps outside, leading to the bronze doors, and then, even steeper, the double marble ascent curving in elegance from the entry hall. Although it was a cold day, they were all heated and panting by the time they had hoisted old Mr. Twite to the top of the second flight.

"Only hope it'll have been worth it, fetching him up here," growled Lemman.

As soon as Aunt Ishie and the unconscious old man had been established in the head librarian's office, Is said, "Now I'll go and look for Mrs. Macclesfield."

She had been exceedingly anxious to get away for the last ten minutes. All the time they had been laboriously heaving Grandfather Twite from step to step, she had been aware, inside her head, of Mrs. Macclesfield's piercing, piteous, continuous cry for help, a soundless moan. Then, suddenly, just as they reached the door of the office, it had stopped. Now what could that mean? Is hated to think. Had the supply of air suddenly run out?

"Yes, do hurry," agreed Aunt Ishie. "Take a candle, you had better . . ."

She had a stock of household goods already collected here: lamps, candles, blankets, and provisions, Is noticed.

Hurrying downstairs with the lighted candle, Is retraced the route along which she had been taken earlier that day—it already seemed a long time ago—by the two guards, down the basement stairs and along the silent passageway among the stacks of books. But now there was no light ahead to guide her. And there seemed to be a dreadfully confusing number of passages to choose from. Is tried to follow a course straight forward, relying on the good sense of direction that she had acquired in Blackheath Wood, but it was hard to be sure that she was keeping to the same route, for she began to think that in the meantime somebody else had been there, disturbing the stacks and shifting them along on their tracks, so that the distances between them were different. If only she could find the opening where Gold Kingy had sat, with the table and chair; but those were gone, the space had vanished. Who could have taken the furniture?

Where are you? I am looking for you everywhere, she sent out in a soundless call to Mrs. Macclesfield. But no answer came back. And the candle, which had been little more than a stub to start, was beginning to burn low . . .

Now there came another disquieting phenomenon. Somewhere, not too far away, Is thought she began to detect a stealthy footstep. At first she had taken it for an echo of her own tread, but it fell at different intervals, it was heavier and slower.

I don't like this place one bit, thought Is; I'd hate to be shut up in here. She stood still and tried to avoid breathing while she waited and listened for the step to sound again. Yes: There it was, closer now. Somebody was following her, stalking her in the darkness. I know a game worth two o' that, thought Is, and blew out her candle. Dark, thick as soot, settled around her. If I keep still for long enough, Is decided, Mr. Footfall can't help giving himself away; I bet I can hold my breath longer than he can.

She was right: after an interval she heard a stealthy shuffle and a suppressed cough. Is, by now, found that her eyes had adjusted to the dark sufficiently to see the upright line of a stack fairly close to where the sound had come from. She put down her candle and, in two tiptoe strides, swung herself around the stack and made a grab with her right hand at what lurked behind it. Unexpectedly, the stack slid sideways in its groove, unbalancing the other person, who fell heavily, letting out a stifled oath: *"S'wounds!"* and dropping something with a clatter. Is, pouncing on this, found it to be a tinderbox and struck a light. To her complete surprise, the person lying on the floor turned out to be Mr. Gower.

"Well, jell me!" exclaimed Is, while he, looking extremely harassed and put out, as much at the loss of his dignity as anything else, picked up his pince-nez and climbed slowly to his feet. "I never thought it would be *you,* mister, playing hide-and-find here in the dark!"

He made no reply to that but, after frowningly scrutinizing her for a moment, demanded, "You were here, were you not, this morning, when your uncle had my sister-in-law shut up in this repellent place?"

"Sure, I was; that's why—"

"Can you remember what number of row—?"

"Ah, now, that's sharp," said Is approvingly. "Yus. Now you come to name it, where Gold Kingy was sitting, at his little table in the middle, that row was K30. I know that's so, 'cos I remember thinking K for Kingy."

He took back the tinderbox from her and lit a candle of his own, holding it up to the nearest stack, which was R17.

"Ah," he muttered, "then I have come by far too far . . ." and began working his way back toward the entrance. Having relit her own candle from his, she followed.

"You come to let her out, then, mister? I thought you was on Gold Kingy's side?"

"My affiliations are no business of yours whatsoever," he snapped.

"Suit yourself, mister. —Now, this was where Uncle Roy sat this morning, for here's a drop o' candle grease on the floor. Somebody musta moved the table, that's what foxed me. Wonder who? And I reckon it was down this way they took Mrs. M—a good long way, till they was almost outa hearing."

But though they followed the row K30 to its extreme end —among dark, rusty, moldy, half-empty stacks, and rotten, sodden volumes—they could find no sign of the imprisoned lady. Mr. Gower called out, once or twice, in a cautious undertone, "Susan? Are you there? Susan?"

And Is sent out her silent mind-message. But neither of these received any reply. Nor, thank goodness, did they come on what Is had feared they might find: poor Mrs. Macclesfield's body, perished for want of air; although Mr. Gower moved all the stacks in turn and hunted with great persistence.

"My wife will certainly expect it," he muttered. "What is that you just picked up?"

"Dunno—feels like it might be a locket."

He lowered his candle and Is exhibited her find. It was, in fact, a small heart-shaped case on a slender chain.

"Yes, that belonged to my sister-in-law. You had best give it here."

"And welcome," said Is, handing it over. "Well, mister, I reckon some other body musta nipped in ahead and unbuckled Mrs. M an' spirited her off somewhere. You can tell your lady at least she's outa the brig."

He merely grunted in reply. It was plain that he had hated his errand, hated the fact that it had failed, and particularly hated being obliged to hold a conversation with Is. Blowing out his candle, he made for the stairs to the hall, which could be seen dimly ahead of them.

Is lingered behind, thinking that she would wait a few minutes until he had left the library before returning to Aunt Ishie and Grandpa Twite. They would not wish their presence advertised.

At that moment something bit her leg and she let out a gasp of fright.

"What?" Mr. Gower said, irritably, half turning.

"Nothing—nothing, mister . . . !"

But she had felt teeth sink in her calf, no question. What could it be: a dog, a wolf, a boar, a wildcat, a giant rat? What other creatures might inhabit this underground maze?

Mr. Gower strode on up the stairs and vanished from view. And then close by, not loud, but distinct, Is heard a familiar sound: the kind of caterwaul—half threatening, half playful—that a young tom makes, warning a stranger off his boundaries.

For a moment she felt desolate, longing for her friend Figgin and her own woods; then she spun around and, with heart beating fast, called softly, "Hey! Who's there? Where are you?"

The sound came again from farther away, and to one side: "Morow—wow!"

Is took a deep breath, gulped, and followed. The course that the creature led her was a jerky and confusing one, zigzagging among the stacks. As she turned a sharp corner, her candle died again, but then, luckily, she began to see a faint gleam of daylight ahead, toward which the beast—person? animal?—seemed to be making. And in fact a few minutes more brought Is out through a side entrance, up a crumbling flight of area steps into an alley. Ahead, to the left, a dark shape was just vanishing around a corner.

Putting on more speed, she went in pursuit.

By now the short winter day was nearly done. And the foggy dusk was made more obscure by a whirl of snowflakes; only the quick, jerky movements of her quarry helped Is to keep him—or her, or it—in view. Across ruined building plots, around corners, over blocks of stone, under tottering arches, up flights of steps, it bounded and gamboled. Showing off! thought Is crossly as she slipped and stumbled in the rear.

Now they were on the edge of the town, in little streets that looked more like country lanes. Soon Is recognized where they were, not at all far from Corso Mill, and five minutes more brought them to the ruined bridge over the millrace. The creature ahead ran out onto the broken arch of bridge and then, with a wild, extravagant leap, cleared the gap and hurled itself across to the other side.

Is measured the distance with her eye. There was a twenty-foot drop below. *I* ain't fool enough to try and jump that, she thought; it'd be downright stupid, plain susancide. I'll jist stay on this side.

"Hey!" she called across the race. "I'm not a-coming no farther. I'm fair tucked up. You come back here!" And she sat down on a bit of ruined wall.

A mocking meow came in reply.

"Listen!" Is called again. "I don't mean you no harm! You must know that by now. Why don't you come back and talk a bit, sensible? I won't even bite you!" rubbing her bruised leg.

She was answered by a chuckle. Now it was too dark to see across the white, racing water.

I'll stay two more minutes, resolved Is; then I'll step into the mill and tell the old gals what's been going on. They'll want to help Aunt Ishie and Grandpa.

"So long, then. I'm off," she announced, after a couple of minutes had passed; and she was standing up to leave, when a skinny black form came flying back over the millrace and a strong hand pushed her imperiously down again.

"Stay! Sit!" commanded a voice that was perfectly human.

Is, with great composure, brought out the stub of candle that she had stuck in her pocket on leaving the library and relit it. By its light she looked at the person facing her.

He was a tall, bony boy. His hair, very thick and shaggy, fell around his face in a kind of ruff, and he had the beginnings of a beard; he had streaked his face with tar or black paint in tigerish stripes, and his jerkin and breeches were made from alternating stripes of brown and gray fur. But what mostly made him seem like a cat was the way he moved: the supple neatness with which he cocked his head, turned his spine, and, as now when he sat down, tucked his hands and feet tidily out of sight.

Is took a long, careful look at his face through the falling snow; then she grinned.

"*You* ain't a cat, boy, whatever you may think," she said. "You're my cousin. You and I are the image of each other. Your da once told me that. You're Arn Twite."

He shook his head vigorously. "No, I'm not! Whatever I am, I'm *not,* and *never* going to be that. If I'm not a cat, then I'm Bobbert Ginster."

"And what kind of an outlandish monacker is that?" asked Is.

"I found it on a tombstone."

Now he had decided that Is was to be trusted, Arn, or Arun, seemed perfectly at ease with her; he pulled a couple of apples from inside his jacket and passed her one. "I reckon what's on a tombstone ain't private property no more and I can use it."

"What's wrong with Twite?" Is, who had missed her noon meal and was ravenous, took a huge bite of the warm apple.

"Who'd want to be that? All the Twites are wrong 'uns."

"I'm not! And Grandpa's not a bad old coot—if he's still alive. And Aunt Ishie's a real one-er." She thought and said, "You might as well say you don't want to be a person."

"Well, I don't. For a long time I *wasn't* a person. And I'm not going back to be one."

"You got no choice," said Is, finishing her apple in another large bite that included the core. "And your dad's dead, grieving for you, and your mom's a-crying her eyes out every night, back in Folkestone. They missed you sore when you left home."

He gave a snarl of impatience. "Why the pest couldn't they think of that when I was alive? Stupid, pig-headed fools!"

"You mean, when they was alive? Anyway, your mom still is alive—so far's we know—and if you don't go back and see her, *you'll* be the pig-headed one."

"I'm never going back," he said. "I'm not saying things are right up here—they aren't, they're as bad as they can be —but at least here I'm me, I'm myself, I'm some *use*. D'you know what they wanted me to do down there—make wigs! I was to be apprenticed to a wig-maker! For fifteen years!

And you say I ought to go back? Are you crazy? Or do you think I am?"

"That's right, your dad did say summat about wigs," Is remembered.

"What happened to him?" Arun asked after a moment or two. "He was healthy enough."

"He got wore out, tracking back and forth to Lunnon. Then the wolves got him."

After another pause she went on, "You might at least write a letter to your mom. To tell her you're alive." She thought of poor King Dick and his lost son. "Did you really know Davie Stuart?"

"Yes. I knew the bloke. He and I came up north together. He wanted to find out about Playland. Thought it was his job to find out."

"Is he really dead?"

"As a tent peg." Arun sat with his chin on his hands for a while, then said, "I carried his button around for a bit."

"It's gone back to his dad now."

"Who sent it?" he said sharply. "They'll miss it at the works."

"I sent it," said Is. "I'd made a promise. But I put my own one in its place. They give me one, back in Lunnon; when I came a-looking for you and Davie."

"You had one too?" Arun turned and faced Is. The candle had long burned out. But perhaps, she thought, he really had taught himself to see in the dark like a cat.

"Yus, I had one, but I gave it to a boy called Col."

After staring at her a moment he said, "Don't you see what that means?"

"No, what?" Is began to feel shaky and sick. She longed

to be in the mill with the old sisters, beside their fire, being given kind conversation and a roast turnip.

"It means that things are going to change. It was said that when somebody else came with another button, that would be the start of things getting better."

"But that wasn't—I mean—you mean—you think *I'm* the cove with the other button?"

"Of course."

"Oh, save us," muttered Is. After another pause she said, "What do you think I oughta do?"

"I expect it'll be laid on you," said Arun. Echoing what she had said to him, he added, "I don't suppose you'll have any choice."

"You ever hear voices, Arn?"

"Voices, what kind of voices? I hear birds," he said. "And owls."

"Ah. Never mind."

"I've been following you for days, you know that?"

"Why?"

"To try and make out your lay."

"It would have made more sense to ask me. And been more civil." Then she asked him, "What sort of a cove was Davie Stuart?"

Arun said: "He was the best. The best friend a person could ask for. Funny, made you laugh, knew a whole lot of things, never in a bad skin—*hey!* Watch out!"

Half a dozen black figures had stolen up and now laid hands on them. Arun sprang away, his eyes flaring. A voice said, "Ech, it's only the crazy cat-boy. Pay no heed—we weren't told to take him up. It's the girl we want."

"You taking me to Uncle Roy?" Is asked, sucking a cut lip, after they had thrown her into a carriage.

"No, we're not!" snapped the driver. "Your uncle's had good and plenty of you; he don't want to see you no more. *Ever.* You're going where you should have gone at the start: into the mines."

10

Every knave will have a slave
You or I must be he . . .

IT GAVE IS A VERY STRANGE FEELING TO FIND HERSELF BACK IN Blastburn station, helpless in the grip of her guards, and to watch the arrival of the Playland Express. So little time seemed to have passed since she had been a passenger on that train herself, but what a great deal more she knew now! She felt like a different, much older person than the Is who had scrambled inside the roll of carpet and escaped on the cleaners' cart. As the great red-and-gold train slid smoothly into the station, and the doors opened, and the whooping, laughing children began to tumble out into the station hall, Is felt like a stranger from a different continent. What I could *tell* them, if I was able, she thought. Poor devils. If only I was able to warn them. But she could not; one of the guards had stuffed a wad of dirty rag into her mouth.

And yet this next part of the victims' journey was one she had not shared. Oddly, she almost felt that she owed it to them, and was not sorry when her guards shoved her in with the group that was being marshaled into the first wagon, outside in the station yard. The children were yawning, giggling, stretching their arms and legs after the long train ride, chattering about what they hoped they'd get for breakfast.

"Five eggs an' a slice o' plum cake!"

"Hot chocolate an' twenty pieces of toast!"

"Hey—pooh—it's a bit cramped in this here wagon, ain't it? You'd think they'd do us better—"

"Miss Twite! *Miss Twite! Miss Twite!*"

Unaccustomed to this form of address, Is took several seconds to realize that the frantic whisper was being directed to her as, among all the other new arrivals, she was pushed and hustled up the ramp and into the wagon. To her astonishment she saw the tall, thin figure of Mr. Gower nearby, feverishly waving at her.

With great difficulty she fought her way to the side of the wagon and gestured to him between the wooden slats that prevented the passengers from either falling or jumping out. He helped to take the gag from her mouth.

"Mr. Gower! What's to do?"

His face was distraught, white as wax; his eyes burned like red-hot pokers.

"My little boy—my Coppy—he has gone—he has vanished. Miss Twite—if you see him in the mine—if you *see* him—"

Oh, my laws, thought Is. Little Coppy being nabbed was *my* fault. I should have held my tongue.

Gower's voice was soon drowned in the chatter of the children and the clatter of wheels on cobbles as the first wagon rolled on its way. Is, familiar now with the streets of Blastburn, knew at once that it was taking the shortest way to the mine entrance, across the dock and through the Strand Gate. Other wagons, she supposed, would carry their cargo of workers to the foundries or the potteries.

Soon the clamor of excited voices began to hush, in the gloom of the underground streets of Holdernesse.

"Rum sort of set-out here, ain't it? Where's this Hotel Joyous Gard, then?"

By the time the wagon reached the big dark square, the equestrian statue of Gold Kingy and the guarded gates of the mine, there was almost complete silence inside it.

"I don't like this place!" wept one small, frightened voice. "I'd rather go home."

The gates swung open, the wagon rolled through, the gates shut behind them with a clang. Several of the children wailed with alarm, and one fairly burst out boo-hooing. To Is, from this point on, the road was unfamiliar and she looked about carefully; but she could see little, as the lights were not very bright and set far apart. It was plain that the track sloped downhill quite steeply, for the cart tilted and the tightly crammed children, all standing, began to slide help-lessly forward.

The ride lasted for rather more than half an hour. Then the wagon drew to a stop, the tailgate was unloosed, and the ramp let down. Stiff and subdued, the passengers began to clamber out, into a stone underground space lit by overhead lamps.

Here there were a great many guards, all large, tough, and armed with truncheons and leather thongs. These, with the speed of long practice, sorted the new arrivals into groups of four or five, and herded them away in different directions. Is, in her group, found herself led off along a passageway that was just wide enough to take two people side by side, and no higher than a short man.

"Where the deuce are we?" asked a boy.

"Where are we going?" wailed a girl.

"When do we get our breakfast?" somebody called out.

"You'll get it at the same time as your dinner—when you've earned it!" said one guard. He was a big, burly man who carried a club and a lamp. "Where are you? You're in the bord, and you're going to the coalface."

"But what is this place?" they kept repeating.

"It's a coal mine," said the escort impatiently. "Ain't you never heard of a coal mine before? Well, now you're in one. And your job will be to get out the coal. If you work, you'll get your grub. Them as don't, won't. Understand?"

A terrified, thunderstruck silence followed his words.

"And don't try to run away," he added menacingly. "Because there's plenty of fellows back there at the gate with clubs and chains and persuaders who'll be happy to teach you that running away here doesn't pay. First, there's nowhere to run to. Those gates we come through are locked, and they stay locked. And that's the only way out."

Now almost all the group was gulping or crying.

"Stow that row," said the man sharply. "It's no use to whine and pipe; you'll just have to get used to it here. Plenty have done before you."

"Where do we live? Where do we sleep?" somebody asked.

"Why, right here in the pit." By now the group had been walking for about twenty minutes and had reached a smaller open space, about the size of Aunt Ishie's kitchen in Wasteland Cottages.

"This is where you sleep," the guard said. There were some wooden bunks against one wall. People were sleeping in them, and on the ground also.

"There ain't enough bunks," a boy said. "Not for all of us."

"Sleep on the floor, then. You ain't the only ones; first come, first served," the guard said. "Besides, there's others working."

In the distance could be heard the sounds of tapping and hammering. Three passages led away from where they stood: ahead, and to right and left. These were much lower—about the height of a chairback. The only light came from the guard's lamp. The ground was wet—as they walked they sank into an inch of slushy, gritty mud—and the place stank with a salt, sharp, dank, disagreeable odor.

"Mind out," said the guard. "Someone's coming with a corf. Stand to the side."

They could hear a rumbling, and in a moment a girl crept from one of the low entries, dragging behind her a basket-work truck on wheels, filled with coal. It was about the size of a wheelbarrow; she hauled it on a chain fastened to a strap around her waist. She was barefoot and wore only a skimpy skirt, nothing else; except, Is noticed, that she had one of Aunt Ishie's pockets strapped to her forearm. She took no notice of the group of new arrivals but went on her way.

"Now, you see that lass," said the guard. "She's a hurrier. She fetches the coal from the heading to where it's taken up to the surface by the whim gin. Half of you new lot'll be hurriers, the other half'll be colliers; those are the ones that cuts the coal on the heading. Got that?"

He lifted up his voice and shouted, "What ho, there! Colliers! There's a new draft in. Come and show them what to do!"

Some blackened, coal-dusty workers appeared, a few of them with candles. It was hard to tell whether they were male or female. Tools and baskets for the new workers were produced from a kind of cupboard in the rockface. The members of the new group were led away in different directions by the old hands. The guard remained in the central spot to see there was no trouble.

A boy called Joe led off Is. "You'll be my hurrier," he told her. "I'm right glad to have one; for two weeks I've been doing the cutting and the hurrying both, and it's slow work. We're told to fill twenty corves a day and they flog you if it's less."

All the time he talked he was hacking away with a slender pick at the rockface in front of him. "The coal comes in a layer," he said, "like the filling in a cake. You can feel it with your fingers. But you have to take out the rest of the rock to get at it. That's what wastes time."

They were in a short passage just wide enough to hold them, and the roof was so low that they banged their heads against it unless they knelt. Joe passed the coal back to Is, who dropped it in a basket. Soon her hands were very sore. When the basket was full she emptied it into the corf, which stood farther back.

Most of the time Joe worked in the dark. "They do give us a ration of candles," he said, "but they're dangerous. If there's an escape of gas, that can blow your head off. That was what happened to my last hurrier."

"Oh," said Is, and then, "The corf's full now."

"Take it back to the whim gin, then."

This proved to be a long way off, twenty minutes' drag, pulling the heavy corf.

The whim gin was situated in a vertical shaft that led up to the surface. Four or five hundred feet above, Is could just see a faint point of light. A continuous double rope wound upward to a pulley on the ground overhead, and the corves were hooked on to it. Two men took her corf from Is, attached it to the rope, and gave her an empty one.

"*Run* with it, you little nippence!" shouted one of them, slashing after her with his cane, and she scurried off into the dark, wondering how she would ever find her way back to Joe.

"Why's it sich a perishing long way from the coalface to the whim gin?" she asked, when she had found him, and begun shifting the heap of coal he had hacked out while she was gone. "Why can't it be closer to here?"

"Why, you nodcock, because we're under the sea here. The whim gin's on the nearest bit of land—Holdernesse Point, it's called, one o' the fellers told me."

"How does it work?"

"There's a horse walks around and around, winding a drum; you couldn't have that in the middle of the sea."

"So that feller wasn't telling truth when he said there's only one way out."

"Ay, but the whim gin's only used for coal. And there's guards by it always, with whips and pistols. No use thinking you could get out that way. *No* one gets out of here."

"You ever meet a cove called Arn Twite? Or Bobbert?" Is asked irrelevantly.

Joe gave a half laugh.

"Oh, *him*! The cat-boy. Yes, it's true, he gets in and out. No one knows how!"

Is went on with her work, thinking about the sea. There it was, up above. If the rock were to crack—if the roof were to give way—it was propped up on thin wooden supports . . .

This is the worst place I've been in yet, she concluded. Grandpa's house was paradise compared. And she thought wretchedly of Aunt Ishie's warm kitchen, of Grandpa Twite yanking and thumping his press in the cellar below. Oh, Grandpa! Whatever happened? Did he die, in the end? Or did he wake up? What will Aunt Ishie do if he dies? At least she's got Doc Lemman to stand by her. One thing about Aunt Ishie: I reckon she'll make the best of things wherever she settles. She don't waste time, she'll be out on her missions again.

Wonder what came to Mrs. Macclesfield? thought Is. I've a kind of a notion that it was Cousin Arn let her out.

And that's one comfort; at least I did find Cousin Arn. She was faintly cheered by the memory. He's a funny one. But I reckon he ain't as touched in the wits as he makes out —not by a long chalk. Wonder if he'll tell the old gals in the mill as I got snatched; that is, if they weren't snatched too . . . What would Gold Kingy ever do to *them*?

Thinking these thoughts, grubbing about in the pitch-black passage to pick up lumps of coal and load them in the basket, Is could not help falling into dreadfully low spirits. If only, she kept thinking. If only Grandpa hadn't teased Uncle Roy. If only *I* hadn't been rude to the horrible bully. If only Davie Stuart and Arn Twite hadn't met in London . . .

But then she thought: If Davie and Arn Twite and I hadn't come up north, it's true some trouble and grief would have been saved, but things up here would be just as awful— Gold Kingy telling his lies, his agents gulling silly kids onto the Playland Express—that's *gotta* be stopped. If I can only do summat about that.

Or I suppose—now I've found Arn—I could go back south myself and tell his mom he's still living; if only heaven knows how) I could get outa here. Only, how *could* I go back to live in our barn on Blackheath Edge knowing what it's like up here? And Arn still away from his mom?

These questions went around and around. And as they did so, all the hideous cold, damp, dark, and horror of the coal-pit seemed to wrap and suffocate and weigh her down, so that she was obliged to sit back on her heels and press her gritty hands together and clench her teeth, in order not to let out a groan of panic and wretchedness.

"Get a move on, can't ye?" said Joe. "You bain't shifting t'coal quick enough."

"I—I'm sorry," gulped Is. And then she felt the Touch, bright-hot and radiant, like a golden skewer passing into and beyond her, coming from somewhere else, invisible, incomprehensible, but immediately connecting her with all those waiting, hoping others. She was not alone. She remembered Mr. Greenaway saying, "You were *Sent*. There be a line from here, stretching northward."

"Where are you?" she called silently to all the others, and they answered together. "Why—we are here! Now you are with us! Now you know about the Bottom Layer."

"Don't I *just*!" said Is. "But what do we have to do, what can we do?"

"Why," they said in simple chorus, "it's for you to tell us that!"

And then the connection faded.

. . .

After what seemed an endless stretch of time to Is, a bell clanged somewhere in the mine and whistles blew; one lot of workers came off shift, another lot crawled from their bunks and went to take up the nonstop labor. A meal of thin porridge and bread was doled out by the guards, but many were too tired to eat; if lucky, they crept into bunks, if not, they fell asleep on the muddy floor. And, through her dazed and hungry slumber, Is felt the Touch come to her again in the form of a dream.

"You have to teach us," the voices said.

"But what, for pity's sake? *I* ain't learned. *I* ain't lettered. Never got no schooling."

"You know more than we do. And we are scattered, single, lost in the dark. We can't talk to each other; only to you. You must join us together. That's for you to do."

Is considered that. First in her dream and then again when she woke in the dark, three minutes before the bell clanged and the day shift (as if there *were* any day) must stagger up, cram down a crust of bread, and bolt off to the coalface.

Working through that shift, Is learned—partly from Joe, partly from observation—that the Holdernesse pit was shaped on a grid form. "It's called bord and pillar," Joe told her. "The coal's spread out in a big, thin patch over several square miles, so they work it in a crisscross honeycomb pattern, leaving pillars of coal everywhere to support the roof."

"Yes, and s'pose the pillars ain't strong enough? Coal's crumbly stuff. S'pose they cuts 'em too thin?"

"Shouldn't wonder but what that *will* happen one o' these days," Joe said gloomily.

The honeycomb shape of the pit meant that the workers had little contact with each other, for the pairs of colliers and hurriers were all working in separate spots, hundreds of little blind alleys, only meeting by chance if they arrived together at the whim gin.

Scrabbling in the damp, dark silence and stink of the bord, Is sent out her thoughts to the Bottom Layer.

"Listen, you lot! Can you hear me? All I can teach you is what I know myself. Agreed?"

An affirmation came back to her like a buzz of bees.

"Well—that I'll tell you and glad to, but one thing you gotta learn, and that's how to talk to each other. Not just to me. That's only sense, ain't it?"

It took them some time to understand what she meant: that if, collectively, they could all be in touch with her, and that if *she* had learned to communicate with *them,* somehow there must be a way of their learning to talk in thought patterns to one another.

"I dunno how it's done," said Is, "but we know it *can* be done, for we're doing it now. So you gotta try, keep trying. I wonder, is there any of you in the pit that I know?"

She felt somehow that if she could address people by name, it would strengthen their identity, give them more power to express themselves. She thought back to her trip on the Playland Express. "Mary-Ann? Is there a girl here called Mary-Ann?" She remembered the yellow-haired girl in the seat beside her. "Mary-Ann from Spitalfields?"

"Why yes!" came a surprised answer. "That's me! I'm here! How did you know?"

"Abel? Tod? Are you there?"

"I'm here—Tod Carter. Abel got killed when the rock fell in on him."

"Tess? Ciss?"

"Ciss tried to run away and the guards shot her," a voice said sadly. "I'm Tess."

"Coppy? Little Coppy?"

"Here I am!" came a furious howl. "They put me in the dark and told me to keep opening and shutting a door. I don't like it here! I hate it! I want my mama! I want my aunt Susan! I want to go home!"

"Don't you fret, Coppy, we'll get you home somehow. Don't cry!" She soothed his wails and said to the others, "Now you see. You've gotta talk to each other. You've gotta get through. You've gotta keep trying!"

"Yes, but tell us something first. Tell us something now. Give us summat to think about."

"Well, I'll tell you about Davie Stuart," said Is, and did so. She told how he was the king's son, how he wanted to see what was happening. "Reckon he thought it was his job to find out, and stop it if he could." She told how he came north, and what happened to him.

Her story was received in total silence. For a while, she thought the connection must have broken. But then she heard a single voice—the voice of Mary-Ann.

"Was that a true tale, you—what's *your* name?"

"Is."

"Was that a true tale, Is?"

"Yus. I know a lot of people who met Davie Stuart in the foundries. And I know his father, who's king of this land."

If the poor old skite hasn't died, she thought.

"Can you others hear what Mary-Ann is saying?" she asked into the silence.

"Yes!"

"There's one that can come through, then. Like I said, you gotta keep trying. Will you think about Davie Stuart? He helped a lot o' people. And his token's still helping them.

—Now I'm tired, I gotta stop and rest for a bit. But I'll tell you some more, later."

Is did find herself staggeringly tired—as if she had been dragging a heavy weight up from some deep, deep well far beneath her. Joe had begun to grumble that he was able to cut out the coal much faster than she could shift it. She hurried to catch up. Moving coal was much easier work than expressing her thoughts to the Bottom Layer. She wondered if Joe had been tuned in to the thought exchanges that had been going on; if so, he seemed entirely unaffected by them, just went silently and doggedly on with his work. Perhaps not every person in the pit could make this contact. But I'm certain a lot can, thought Is; it feels like hundreds and hundreds of 'em coming through.

Later on, when she had given her mind a rest, she told the Bottom Layer about Aunt Ishie, and got a very strong response.

"I know! I heard of her! I've got a pocket she made—I've got one too! And I have!"

"Who gave you those pockets? How did you get them?" Is called back.

"The cat-boy gave it to me. The cat-boy. The cat-boy . . ."

Aha! thought Is. I wonder how he gets in and out?

She asked, "But who gave them to the cat-boy?"

Tess answered, "A lady who lost her daughter."

"Mrs. Macclesfield!" Then Is had a thought. "Anyone here called Helen—Helen Macclesfield?"

A faint, exhausted thread of reply came through. "Yes . . . that's my name . . ."

"Helen! It's your little cousin Coppy who's just come—Coppy Gower. Can you talk to him?"

"Coppy?" came the whispered thought. "Can you hear me?"

"Yes!" he howled back.

"Good, Coppy! Just keep your hopes up. Being in the dark isn't so bad if you can talk."

But hope for what? wondered Is. Still, she did feel that progress was being made.

"Now," she said, "I'm going to tell you some of the tales that my sister Penny used to tell me."

And she told them the one about the mysterious barricades, and the one about the lost five minutes.

11

*Little man in coal pit goes knock, knock
Up he comes, up he comes, out at the top . . .*

AT THE COALFACE THERE WAS LITTLE POINT IN TRYING TO remember about nights or days. Very soon the workers had lost any idea of whether, in the world up above, it might be dark or light; they thought in terms of shifts. On Sundays they received a lump of cheese with their bread and gruel; this was the only change marking the passage of time in the days and weeks of blackness and silence.

After Is had been talking to the Bottom Layer for twenty or thirty shifts, she had told them, many times over, all of Penny's stories, and one that Dido had told her once about a king who lost his keys; she had even begun to make up some stories of her own. She had recited as many of Grandpa's riddles as she could recall, and given them a lively description of Grandpa: how he was sensible and a skilled printer when sober, but turned into a dangerous lunatic when drunk.

This fetched a lot of response from the Bottom Layer.

"Ah! My dad's one o' that kind! Used to lay into us with the fire tongs! That's why I run off from Clerkenwell."

"So did mine, anytime he was on the gin!"

Then Is told them about her dad, also one for the gin, and how he used to make up tunes. Many of these they knew already, and at the mention of each song a wave of inaudible music would pass through the mine, like the ripples of prayer that pass outward from a minaret.

Is worried sometimes that she ought to be teaching the workers something more useful than stories and songs and riddles, but the main thing, she supposed, was to keep talking; to keep the channels open and responses flowing along them. And she knew that she was getting stronger responses; shift by shift, new voices made themselves heard.

One day Joe suddenly spoke up, in the bord ahead of her.

"Is that *you,* buzzing away back there? I thought it was a swarm of bees got into the pit . . ."

Is found this very funny.

"Oh, Joe! Didn't you ever know? I told them who I was, ever such a long time ago."

"I didn't hear that. I didn't know your name was Is. You never told *me!*"

After that, she and Joe talked to each other in thoughts, more often than they used words.

And time went on . . .

Emptying her basket into the corf one day, Is felt something brush against her leg and bite her ankle. She let out a startled gasp.

"Don't fret, it's only me," said the teasing voice of Arun Twite. "And a pest of a time I've had finding you!"

"Arun! It's really you! Am I glad to hear your voice!"

"Listen!" he said. "There's danger! I've come to warn you. Aunt Ishie—"

"Oh, Arun! Have you been to see her! I'm glad! How is she? Did Grandpa die—?"

"Never mind that, this is urgent. Ishie and the old gals at Corso put their heads together—they all reckon there's terrible stormy weather coming soon. They're weather-wise, you know that. A big mountain, they say, a mountain called Hekla on an island hundreds of miles northwest that's going to blow its top off, and send huge waves chasing over the sea, and *that's* liable to smash in the roof of this pit like you'd smash an egg with a spoon."

"Lord-a-mercy!" said Is. "When's this going to be?"

"Soon. Dunno when. In a few days, they think."

"Then we gotta get the Bottom Layer out o' the pit. Arun —how in the name of goodness do *you* get in?"

"Same way I first got out," he said. "I swim. And that's how I go to and fro with the pockets Ma Macclesfield gives me, in a wetproof bag."

"Swim?"

"There's a cave down in the cliff at sea level on Holdernesse Head. That's how I found my way out when I was a collier. But it's a half-hour swim around the point before you can get ashore; the cliffs are too sheer to climb."

"Then that wouldn't do for the Bottom Layer," said Is.

"For I'll lay most of 'em can't swim. No more can I, for that matter. We'll have to get them out by the whim gin."

"What about the guards?"

"I think I can fix 'em," said Is thoughtfully. "Or some. That ain't the main snabble."

"What is?"

Joe suddenly broke into their talk, coming through to Is on a thought wave.

"What the plague's going on? Who are you colloguing with, back there?"

"Oh, Joe! Listen. My cousin Arun's here—the cat-boy . . ." And she told Joe what the old ladies were predicting.

"Ah," he said thoughtfully. "Yus. That's what I've allus been afeared of. A few real big waves up above would break the pit pillars down here like parsley stalks. And no use to tell the guards about it and try to get 'em on our side; they're locked in with us. The chief mine manager out in the town, he keeps the keys. So what do you reckon?"

Is told him her plan.

"What we got to do," she said, "the hard thing, will be getting the people out *in turn,* so they don't panic and jam up and squash together like bullocks at a gate."

Joe said: "The way to do it would be to have the ones closest to the whim gin go first. Then the ones a bit farther off move in. Then them farthest of all; they can all be moving in closer while the others is going up."

"Yus," agreed Is. "That's the way to do it, no question. But how do we explain, how do we get that plan into their noddles?"

"The bords have numbers," said Joe. "If they don't know their number, they gotta find out. Then it'll be easy, for the lowest numbers are closest to the whim gin, where they started digging. Here we're in number thirty-two. A long way back."

"I see," said Is. "How'll they find out their numbers?"

" 'Times it's stuck up at the end of the stall on a bit of board. If it ain't, they'll have to ask the overlookers at the whim gin."

"Won't that make those coves smell a rat?" said Arun.

Is chuckled. "They can say it's for a lottery. Winner gets an extra lump of cheese on Sunday."

Joe said: "But how about the coves up at the top of the whim gin? How'll we fix them?"

"I can take care of that," said Arun.

"And how are you going to let us know when we're to go?" Joe asked.

"Can you send a thought message, Arun?"

But this Arun could not do.

"Well, can't be helped," said Is regretfully. "We'll just havta start work right away on getting them ready. It'll surely take a while. We can't afford to wait. You best go off, Arun, and fix the coves on top. —But wait, is there any other news? About Grandpa, and Aunt Ishie?"

"Eh? No," he answered rather hurriedly, and then, "Well, there was a message, Miss Sibley said, from Ishie. She'd seen Captain Podmore and he had asked her—this was important —to tell you that someone you know of had died."

"Someone I know of—my stars!" muttered Is. She drew a long breath. "Someone I know of. Oh, my cats alive." Poor old King Dick, she thought. That sad news about his son was the last straw for him. "Weren't there no more than that?" she asked after a moment.

"Yes, there was. Wait till I think." In the darkness, Arun

scratched his head; if he'd really been a cat, Is knew, he'd have suddenly washed an inch of fur behind his elbow.

"This was the other bit," said Arun, after he had done thinking. "Someone you know of didn't have any other children, Captain Podmore said. So his cousin was going to take over his job."

"His cousin?" Baffled, Is wondered who King Dick's cousin might be. How would she be expected to know a thing like that?

"I'll be off, then," Arun said, and left, promising to put in hand his scheme to nobble the upper-level operators of the whim gin in about two days' time. If anything went wrong with this plan, he would try to drop bunches of heather down the shaft as a warning.

And Is addressed herself to the task of telling the Bottom Layer that they must now get ready to escape from the pit. It was a hard and complicated process. First she had to reassure them, over and over. Don't panic. Don't panic. This is a real early warning. The flood won't happen for days and days. But it will come, it's bound to come. And it's going to take a precious long time for everybody to clamber up the whim gin; we gotta do it sensible and orderly, so's not to start a stampede and make a louse ladder of the business.

First you gotta find out your bord number. Then call in and let me know what it is.

This part of the affair took a nerve-rackingly long time. Very few knew their numbers. Some of the older bords had names—Dead Man's Lane, Shelly Bottom, Echo Level—but hardly any of the workers knew where they were in relation to the other workers with whom they had begun to form thought connections. All this took several shifts to sort out.

Is talked to them tirelessly, hour after hour, going over the details.

"First number three, Alice and Tom—then number four, Mick and Fred—then Sol and Sim—then Ann and Sue—then Dick and Peg. Just remember who comes before you, that's all you really have to learn. Don't forget to bring your corf with you—*empty*. I'll be at the foot of the whim gin, and I'll call in the first ones, jist as soon as we're ready to start moving. I'll be there first, and I'll stay there all through, I promise."

All the days of practice conversation—the stories, the riddles, the back-and-forth responses—had been worth it, she realized; the Bottom Layer was calm now, and ready to trust her.

Just the same she had a last-minute flash of panic, wondering: suppose there's some folk in the pit that have never switched in on our thought channels? Will they understand what's going on? Will they run amuck, or will they get left behind and caught in the flood? Or suppose Arun doesn't manage to nobble the coves at the pit head? What then? But it was no use dwelling on such anxieties.

When all the workers had been sorted into a rational order of escape, and the order had been practiced and recited over and over again, Is dragged her corf down to the whim gin with Joe close behind her.

"Now, Joe, you gotta make a ruckus up the passage a way, while I fix t'other guard," she told him.

So Joe began to yell out lustily, "Help! Help! The roof's a-caving! I'm caught! I'm trapped!"

One of the two guards went with caution to investigate. The other, following fixed orders, stayed by the rope and the baskets with his hand close to his pistol. But Is, who had brought a stub of candle with her, lit it and walked up to him.

"Mister!" she said urgently. "Look at this candle! Look at this light!"

"Well? What of it? What the deuce are you playing at?" he growled, as she moved it gently to and fro.

"You are walking down a cool, grassy path to a river," she told him. "Now you are walking into the water . . ."

His eyes wavered. Oh, Lord-a-mercy, thought Is, *what if it doesn't work?* What'll I do then?

But it did work.

His eyes became fixed, his breathing grew deeper and slower. His hands relaxed. The pistol fell to the ground.

"You are fast asleep," she told him. "You are going to sit down comfortably with your back resting against the wall, and you will not wake up again until you hear a rooster crow."

At this moment Joe appeared, panting and triumphant, dragging the other guard, whom he had knocked unconscious with his pick handle. "It was easy as pie!" he said, astonished. "Why didn't I do it months ago? But how in the world did you ever manage to nobble your fellow?"

"He'll be out for hours. But you better tie yours, if you can find a cord."

While he did so, Is began sending out her call. *"We are ready to go. Now we are ready to go. Alice and Tom, you are the first, come now; then the others, in the order we planned. Mick and Fred, Sol and Sim, leave your places and come as fast and quietly as you can. We are ready to go. Don't panic. Don't rush. Just wait for your turn, then come. Tell your names to the others, give your number as you leave your bord. Just come . . ."*

In less than four minutes, two grimy figures appeared at the whim gin: Alice and Tom.

"Two into a corf, that's right," said Joe, and helped them start the slow, dizzy, swinging ascent. There was no spark of light to be seen overhead now, Is noticed, which must mean that it was nighttime in the world outside the mine. Just as well; she hoped it might be early in the night, so that they would have all the hours of dark ahead, time to empty the whole mine of its workers before anybody up above realized what was happening. She knew now, from counting names and bord numbers, that there were well over two hundred workers in Holdernesse Pit. They had a long job ahead of them.

In fact the evacuation took over five hours.

Is found it strange, meeting people face-to-face who hitherto had been known only by their thoughts. A boy called Desmond, who in his thought shapes had come over as forceful, strong, and highly intelligent was revealed as a thin, small, shy figure with a crooked shoulder; Mary-Ann, the yellow-haired giggler of the Playland Express, turned out to be a most efficient organizer, bringing several workers who had not tuned in to the transmission of thought. And, for their part, many of the Bottom Layer were startled, almost incredulous, at their first sight of Is, whom they had expected to be big and bossy and fierce.

At the very end came Tess with little Coppy, who had been left out of the number roll because he was not in a bord at all, but had been given the job of trapper boy, obliged to sit all day and night beside a ventilation door which he had to keep opening and shutting. He was wailing and furious at being left behind, but Tess carried and comforted him.

"Soon we'll be out. See, we're going up in the basket—like the old woman who went over the moon."

"Right, that's the lot . . ." sighed Joe, stretching his shoulders with immense relief.

"Let's *hope*—" said Is. She sent out a thought call through the mine: "Is there anybody left, is anybody still working?"

No answer came back.

"Best us go now; my cove's beginning to stir," said Joe.

"Hold on a moment, then."

The guards had a slate on which they kept the tally of the corves and which hurriers had brought them; Is wiped it clean and wrote: WEVE CLEARED OUT AS PIT IS DUE TO FLOOD YOU GOT SENSE YOULL CLERE OUT TOO, while Joe undid the rope around his man's wrists.

Then Is joined Joe in the corf and began the slow creep up the black well. Suppose the rope breaks, she thought. Well . . . it didn't for the others, why should it for us? And Joe and me don't weigh so much as a basket of coal. But just the same . . . suppose it did? She thought of the black depth underneath.

"Joe," she said, "can you crow like a rooster?"

"If you want me to," said he, and did so, hanging over the side of the corf. *"Cock a doodle doo!"* Is thought of the woods at home, and the faraway cock on the Kentish farm.

"Wonder what we'll find when we get to the top?" said Joe. "D'you reckon the others will still be there? Or will they have bunked off?"

Is had been wondering the same thing, and had been worrying about it. For it was all very well to devise a means of getting the workers out of the mine. But what was to be done with them next? There had been no time to make further plans. They would need clothes and food; most of them were half naked. Most would probably want to go back to their homes in the distant southland—but a big obstacle lay in between, and that was Gold Kingy. He's gotta be dealt with now, thought Is, but how? In the wide world, *how*?

The upper mouth of the whim gin, when they reached it, was not large: a hole about eight feet across. Dim light of dawn revealed the bulky wooden structure; the big winding drum up above; the shaggy, patient horse plodding around in a circle.

"Right there, Dobbin, you can stop now!"

Is climbed out of the corf basket with suddenly buckling knees, and had to grab one of the wooden posts to support herself. Next moment she found herself wrapped in the bony hug of Dr. Lemman, and was dazed and astounded to hear a wild shout of welcome from hundreds of hoarse voices all around.

"Huzza for Is, who fetched us up outa the dark. *Huzza!*"

Is gulped. Stupidly, she felt she could almost have boo-hooed, even louder than little Coppy. Instead she swallowed a couple of times, and spoke, after a moment, in thought language: "Thanks, cullies! But we ain't outa the wood yet, no how; we gotta find somewhere to lodge you and feed you till we get you shifted from here. So don't hollo too loud yet!"

"What's that message you are sending out to them?" inquired Lemman, who still grasped her arm and was looking at her with close attention. She told him in words.

"I say, dearie, that thought-transit system of yours beats semaphore any day of the week! But don't you fret; we're going to get 'em under wraps down there in the old post office; your aunt Ishie and the other good ladies have been boiling turnips and making britches out of mail sacks for the past twelve hours. The colliers wouldn't start down the hill until they saw *you* come up safe and smiling. But now I reckon it's time for them to trudge; if you'll just give 'em the office to start. Father Lance will show them the way."

"Will you all follow the old bald gent in the black petticoat!" Is told the Bottom Layer, the grimy hopeful throng around her on the hilltop. "And he'll take you where there's vittles and togs."

Relieved, grateful, and shivering, they trooped off down the hill.

"How did you and Arun nobble the whim-gin winders?" Is asked Lemman.

"Oh, all I had to do was offer them a dram, and lace it with a drop of laudanum. They're asleep in the workshop yonder." He nodded toward a shed at one side of the coal yard where they stood. From it a rail track ran down the side of the headland diagonally to the docks and foundries below.

"The foundries!" cried Is in a fright. "What'll happen to them in there when this big wave comes? They're at water-level, on the dockside—"

"That's all rug, dearie. Your pal the cat-boy has been down and warned 'em."

"But if it comes sudden—" began Is.

"Well, you can only do so much, dearie," said Lemman. "You can't save the whole *world*, you know! —What's up?"

She was looking past his shoulder in astonishment. Most of ruined Old Blastburn lay visible below them, fringing the landward side of the headland, with its mangled townscape and broken buildings. A dark and windy day had declared itself, with smoke from the foundry chimneys streaked by tails of snow like strips of grimy tattered rag gusting inland. Dimly visible through the smoke, between the broken roofs of Old Blastburn, through its ruined streets, wound something that resembled a black and flashing snake.

"What's *that*?" said Is.

"Oh—that—" answered Lemman, rather awkwardly for him. "That—I fear—is your great-grandfather's funeral procession. Gold Kingy decided he must have the old gentleman buried with full military honors; as Grandfather of the State, or some such nonsense. I reckon that way Roy hopes to sugar over the fact that he hastened the old boy's end by flattening his cat and wrecking his home and generally harassing him. Your aunt, I need hardly say, does not see eye-to-eye with Roy over this; although she was offered a black-and-gold landau and a leading part in the procession, she chose to absent herself from the ceremony. As I said, she is in the post office cutting up mailbags."

"So Grandpa did die."

"Not immediately," said Lemman with a grin. "He contrived to linger for six weeks in a coma; no one can say if he did it on purpose to drive Gold Kingy wild, but it certainly had that effect. Yes. If he wasn't crazy before, he's on the edge of it now. *You'd* best keep out of his way, dearie. Captain Podmore says he'll be glad to take you on board—"

Is hardly heard Lemman. She was watching the spectacle of what must have been Gold Kingy's entire army, with bayonets flashing, musket barrels swathed in somber chiffon, bright standards at half mast, and all those black chariots and black-plumed horses, winding slowly among the ruined streets, making for the main entrance to Holdernesse town and, presumably, Twite Square.

Poor old Grandpa, thought Is; wonder where they'll put him? Is there a cemetery in Holdernesse? I'm real sorry the old boy's gone, I'll miss him considerable, but how he would laugh to see what's happening now! If he's up above (and I'm sure I hope he is, for he never meant any harm, and in his time he must have been useful to lots of folk) he must be splitting his sides at this very minute. She chuckled in sympathy.

But then, clutching at Lemman's arm, Is cried out, "*Murder,* Doc Lemman! Look there!"

Down the coast from the north came rolling a wave. But what a wave! It was to the ordinary lace-crested breaker what a killer whale is to a tadpole. It marched along the coast, steel-gray, iron-blue, large as a mountain, calmly and majestically chewing off whole landscapes of cliff or sand dune as it proceeded. Behind it came eight others, equally huge.

Off Holdernesse Head the leading wave performed a gentle curtsy: as a person might tread on soft ground over a mole run, sink, stumble, then gracefully recover and move on without breaking step. The following waves eddied and dipped likewise, but then traveled calmly on. That's the mine smashed in, thought Is. Now the procession of waves approached the docks of Holdernesse town; they swept over the foundries like a bucket of water demolishing an ants' nest; a plume of steam flew up and a distant explosion rocked the hill. A back wave careered up the estuary and swept away the inky funeral procession as if it were a handful of coal dust, entered the gateway of Holdernesse town, and then withdrew again. Its eight attendant waves followed the same course—up, back, in, out—then all of them slid away down the coast, on their southward road toward London and France.

"Heaven help us!" said Lemman soberly. "That's the end of Holdernesse town."

They could feel the hillside slipping and shuddering under

their feet, like a sandcastle when its foundations are washed from under it. Lemman started running down the hill toward the foundries and the dock area. Is followed. Arun and Joe, at the tail of the procession of colliers, guessed their intention and came racing over to join them.

"Perhaps somebody can be saved," Lemman panted as he ran.

But when they were halfway down the hill, at an elbow in the road, the doctor stopped and threw out his hands with a gesture of helpless despair. For below them there was now nothing but water; the sea had risen and covered the docks, the foundries, all the area at the foot of the headland; both arched gateways to Holdernesse town were completely submerged. All that could be seen was some wreckage tossing about, and the tops of one or two foundry chimneys.

"There *can't* be anybody left alive in the town—can there?" croaked Is.

Lemman shook his head. "Not a ghost of a chance, dearie —see what's happening to the hill."

It was plain that the cave roof over Holdernesse had collapsed.

"Stove in like a busted egg," said Arun. "Lucky we didn't wait any longer to get out the colliers."

Is thought of Grandpa Twite's funeral procession, and shivered. Where was his coffin now? Washing about in submerged Twite Square among the bodies of Gold Kingy's army? Where was Gold Kingy?

"And what about Lunnon?" she asked, clutching Lemman again in horror. "Lunnon's low-lying too!"

"What about the coast of Kent?" from Arun, suddenly anxious.

"Well—maybe the waves will have reduced in size by the

time they get farther south," said the doctor. But he did not sound too hopeful.

"Let's go to the post office and help Aunt Ishie," said Is. "That's summat we *can* do."

To get there, they had to climb over the hill again. There was no way around. Descending the landward side, they found that Corso Mill was now within a quarter mile of the new coastline. The lower streets of Old Blastburn were awash, but the upper ones, with library, post office, and rail station, were well above water level.

Passing the library they saw on its steps the Gower family —Mrs. Macclesfield, her sister, Coppy, a girl who must be Helen, and Mr. Gower. He was white, drenched, and shivering, but with a look on his face Is would hardly have believed it could wear.

He ran down to her and gripped both her hands.

"Miss Twite—I cannot tell you—I do not know what to say—my boy—my niece—all restored to me . . ." He stuck there, with his mouth twisting uncontrollably.

"Oh, well," said Is gruffly, "that ain't no big grig—it's jist lucky we was able to get 'em all out in time. —See here, Mr. Gower," she went on, a sudden excellent notion coming into her head, "are you in charge here now? Is my uncle Roy a goner?"

"I—I scarcely know," he said, startled. "No one has seen him. It seems likely indeed—he and the whole funeral procession were inside the city, or entering it, when the first wave struck. I went down in a boat to reconnoiter, but any attempt at rescue is out of the question; huge masses of water are still washing about inside and, indeed, everybody in there must have been drowned at once."

Well, Uncle Roy's no loss, that's for sure, thought Is. She

went on, "Seems to me, Mr. Gower, the least you can do is to ship all these colliers back home wherever they come from."

"That's a capital notion, dearie," agreed Lemman. "Though of course we must bear in mind that their homes in the south may also have been flooded. Don't you agree, Gower, that they should be sent home? There's naught for them to do here, with the foundries awash and the mine full of water."

Mr. Gower looked much beset and moithered at having these large responsibilities thrust on him, but Arun, very unexpectedly, suggested, "Why not pack the lot of them on the Playland train and send it back?"

"Ay, but what about the track farther south? It may have been flooded."

Gower was full of doubts and possible objections, but Lemman said, "Just the same, that's a decidedly happy notion, dear boy; why don't you go around to the station directly and discover what kind of trim the train is in."

"What about a driver?" said Gower fretfully.

"The boy can look about for a driver at the same time."

Arun nodded and ran off. He was beginning to look, Is thought, less like a cat, more like a person. I must talk to him some more about Davie, she thought, when we've time. I want to hear as much as I can about Davie.

They went on toward the post office, accompanied by the Gower family. Mr. Gower, now that he had run into Lemman, seemed reluctant to lose sight of him, and asked him continual questions.

"What should we do about the drowned people? All that destroyed property—houses, stores, manufactories? Should we try to compile a list of what's gone—a list of the victims? What is your opinion, Doctor?"

"Why," said Lemman rather impatiently, "our main duty, as I see it, is to care for those who remain alive. And here we have them," he added as they walked into the sorting office.

This presented a scene of brisk but orderly activity, with Aunt Ishie and her friends very much in control. Soup, cheese, and bread were being distributed in flower pots, pewter bowls, seed pans, crocks, jugs, baskets—any vessel that could be found and brought into use. Shirts, skirts, and breeches were being cut and pieced together from the old mailbags, stitched with expert speed, and eagerly received by the shivering mine workers. A few of the Bottom Layer were already engaged in useful activity, helping their elderly hosts sort mailbags, pour soup, or fetch fuel for the great iron stove; but a large number of them appeared utterly exhausted and shocked by what they had been through, and could do no more than huddle together and tremble. Most of them could hardly see in daylight, for they had been so long underground that their eyesight had become dimmed.

"Poor dears, it will take them days to recover, I fear," said Aunt Ishie. Then she gave Is a hug and a warm commendation: "You did well, dearie! You did really well! I'm proud of you, and so would Grandpa have been."

"Aunt Ishie, did you know all along that the cat-boy was my cousin Arun?"

Ishie shook her head.

"I understood that his name was Bobbert. And then yesterday—to my astonishment—he comes and tells me who he is—asks for help in providing for the pit workers—"

"*Did* he, now?" Is tucked this fact away, to be thought about when she was not so busy.

Dr. Lemman was methodically making his way back and forth among the grimy crowd lolling on the flagged floor—which also included workers from the foundries and the potteries—asking them questions about their state of health.

"Carrots: They must eat raw carrots for their poor eyes," said Aunt Ishie briskly, and dispatched several of her aged helpers (more and more old ladies seemed to be emerging from their secluded moorland dwellings as news of the flood spread about the countryside) to search for wild carrots and healing herbs in woodland or fellside or people's abandoned gardens.

"I reckon they'd all perk up a sight quicker if they had summat to look forward to," remarked Is, and she sent out a thought message: "How many of you 'ud like to go back home, if we can fix up some way to get you there? Any offers?"

She was almost knocked over by the volume of the answer that came back: "Yes, *yes*! How soon can we start?"

"Well, we gotta get you on your feet first, cullies, haven't we? So you eat all the carrots Aunt Ishie can find while we work at fixing up a way to shift you." She thought a bit, then added, "And keep on talking to each other in thought language. I reckon that's valuable. Us pit workers may be the only ones that can do it. We don't want to lose that, do we?"

"Never!" came the heartfelt agreement.

"Talk to each other—and tell the coves from the foundries and potteries—get them started too. Maybe we can teach everyone in the world."

"I could tell 'em all some funny jokes," volunteered Mary-Ann, who was cutting up mailbags with professional speed. And several more came through with suggestions for entertainment and instruction: Desmond had made up some arithmetical puzzles; Tess knew rhymes; Mrs. Macclesfield unexpectedly said that she could teach them some history. She seemed to be the only adult who, so far, had picked up the trick of talking in thought waves. "It was because of the strength of my link with Helen," she said. "When she was taken into the mines she called to me and I heard her."

Helen Macclesfield, who had been in the mines longer than almost any of the other colliers, was one of the worst sufferers from day blindness, and was pitifully thin; her arms and legs were like knobbed twigs, her hair and skin were paper-white, but such a huge joy vibrated from her that it was warming just to stand beside her. Already she had a pair of wooden needles and skein of wool and was halfway through making some garment, for, as she said, "You don't need sight for knitting."

Halfway through the first day, Aunt Ishie suddenly broke into thought language. "It's like skating!" she said in de-lighted amazement. "Why did I never do it before? How wonderful to learn a new skill at my age!"

And she told them a long story about the witch-queen Dahud, and the submerged city of Is, off Cape Finisterre, where the people are transparent and can see right through each other.

"Like us," said Is.

Now Arun reappeared with a limping, one-eyed man; he seemed vaguely familiar to Is, and then she remembered that she had seen him in the driver's cab of the Playland Express.

"This here's Mr. Stritch," Arun told Lemman and Gower. "He's the only train driver left."

And a right shravey cove he looks, thought Is, studying him with disfavor.

Dr. Lemman evidently felt the same.

"Is he the best there is? What happened to the others?" he asked, coldly scanning Mr. Stritch, who threw himself into a paroxysm of nods and bobs and bows and grins, twisting his face up like a paper bag.

"Oh, my dear stars, yer honors, ain't it jist a treat to see all them young 'uns having a lay-easy and a feast, poor young mossels, instead o' having to work for their living. It do my old 'eart good—that it do!"

"What happened to the other drivers?" repeated Lemman, without troubling to congratulate Stritch on his benevolence.

"Well, yer honor, two was pressed into service in the army. Gold Kingy was runnin' short o' men, see? Me they wouldn't take, acos of me gammy leg and missing peeper. Otherwise, nat'rally, I'd 'a bin prard to serve me country—"

"Never mind that. What about the rest?"

"Two run off, time we done our last run to Lunnon town; said they was sick o' the job. So now I'm all on me loney," said Mr. Stritch sorrowfully, "but ready *an'* willin' to assist yer honors any way I can."

"Could you teach four or five of these youngsters to drive the train?" asked Gower.

"Well, Mr. Gower, sir," said Stritch humbly, "train-drivin's 'ard, dangerous, difficult work—that I will not deny —'tis more of a job for a able, strong, clever, growed man than for these puny little pit sweepings . . ." casting a disparaging glance at the Bottom Layer. But then, hastily recollecting himself, he added, "Still I dessay some of 'em's as clever as they can hold together; if we takes it by slow stages I don't doubt a few of 'em'll be able to manage well enough— under my supervision, o' course."

"Very well. Do we have any volunteers?" called Lemman. A dozen hands shot up. One of them was Mary-Ann's.

"Driving a train 'ud be a sight better trade than going back into the millinery," she said.

"My poor drowned mates'd be right happy to know you think so, missy," retorted Stritch, giving her an unfriendly look. "Ah, dragged down by Neptune's sheep, my poor cullies was, along with our beloved leader. With my very own eyes that sorrowful sight I saw, and never did I think that our beautiful train 'ud be under the charge of a passel of rapscallions and females—"

"You say that you actually witnessed the death of my nephew?" interrupted Aunt Ishie, who happened to be passing him at that moment with a bundle of canvas. Mr. Stritch started in fright at her proximity and gave an anxious, ingratiating bob of the head, backing away.

"Not to tell a lie, I did indeed, ma'am; I was the witness of that fatal end. See, I were sitting on a wall in James Street to watch the percession go by that was to lay your sainted and revered old gent in 'is last resting place in 'Oldernesse town (I wonder where 'e is now, by the by?)—an' there was a troop of 'ousehold cavalry bringin' up the rear, an' two big old cart horses a-pulling of the gun-carriage with the coffin on it, an' be'ind it, Gold Kingy a-riding in 'is chariot. My two mates was on the cart horses, them not bein' accustomed to 'orseback. An', just as they come by me, down heaves this perdigious great wave, 'igher than the 'ole of Mount Snowdon, I give you my word, an' tosses 'em all abart like fishbones. And Gold Kingy shouts out real loud: 'I kin walk on the water!' 'e yells. 'No flood can drarn me, I kin walk on the water.' "

"And could he?" asked Aunt Ishie with deep interest.

"Lord bless you, no, ma'am, that 'e couldn't. Down under the watter 'e went, same as the rest. All of 'em got washed down James Street and into the entrance to 'Oldernesse cave —like sand down a sinkpipe."

Is shuddered at the thought of what it must be like, now, inside Holdernesse town.

"So now we are fairly certain that my nephew is dead," calmly remarked Aunt Ishie.

Mr. Stritch threw her a remarkably sharp look, then assumed a doleful expression and replied, "That we are, ma'am, and a sore loss for you, let alone this 'ole country of ours—" edging away from her as fast as possible all the time he spoke. When he was a safe distance away he pulled out a large leather snuffbox and helped himself to several massive pinches, at the same time making a quick gesture with his left hand as if to dispel her baneful influence. Indeed the whole atmosphere of the sorting office and the old ladies going about their tasks seemed to make him wretchedly uneasy.

"I'll be taking the lads back to the station, then, sirs. And, come dinnertime, mebbe one o' the young lasses can bring down their grub, and a bite or two for me. There'll be plenty for them to do down there, a-working on the ingine."

"I wouldn't trust that fellow with a tin halfpenny," said Lemman, when Stritch had taken off his band of apprentices.

"Agreed, but he's the only one we have."

"Mary-Ann'll keep an eye on him," said Is.

12

This is the key of the kingdom . . .

IS, HAVING BETTER EYESIGHT THAN MOST OF THE OTHERS, NOW
went out daily over the nearby hills on a search for wild
herbs and roots. From her life in the woods with Penny she
had already a rough knowledge of the more commonly used
herbs and simples—foxglove, feverfew, marigold, rosehip,
sorrel—but under the tuition of Aunt Ishie and Miss Sibley,
who made careful little drawings and described the kind of
locations where the rarer plants could be found, her knowledge soon became more comprehensive. Arun often accompanied her, since, from roaming and wandering during the
time of his cat-hood, he knew the country very well; and he
was of great help in scraping away snow or digging for deep
roots.

At first very little was said on these excursions, for Arun

had lost the habit of much talk (if indeed he ever had it), but Is felt comfortable in his silent company, and he appeared to feel the same with her. Sometimes he appeared to her more boylike, at other times more catlike. She could not tell what caused these fluctuations, but on the whole, she thought, the human periods began to last longer and come oftener.

"Arun, what turned you into a cat in the first place?"

"It was after Davie died, and they sent me back from the foundries to the mines. I felt like a cat; I *was* a cat. And I knew a cat could get out of the mine, and I did."

That was all he would say.

"Your dad said you used to sing and make up songs," she said to him one day. "Don't you do that no more?"

"No," he answered, with a shut face. She did not pursue the topic any further. Nor did she ask if he had had any more thoughts about going south. Let's leave him be for now, she felt.

He was good at the work they were engaged on, visibly pleased when they uncovered a large patch of wild spinach, a good birch-bark tree, some large bracket-fungi, or a plentiful growth of comfrey ("so *sovereign* for low spirits," said Aunt Ishie).

One day, a mild day of thaw, when they were digging out evening-primrose roots, Arun began to tell Is more about his friend Davie. He talked thoughtfully and easily for a long time. In after days, Is could not remember the exact words he had used, but the picture he made was so clear that she almost felt she had met Davie herself, and regretted all the more that she had not. Davie had been the kind of person, Arun said, who made you glad to be alive; made you feel there was some *point* in being alive.

"There aren't many like that," he said seriously.

"No, there bain't," Is agreed.

Davie, said Arun, had not thought about himself *at all;* his concern was always for other people, how he could help them. And yet he had not been at all priggish or saintly, but always the best of good company, full of jokes and seeing the funny side to the worst situations.

"It was in the Strand, in London, that I met him first off," recalled Arun, looking back, "and we got talking—about birds, I think it was. Then we used to meet and walk about together. Then he told me he'd heard about the Playland Express and how all the kids was going on it. And he wanted to find what happened to 'em. And he said, 'Are you game to come with me?' so I said yes I was."

The gentle, reminiscent note in his voice prompted Is to say—rather rashly—"Arun, have you thought any more about writing a letter to your mom?"

Of an evening, in the sorting office, Aunt Ishie had set the Bottom Layer—those few of them who could read—to sifting the huge heaps of dead letters into batches, arranged under destination, ready for the day when the mails might begin to move again. While they did this one of the old ladies, or Mrs. Gower, or Mrs. Macclesfield, would often read aloud from some dusty leather-bound volume fetched over from the disused library. At these times Coppy sat wedged between his parents, and Helen Macclesfield, curled on the floor, would lean her head against her mother's knee. Is had once observed Arun watching these family groups with what seemed a look of incredulous envy.

"It must be lonesome for your ma now your dad's gone. When I go south on the train I could take your letter, and then carry it on to Folkestone. That ain't too far from Blackheath Edge. She'd be right pleased to hear from you."

Without answering the question, Arun said, "You reckon to go on the train?"

"I might."

"What about Captain Podmore?"

"I've a notion his vessel musta been swamped by the flood," she said sadly. "Otherwise we'd surely have heard from him by now."

Arun made no reply, but dug up six more roots.

"Your dad walked to London thirty times, looking for you," Is said neutrally.

He burst out in irritation. "Yes, when it was too late! What use was that?"

Now it was her turn to remain silent.

Next day Arun stayed in the sorting office helping Mrs. Crockett pound up the evening-primrose roots, while Is went out on her own to search for wild garlic. This was always easy to find, for it grew in hilly bottoms around the source of springs, where the snow had mostly melted.

She was kneeling in some dead leaves, listening to the babble of the brook, peacefully grubbing up a handful of roots and feeling quite cheerful, since the Bottom Layer was making visible daily progress while good reports came from the apprentice train drivers, when two hands holding something potent and choking closed over her nose and mouth. Simultaneously, a violent blow struck her on the back of her head. The snowy copse faded from her view, and she fell down into bottomless dark.

When she came back to consciousness it was still dark. And a long time had gone by, she felt certain; though it was hard to be certain of anything, because the effect of whatever had drugged her was lingering still. She could smell its harsh sweetness, and her tongue, throat, and mental workings all seemed unnaturally clogged and slow. She tried to speak, tried to call for help in thought language, but could do neither. She must, though, have made some sound or movement, for a voice said in satisfaction:

"Good. She's stirring at last. You gave her too much."

"What happened?" Is crossly tried to say. "Why can't I budge my hands?"

Impotently, she tried to move. No sound but a croak came from her lips. And her hands seemed to be chained behind her.

Someone struck a light. By the quick flash, Is could see stacks of dark books. I'm in the library, then, she thought. I came to rescue Mrs. Macclesfield . . . but she ain't here. No—that was before. That can't be right.

The light grew and glimmered. Somebody had lit a candle.

"Be that sensible, guvnor?" doubtfully asked a voice—a vaguely familiar voice.

"Deuce take it, of course it's sensible. Just because you pulled me out of the water, don't think you can teach me my business," scornfully retorted another voice, even more familiar. "They're all eating carrots—sorting dead letters."

"Uncle Roy!" croaked Is, with immense difficulty finding her tongue.

"Well, girl? Woke up at last?"

"I thought you was supposed to be dead. Drown-dead."

"And you're wholly sorry I'm not," he responded sourly.

She could hardly deny this. "Why—why—what are we doing here?" she mumbled with difficulty. "In—in the library?"

"Hah. You worked that out?" He moved the candle and she could see his face—angry, aggressive Uncle Roy, mud-stained, bloodstained. Plainly, although not drowned, he had had quite a struggle to remain alive. I suppose Stritch saved him, Is thought. And got small thanks for it.

"Grandpa had the laugh on you in the end," she uttered slowly.

"The old devil!" he burst out. "And that's why *you're* here, my girl. You're going to tell me his secret, before I go off westward. You and Ishie are the only two who know it." And you're afraid of Ishie, Is thought. He went on, "If you don't tell me—you'll never leave here."

"Like Mrs. Macclesfield? But Mrs. Macclesfield did leave, Uncle Roy! Did you know—did you know—" Talking was frightfully hard work, it was making her throat ache; what frightful potion could he have given her? —"Did you know, Uncle Roy, that we can all talk to each other in thought language? Mrs. Macclesfield, Coppy, me, and all the Bottom Layer—"

"Be silent!" he shouted furiously. "I don't want to listen to your crazy ramblings. I ought to be on my way to Cokehouses—now—I've money in the bank there, I can start again. I only want one thing, I want you to tell me—"

"If you please, guvnor, *don't shout!*" implored the other voice, which now Is was able to identify. It *was* that of Mr. Stritch the train driver. Lemman had said he wouldn't trust the man with a tin halfpenny, Is recollected. He was dead right. "You ain't popular around here no more, you know that," humbly reminded Mr. Stritch.

By the candle's light Is studied Gold Kingy's face. He allus did have a screw loose, she decided, and now he's come downright untwisted. Don't Stritch know that? But Stritch is none too bright either; maybe he thinks helping Gold Kingy is better than teaching a passel of kids to drive a train.

"Listen!" said Gold Kingy, bringing the candle closer to Is. "You know what I want. If you don't tell me—and I'm not joking, I never joke—you'll not be Is no more. You'll be *Was*. First I'll set fire to your hair; then I'll set fire to the library. And after, do you know what I'm going to do? That train—my Playland Express—that train you're so set on sending back south, with all those scrawny kids aboard that should be down below digging out the coal, *my* coal—scalp me, when I think of the trouble you've caused me, girl, one way and other, it's all I can do not to split you like a haddock—"

"Don't get frantic, guvnor, *don't*!" implored Stritch again. "Jest ask what you want to know and let's be on our way to Cokehouses. Those kids make me nervous. If any of the colliers or the foundry workers get a sight of you, they'll toss you in the Wash River."

"That train—" repeated Gold Kingy furiously, without taking the least notice of Stritch. "There's a hand-basin full of dynamite packed aboard, ready to blow it all sky-high as soon as the train leaves the station. If they don't work for me, they shan't work for anybody else. So you better tell me fast—"

"But, Uncle Roy—"

Almost, Is felt sorry for the poor crazy creature. Though at the same time she was mortally afraid of him. He looked as dangerous as his own dynamite—ready to blow up at any moment, and blow up everybody else at the same time.

"Uncle Roy. *Listen*. Grandpa told you himself. It was the last thing he told you. Remember the rhyme? 'As backward you go—' How did it go on?" She thought hard, slowly remembering.

> "As backward you go, take a turn around the pond
>   If threescore-and-ten you would pass beyond."

"What the flaming fiend are you going on about, girl?" he almost screamed at her. "Don't mumble that old monster's gibberish to me!"

"But he was telling you, Uncle Roy! 'As backward'—that's S-A. And 'a turn round the pond', that's P-O-O-L backward—so the whole thing gives you saloop."

"Saloop? What the plague is that?"

"Don't you remember, Grandpa used to drink it every day. Ask *me*," said Is, "*I* think Grandpa was just a tough old codger. I don't reckon it was the saloop so much as his own ginger that kept him going; but maybe it was the saloop. Who knows? Anyhow, that was what he told you, his own self. Before he died. So you better believe it."

Uncle Roy was almost frothing at the mouth with fury and frustration.

"I *don't* believe it!" he shouted. "Is that all? There *must* be something else—anyway, what *is* saloop?"

"Guvnor, guvnor!" implored Stritch.

"It's a kind of warm, milky drink. Made from powdered orchid roots, Ishie said."

"Orchid roots? Where am I supposed to find *them*?"

"Grandpa used to get his own. Maybe you'd get 'em from an apothecary," Is suggested.

She was ignored. Roy turned on Stritch.

"You get me some! You just go out now, this instant, and

find me some. Before we start for Cokehouses. And make haste."

"But, guvnor! What the plague do I know about orchid roots? Digging up roots? What kind of a job is that for a goodhearted, sensible, able man?" protested Stritch.

Uncle Roy's answer came in a cold, terrible, crazy voice.

"If you can't dig up orchid roots, you're no use to me."

There was a swift movement in the dark, beyond the candle flame, a fearful scream from Stritch.

"Aaaaagh! Guvnor—" The scream was abruptly cut short.

Uncle Roy turned toward Is. She saw the red light reflected in his eyes, and on the blade that he held in his hand. "Now you—" he began.

But at that moment there were voices and footsteps close at hand. Thought waves began to flash, almost unbearably loud—Is tried to clap her hands over her ears, failed, then almost laughed at herself, realizing that the sound was *inside,* not outside. But there were spoken words as well.

"Is? Are you there? Is that you?"

"Yes, yes, I'm here!" she called back shakily, and sent out rusty thought patterns to give them her direction.

Uncle Roy turned, glared, the blade shook in his hand— then he suddenly vanished into the dark, sideways, crabwise, stooping; with the candle in his hand throwing grotesque shadows, he looked like a black dwarf. Next moment he was gone.

Another light approached. The glimmer of a lamp carried by Helen Macclesfield. With her came Coppy.

"You're alive! Oh, what a relief!" Helen gave her a warm hug, and Coppy danced up and down.

"But you'll have to undo my hands," Is said. "They're clamped on to the stack behind me."

"We all thought you must be dead," Helen said, grappling with the chain, which was hooked over a bolt on the stack, while Coppy held the light for her. "We'd had no thought messages from you—nothing—we were so terribly worried; everybody thought you must have been drowned in a spate or buried in an avalanche."

"How long have I been here?"

"Days and days! All the search parties had given up. Then Coppy began to get faint, peculiar messages— There! That's got it undone."

The chain pulled loose, and Is was able to rub her cramped hands.

"Ugh!" said Coppy, jumping back. "There's a man on the floor here."

"Oh—yes—Stritch—poor stupid cove. But what's worse —Uncle Roy's on the loose around here, and he's mad as a weaver. We'd best get outa here right away. He ain't safe."

They hurried out of the dark basement. Coppy led the way. Outside, it was broad day. Is could hardly believe that she had been unconscious for so long.

"Though it was mighty strong stuff, whatever they used to hocus me—I felt as if I'd been dead. Where are you ever taking me?" she asked shakily as Helen and Coppy, instead of making for the post office, turned uphill.

"We thought you'd want to see the train go. There won't be time to get to the station—but if we stand on the foot-bridge we can see it go by."

They were leading her up to a point where a narrow footbridge, high above the track, spanned the deep cutting between embankments through which the railway track ran out from Blastburn station before it crossed the Wash River bridge.

"The train's going *today*?"

Is felt almost cheated. To send off the southbound train had been her idea—well, Arun's—and it seemed terribly unfair that the event should have been planned to take place in her absence. "Without me there?"

"Don't you see, everybody thought you must be dead. They were all dreadfully sad—they'll be so relieved to know you are alive!" Helen assured her. "There is a big ceremony down at the station, going on at this minute. Coppy was to have cut the ribbon, only then he began getting thought waves and dragged me off to the library—didn't you, Coppy?"

"Iss!" he said cheerfully. "Better find Is than cut a ribbon!"

Is suddenly stopped still in horror.

"But it mustn't start! It *mustn't*! Oh—not because I'm not there—that don't matter a button—but we must warn them, we must stop them! We've gotta run down—Coppy, you can run better—oh, plague take it, why am I so weak and wobbly—I can't even send a proper thought wave—"

"Why? What's amiss?"

"Uncle Roy fixed a load of dynamite to blow up the train when it starts."

Helen turned even whiter than her natural pallor. "Come, Coppy, we'll both run. Is, you stay here . . . we'll come back—"

"Send a thought wave to someone!" said Is. "I can't, my head's too muzzy yet—"

But the cousins had raced off down the embankment, diagonally toward the mouth of the station, which could be seen in the distance with the red-and-gold engine just protruding from it.

Maybe there's still time, thought Is. There must be.

Then she saw somebody—two people—climbing up the steep slope toward her. A long, skinny boy and a man: her cousin Arun and Dr. Lemman.

"The train's dynamited!" she shouted with all her strength as soon as they came within earshot.

But they shook their heads.

"Don't you fret, dearie; the boys found your uncle Roy's little surprise packet," said Lemman, striding up to her. He gave her a hug, and so did Arun. "They found it last night when they were giving the number-one engine its final polish. Old Roy will just have to be disappointed. —But, dearie, are we pleased to see *you*! Everyone thought you must have tumbled into a torrent, because the thought waves were turned off. Aren't we glad that you didn't!"

"Look," interrupted Arun seriously. "There she goes."

With a tremendous yelling whistle of triumph, the Playland Express pulled, in a series of jerks and clanks, out of Blastburn station.

"There's five drivers on board, plus Gower with a message to the London government," said Lemman cheerfully. "They ought to do well enough—if they don't run into floods, that is."

Every window of the train was full of arms, legs, and heads; weaving, screaming, yelling, cheering.

"It's like a Wakes train," said Lemman.

Is could not help feeling a little sad. All her friends—the Bottom Layer that she had brought out of the dark—there they went. She might never see them again.

But that don't matter, she thought then. We can still talk, however far apart. And indeed a tremendous wave of warmth and friendship came up to her as the train approached the bridge, and she leaned over the rail, tossing her good wishes back and her love for all of them. It's a huge family, she thought. It's us! All over the country. And there'll be more . . .

"And they aren't *all* going," said Arun, astonishing her by suddenly breaking into thought-speak. "Quite a parcel of them decided to stay here for a while at least and help rebuild Old Blastburn."

"Arun! You are talking in thoughts!"

"Everybody else seemed to have the knack, so I reckoned it was time I began." He gave her a teasing grin.

"Oh, heavens! Look! Down on the track—" Is clutched Lemman's arm in horror.

Down on the track was Gold Kingy, almost black-faced with rage, dancing, shouting and screaming inaudible curses, shaking his fists at the train, which came implacably toward him.

"Stop! I order you to stop! I command you to stop!"

They could see him mouthing the words, willing the order, as he had willed himself to walk on the water.

The train did not stop. It was going too fast by now for braking to make the least difference. The train tossed Gold Kingy indifferently to one side, and he flew through the air, over the parapet, and into the Wash River.

Lemman ran down to look over the wall, then shook his head, and began walking slowly back.

Now he'll never be able to try saloop and see if it works for him, thought Is. But my guess is that it wouldn't have. She could not feel the least regret for the death of her uncle Roy; he had caused too much harm and misery.

· · ·

Arun was saying something about Captain Podmore.

"Ship turned up last night. He'd been down at Plymouth; missed the worst of the tidal waves. We could sail with him tomorrow—he sometimes puts in at Folkestone, he says. He told me to tell you the king's cousin—the new king—is a cove called the Duke of Battersea. Podmore thought you might be pleased. He'll be King Simon the First."

"Oh, Arun, that's right good news! Simon! Yes, he'll make a prime king—he's got real good sense. Funny, I knew he'd high-up connections, but I never knowed he was the king's cousin."

"So what Davie did won't have been wasted," said Arun.

"We gotta *see* that it wasn't wasted," said Is. And she started wondering where the token might be now.

"And I'll tell you another thing," said Arun, putting a comfortable, brotherly arm around Is, who still looked and felt very sick and shaky. "They're starting to rebuild Old Blastburn, and they've decided to change the name. And they're going to call it *Is*—after that city Aunt Ishie told of, that once got drowned in the sea. Why, dearie!"—he had caught the trick from Lemman—"why, dearie, what in the world is there in *that* to make you start crying?"